ALL FOR GRACE

Praise for *All for Grace*

"*All for Grace* is truly a wonderful book. A real page-turner that I read in two days! It is a beautiful mix of spiritual and fiction and the writing is entertaining and uplifting. I highly recommend reading it. The last time I read a book this fast, was when I came across *Conversations with God.*"

– LILY HOLISTIC, Ireland (www.lilyholistic.com)

"A grace-full debut from a talented and inspirational author. It's not often that a book like *All for Grace* comes along - an uplifting story that doesn't answer questions, but simply asks them, and lets the reader come to his or her own conclusion.
Mairéad Whyte has a natural flair for characterisation, matched only by her ingenious ways of captivating her readers' imaginations.
In a world filled with the likes of James Patterson and JK Rowling, it's not often that a book makes you stop, think and then, after you've thought for a little while, think some more. *All for Grace* is such a book."

- BECKY GRICE, Editor, *East Cork Journal*

"*All for Grace* is a clever, thought-provoking book. On the one hand, it's a novel about love and life; on the other, it's a personal-growth guide, offering life lessons and advice which the reader can take to heart. I thoroughly enjoyed it."

- JOHN DOLAN, Features Editor, *Evening Echo*

"*All for Grace* is a magical, life-enhancing story that is fun and up-lifting and takes you on a soul journey from the ordinary to the extraordinary. It evokes laughter, sadness and deeper thinking that will certainly stir debate."

- SHERRON MAYES, Journalist and Author of best-selling book,
Be Your Own Psychic

"*All for Grace* is a fun and inspiring novel that takes the reader on an extraordinary adventure. As a busy Mum, I haven't read a book in a single sitting for years - but this is a real page-turner and I just couldn't put it down. The idea is unique and what I love about *All for Grace* is that not only do you get a fantastic story with brilliant, thought-provoking characters - you also learn so much about yourself and your family. Every home should have one."

- LORRAINE THOMAS, Author of *The Mummy Coach, Get A Life*
and *The 7-Day Parent Coach*

"*All for Grace* is a great book that teaches important life lessons in a fun and unique way. Simple to digest and engaging throughout, Mairéad Whyte has written a great story that entertains, informs and enlightens. I wholeheartedly recommend it."

- BRIAN MAYNE, Global speaker on success and Author of the
best-selling book, *Goal Mapping* and *Life Mapping*, and *Sam the Magic Genie* (www.liftinternational.com)

ALL FOR GRACE

MAIRÉAD WHYTE

ORIGINAL WRITING

978-1-907179-90-7

A CIP catalogue for this book is available from the National Library.

Published by ORIGINAL WRITING LTD., Dublin, 2010.

Printed by CAHILL PRINTERS LIMITED, Dublin.

For my father

And

For my mother

CHAPTER ONE

Screams echoed from the end of the tunnel and I estimated less than an hour to get there. It was my umpteenth time taking this journey so I considered myself a veteran, but it was a first for my twin brother and he had spent most of our last few weeks annoying me about what we should expect when we crossed the finishing line. I had told him that everyone on earth had travelled this course at least once and every solitary soul had gasped for air while simultaneously being overwhelmed with joy on arrival. He did not believe me, knowing my tendency to change my mind for no obvious reasons.

Through blurry vision I had suspected my brother looked like a mandolin, with a wrinkly face and matching neck. When his haphazard chatter irritated me, I told him so. Innocently, he told me my face looked the same even though he had never seen a mandolin; I can only suppose I looked stressed from the constant torment of his naive questions.

Quite frankly he had nothing better to do, and when he was not asleep he had spent most of his time talking and playing, I spent most of my time day dreaming and it had been a trying routine lying there to hear him clock up his speech mileage which was an interruption to my thoughts. But there was nowhere to escape since we had been confined and unable to move freely, locked up together in a tiny vessel. It was a journey that typically lasted nine months, but had only taken us eight. We were early. I had seriously hoped we were prepared.

It was just after seven AM on Friday March thirteenth, in the year 2172, on our last day in that dark and stuffy chamber. My brother had awoken gently with a slight stretch as he yawned; he had appeared refreshed and oblivious to the external commotion having slept easily for the previous five hours through the constant shrills of the apparent agony on the outside. His antics had no longer surprised me as it was beyond question that he could oscillate with no bother between sleeping soundly to an enthusiastic, purposeless speech. I reckoned it was all his talking that made him so tired.

"Are we there yet?" he asked with excitement.

"You tell me, you're going first," I let him know.

"But, you'll be hot on my heels – right?"

"Of course I will," I lied. I had planned at least twenty minutes alone to reflect and contemplate my next move. Appearing irritated, Fragrance was onto my premeditated plot as she announced firmly, "stay true." Fragrance and I had an agreement but when she reminded me of my morals and obligations, it was enough to induce a headache onto an aspirin. I had my reasons.

Fragrance was always on standby whenever we beckoned her. She was our guide and our coach from the Realm where we had originated. It required vast labour being born into the world, and once we were delivered safely, Fragrance would leave us. She would only return to us during our final days, during the inevitable human process of dying. Dying is certainly no picnic but I knew from experience that it was a piece of cake in comparison to the long journey to incarnation. And as I had then believed, it was my proposed punishment that I was embodied in human flesh, soon to enter the human world and starting again with a blank template. Once I was born I would remember nothing; nothing of our long journey, nothing of the Realm and equally nothing of my previous lifetimes. We were about to emerge on a blank canvas. Our memory bank would become a vacuum.

Faint light had entered the opening of the tunnel and we were curled together side by side with our heads directed towards the protruding beam of light. The rays seemed to expand, encouraging more light to enter and also inviting more noise from the several voices on the outside. The exaggerated piercing sounds still came from the same person, I could recognize her noise from anywhere; I had wondered several times if my new mother was a drama queen. She was the person we had most listened to over the previous eight months, not by choice but due to the fact we could not get away from her; and at times she was less coherent than others. She had a tendency to get excited at the least little thing. And when she got hyperactive everyone knew about it.

* * * * *

When she had first discovered she was pregnant, we had only been there four weeks and she spent the entire day on her transmission phone, recalling the story in exquisite detail again and again and each time she exaggerated a different fact, over-hyped or added new detail to make the story more interesting.

When transmission phones had become widely and cheaply available in the mid-twenty-first century, allowing people to automatically appear as holographs to each other during call connection, this presented another problem to us. It had taken me the entire four weeks to work out exactly what she had been doing. And since I had nothing better to do at that early stage, I adapted the persona of detective. I deduced our mother spent hours grooming her appearance before any transmission calls, which made her story telling process even more painful. The evidence came from hearing her overly eager phrases such as, "you'll never guess what.." or, "you won't believe this now but.." or, "some people would not believe this but I saw it with my own eyes..." repeated over again in different tones with no one responding, and in the background I could hear sounds like hair dryers, running water and some utterances of, "crap, I have to redo my makeup." And sure enough, sooner or later I would hear her connect on her transmission phone and start the whole rehearsed story but this time someone on the other end would respond. Since I had no other theories and it was not the most interesting of investigations, I decided to believe that she loved to practice her excitement in several rehearsals before the event so that she could maximize on the feeling before and during each conversation.

The feeling was not as thrilling on the inside as the more excited she got the more her flitting stomach seemed like bangs of thunder bombarding the top walls of her womb; our inner

3

chamber. Sometimes we had kicked back in response which had stopped her in her tracks for a bit, but as soon as we started to understand her addiction to a hyperactive state, we stopped our kicking also. It had become obvious to us that she even manipulated the purpose of our kicks to add more drama, with her theories that certain foods did not appeal to us and what fussy rascals we were.

It was a call that she had made to 'Psychic Pregscan' that revealed her pregnancy at that early stage. I found the term 'pregnant' insulting since there were two of us in there. Two unique Realm One souls about to enter earth, and like every other Realm soul we held a database of knowledge greater than any human could ever possibly comprehend. Though, fearfully, I had known that would be wiped within seconds of birth, one of the most frightful experiences of being born.

"Look on the bright side," my brother had said chirpily; clearly thrilled she was aware of the existence on her insides. Though he had no idea with whom our mother had been conversing, and even if he did, he had no understanding then what the 'Psychic Pregscan' helpline was. Moreover, he did not know at that early stage the significance it held for me in my memories and past associations with them.

"For pity's sake, they can do better than that," I burped out with frustration.

"Oh my God, oh my God, oh my God," our mother had shouted in more excitement. "The baby just burped, I heard it; I heard a little burp." She had started crying, it seemed like happy crying. It was ridiculous; she could not have heard a four-week-old unborn burp. I was thinking hard. Unless of course, nah, it could not have been that – could it? I then dismissed those thoughts.

"Excuse me," I coughed up with the disgust of being categorized as a baby. "My name is Ariel and I have originated from Omega, the inner city of the district 'Realm One'." I had barely started my sermon when the 'Psychic Pregscan' lady over-spoke me. "The baby is clearly excited that you know about its existence," she said. What a weak response and a poor prediction

4

she had made, and what a cheek they both had, talking about me as though I could not hear. And they had also seemed to overlook the presence of my brother, Morcan, as they referred continuously to us both collectively as 'the baby'.

'Psychic Pregscan' was an organization of psychics operating from San Diego, California. They were no ordinary organization of human psychics, they specialized in providing details of pregnancy, predicting not only the sex of the baby or babies, but the baby's sexual preferences, choice of profession, IQ, level of wealth and success and emotional intelligence. They operated a huge internet business targeting all new 'mothers to be' in all corners of the earthly globe and had huge neon signs in most of the so called earthly spiritual centers. Their website roped in the new mothers with adverts of a free psychic scan, and in essence they were no different than any other money-making internet marketing sites that gave women 'free' scans in return for the woman submitting all her personal contact details; then they could target each mother to pay subscriptions to get more information on her unborn. They claimed they could also advise any mother of any upcoming health issues the child may experience, and they offered pricey insurance policies based on their predictions; along with an enormous amount of baby garb adverts they bombarded the mothers with in the months leading up to the birth. The organization as a whole placed subtle adverts playing on the fears of unsuspecting mothers, mothers who wanted to 'get it right', mothers who wanted to do all the correct things for their new unborn babies and be the perfect parent. Souls in Realm One knew there was no such thing as the perfect parent or the perfect upbringing, in fact we chose our earthly parents in advance and generally we picked them based on their imperfections. However, knowing about their imperfections in advance and experiencing them on earth are two entirely different stories.

Despite the organizational goals, most of the people working for 'Psychic Pregscan' were empathetic humans with a genuine interest in supporting women through pregnancy, and they sought their guidance from a carefully selected alliance with a Realm One soul. Even though I did not agree fully with the marketing techniques and money-making bank of the 'Pregscan' organization, I had once been one of those souls with whom they communicated and I knew the ins and outs of this earthly organization in detail. Although it was an 'Undercover Movement' and illegal to contact humans from the Realm, we all had our own reasons for working with earth psychics, risking the Realm consequences in the event we were found out. Realm One souls gave the human psychics the information they needed and in return we asked for a few favours ourselves. It was a two way street, let's face it - there is no such thing as something for nothing, not even in the Realm.

During those earlier weeks of the unborn process, I had often wondered which Realm One soul was working with the lady my mother had been conversing with, or more importantly whether these souls were still communicating with earth. I questioned whether this psychic lady was actually genuine. It was interesting for me to know.

"Careful now," Fragrance had responded in a scolding tone, obviously keenly listening to and reading those thought processes. Whether I had allowed my thoughts to be transmitted or not, Fragrance held special permission to override them, which was a privilege for all coaches who guided souls on their journey to and from the earth.

"Oh come on Fragrance, I was only wondering, cut me some slack here, will you please, it's not like I was trying to communicate back to the Realm," I replied defensively.

"Ariel, you have been blocked from any communications," Fragrance had reminded me. "Though I suspect you will no doubt try. Why can't you be a clever soul and just enjoy your journey?"

"I'm only reminiscing on my days in the Realm, while I still can," I said as honestly as I could.

"Your days in the Realm were not spent wisely. Do you still choose to reminisce on that unwise behaviour?" she asked, reminding me again of what I believed to be my so called punishment.

"All I want to know is whether some souls still communicate with earth psychics, you can't really blame me for wondering that, it's not like there's a whole lot for us to do in here, except wonder," I said.

"Forget your new mother's business. She is on her own journey. It is her choice to believe what she decides in any given moment," Fragrance replied firmly.

"That's true, it says so in rule twenty-two of the Realm bible," Morcan added eagerly with innocence. I frowned at him but his big, saucer-sized eyes only reciprocated a sense of confusion.

"So the movement continues then, Realm One souls are still contacting earth people?" I persisted to ask, slyly seeking confirmation from Fragrance, but I had already suspected that she would respond with a politician's non-answer and avoid the question.

"You can no longer have information about the Realm during your journey," she replied on cue.

"Yep, that's true, rule sixty-eight of the Realm bible," Morcan added again, possibly trying to impress Fragrance with the intricate detail of his studies. I ignored him.

"Okay, forget the Realm, what about earth since that's where I am heading, can humans still contact Realm One?" I then asked, cleverly turning the situation around.

"No, you can't know that either," Morcan piped up instantly, "that's rule sixty-nine, we can't have information from earth either on this journey." I had wanted to strangle him. "Fine then," I decided, "we cannot have current information about the Realm or the earth during this journey." I sank back into my section of the womb as I mentally created a clear division line separating Morcan's living quarters from mine, a line that I would dare him to cross.

Fragrance smiled in Morcan's direction and he was thrilled as though he had just earned brownie points. Irrelevant brownie points, because none of this would matter when we were born. Fragrance's energy presence faded as though she was letting us argue it out for ourselves and I was a bit annoyed with myself for falling into this trap; I should have known most of the rules, after all, I had several Realm years of breaking them.

"Okay, let's give our mother and the lady on her transmission call a clue," I sighed towards Morcan's side of the womb, "let's both cough simultaneously, unless there is a rule against that also."

"Why?" he responded simply.

"To let them know there are two of us in here," I said, frustrated by his question.

"It doesn't really matter."

I coughed despite him.

"Go on; your go now, your turn to cough," I instructed him.

"No, I couldn't be bothered, you're up to something," he said in a suspicious tone.

I coughed again.

"I think the baby coughed," my mother announced joyfully while still sobbing. And unless there were human technological advances I did not know about, there was only one way that she could hear any noise from a four-week-old unborn. Morcan appeared unaware of this as he bounced around the section I had assigned him, content in his own oblivion.

"Did you hear her? Our mother is communicating with me, isn't that amazing? Don't you want to communicate with her?" I asked him in a slightly manipulative way.

"Yes, but no, I mean yes, but I'm not sure if we're allowed," he said innocently.

"Are there any rules against coughing?"

"No, I don't think so, but it may fall under rule sixty-eight or sixty-nine, getting information from earth while in transition. I'm not sure," he replied.

"Don't be silly, those rules only prohibit us from asking for information, and even Fragrance confirmed that," I said.

"I don't know, I don't think it is right," he said quietly.

"It's like a game, you like games – don't you?"

"I love games," he said enthusiastically. Result at last.

"Okay, on the count of three let's cough together, one.... two... th.."

"Hang on," Morcan interrupted, "hold your horses, and let's go through all the rules to be sure."

"There are thousands of them, it will be too late, mother will have finished her call with the lady by then, come on, we know it's safe, if it wasn't Fragrance would be on to us again by now, isn't that true?"

"I knew you were up to something. Why is it so important for us to do this while mother is still on the call?"

'So I can deduce whether the Realm 'Undercover Movement' is still in operation, and check out if the psychic does really have detailed information about us, because if she does she must definitely be communicating with a Realm soul,' I thought to myself in frustration. I had approximately eight months left in there at that point and I thought it was as good a way as any to spend it, and it would prove useful for my memory bank when I would again return to the Realm. I had hoped to get back to Realm One sooner rather than later, but that plan would not be put into execution until Morcan was safely delivered to the outside. I had known Fragrance was onto that plot also and I would deal with that at a later stage. Fragrance had a habit of only challenging me on my thought plans at a time convenient for her.

Even though I was certain Morcan did not pick up on my thoughts, I took care not to transmit any just in case there was some remote possibility, because it is fact that thoughts with strong emotion tend to manifest themselves no matter where you are on the universe.

"We should cough together because it will be great hearing mother talk about us both," I replied instead. "If she finishes the call and then hears two distinct coughs simultaneously she has no one to immediately tell, and by the time she prepares herself to transmit a call to one of her friends to tell them about us, you will have fallen asleep. It's only harmless fun, and you don't want to be asleep when she tells someone, isn't that true? And I know you want to have fun and maximize your journey; don't you?"

"Yes I do," he responded. Of course he did, there was no other way to respond to a question that could only have a 'yes' answer, a tactic I had learned from a solicitor in a previous lifetime.

We both coughed.

"I think the baby coughed again," our mother announced joyfully.

"I believe the baby is trying to communicate with you," the 'Psychic Pregscan' lady added in a lame attempt at encouragement.

"Two of us trying to communicate," I stated firmly. We both coughed again and Morcan seemed to love the game.

"It feels like a little party in my stomach, my baby seems happy," our mother said.

"Yes, it is a celebration," the psychic lady said. "In fact, I think I have some new information that will thrill you, however since this is a free scan only, you will need to subscribe for more details. Would you like more details about your baby?"

"Two babies, if you must call us that," I responded. "Oh go on mother, subscribe, get the info, you know you want it," I added in appeal.

"Yes mother, please subscribe," Morcan also said to copy me, before he asked, "subscribe to what?"

"I donno," I lied, "but it sounds like it's something important she must do to get information about us."

"Does this have something to do with your conversation with Fragrance about human and soul exchange of information?" he asked, and I started to sense his fear of rule-breaking return. I had known that he did not want to jeopardize his journey in any way; he had been clearly excited about his first experience on earth. We all had been when it was our first time. We all eagerly anticipated it. New-born souls had a wonderful innocence so I could not find it in me to deceive him further.

"It's okay, I'll level with you," I said.

"I do really love the coughing game," he said, as though I had a need to be convinced as he bounced up and down enthusiastically. "It's brilliant fun!" And then he pounced practically on top of me as he stared into my eyes, "but I'm afraid of what they'll do in the Realm if we break the rules."

As he spoke, I felt immense pity for him. "They won't do anything; you are not breaking any rules, all is okay. On earth some humans believe that constant rule-breaking sends their soul to hell and we know that all souls return to the Realm no matter what their human conduct was, correct?"

"What about limbo?" he asked with worry. "Oh God, please help me," I cried. How could I have explained limbo to him? But I knew I had wanted to be somehow truthful while treading carefully on what he had been taught and what he had learned to believe. It was not the right time to start dissecting his beliefs.

"Limbo is only a word, it is common to refer to our transition as limbo, the state we experience on our journey to earth, and also our state when we are rehabilitated back into the Realm at the end of our earthly lives, but you know that, don't you?"

"Yes, I know what it is. But what if the Realm guides decide to keep us in this limbo and we never get out?"

"Then our mother will have two huge overgrown babies when we eventually do," I said as I transferred a smile of encouragement towards him.

Morcan's voice had started to shake, "I know you are trying to comfort me, but what if they really do keep our souls in limbo?" he persisted to ask. I had wanted to shout and tell him that it was not possible to get stuck in limbo, limbo was not a place, it never existed, what part of 'limbo is only a word' did he not understand? Limbo was only referred to as a place by the guides in Realm One, a fictional place, so that we would not break their rules out of fear of being sent there. Limbo was a state of being, a state of experience from the Realm to earth and back again. No more, no less. I wanted to scream and tell him the guides on Realm One were no different from some of the preachers on earth, instilling teachings about hell and the rules to obey so that humans could save their souls for fear of being sent to that evil place of eternal torment. But I guessed that is what the term 'human nature' must have meant; the human ability to follow the thought train of the majority and failure to think on their own, denying any questioning curiosity which may not be deemed acceptable.

Realm One souls knew the fact that hell did not exist, however most did not apply the same logic to realize that limbo was equally imagined by the Realm guides as the dismal place where a soul could be sent for eternal punishment if they acted contrary to any of the Realm rules. I knew this because I had infringed on far too many rules myself in the Realm and I was not experiencing eternity in limbo. It proved that limbo did not exist.

"Two things can happen, we are born in these human bodies and we spend a life on earth for a period of time, or we are not born and we go back to Realm One," I explained calmly. "Now, if you still believe there is a place called limbo on Realm One and you believe that you could be sent there, remember that you only get sent there if you disobey the rules, and you are not breaking rules. We are not asking for any earthly information. We are not asking for new Realm information. We are happy in our transition state playing with our mother and I am sure that is what the unborn are meant to do."

"So what are we asking our mother to subscribe to then? Assuming it's not breaking the rules," he asked.

"Our mother is talking with another human who I suspect is communicating with a soul from Realm One," I responded, and I was unsure how he would take the news.

"Oh my God, that is why you asked Fragrance those questions. I thought you were up to your old tricks and wanted to annoy and tease her."

"What do you know about my old tricks?"

"Finish answering my question first," he squeaked.

"I just want to know if that lady is really communicating with a soul in the Realm, there is nothing more to it."

"That is illegal."

"It's not illegal for us, we are not contacting anyone! We are playing with our mother."

"Playing with our mother to get the information and it is a rule break to start looking for information while we are here."

"We are not asking for information, the rules state you cannot ask for information about the Realm and the earth while in this state, we have been over this twice already. If mother subscribes to this 'Psychic Pregscan' she will get more information about us and she is happier, you are happier because then she will know you exist also when she stops referring to us both as 'the baby', and I am happier because I will know whether the psychic lady is able to communicate with a Realm soul to get the information. I would not be asking for that information, I will have easily deduced it for myself. And there is no rule that bans us from deducing the information for ourselves. It is really that easy. We have asked for nothing. We disobey no rules."

"I'm not sure," he responded.

"A minute ago you wanted her to subscribe to get more information on us," I reminded him.

"Yeah I know, but it doesn't feel right."

"Everything said has been open, if there was a loophole in anything I said, Fragrance would be down on us right now."

"Yeah, okay, fair enough," he said finally with content, "let's give it a go again."

"By the way, what was it that you know about my apparent old tricks?"

"There's no time for that now," he said as he skipped towards me and his big eyes overstepped the line into my space, "enough time has been wasted, as you said, this is fun. And I know you want to have fun and maximize your journey, don't you?" He snared me on that one, I had taught him well.

We started our synchronized coughing. Then we paused; and waited for the response from the external conversation. It was not long before our mother spoke, in a fonder tone this time, "oh! I am starting to hear little coughs again."

"Good - how many?" I asked excitedly, as Morcan and I huddled together waiting for the response.

"As I explained, she really is a very gentle soul," the lady said.

"Huh? Who are you talking about? Who is 'she'?" I asked in confusion. Morcan mirrored my confusion. It was not the response we expected. We were overwhelmed with surprise.

"Oh, I had better go, she seems to be a little upset, thank you so much for all the information you have given me, it has really been invaluable. I feel privileged," our mother said as though she was about to terminate the conversation.

"No, wait, hang on, what information? Who is 'she'? What about us?" I asked frantically.

"I am glad this call has helped you. You know you can still opt for a monthly subscription and I will deduct the one -off payment you made for today's detailed information," the lady said.

"What detailed information?" I asked, concerned. Morcan shrugged his shoulders.

"I understand, thank you, all the information you have given today is enough for now, I feel overjoyed; I think I need to rest now, and I feel the little one in my stomach needs a rest too," our mother said. She was right about that for certain. Everyone was overwhelmed and there was certainly more confusion on the inside than on the outside.

"It has been a pleasure speaking with you today, if we do not speak again I wish you a wonderful pregnancy and I am sure the birth of your little girl will bring you immense joy," the lady said, and then the transmission ended.

It was over in a shot. Both Morcan and I stared blankly into space.

"She thinks you are a girl," Morcan said to finally break the ice. I had sensed he found humour in that.

"And she still doesn't know that you exist," I reminded him curtly.

"I am sure when she does find out, she won't call me a girl," he sang.

"Be quiet for a minute, I need to get my thoughts straight," I barked.

"You are not any wiser, are you?"

"I would have been if I had the chance to listen instead of answering your stupid questions about limbo. It's your fault, you know, we missed the conversation and it's your fault," I retorted, driven by self-pity.

"What was the point anyway? We know the result. Mother thinks she is having one baby girl," he said in a totally amused tone. I was shoving him back to his side when Fragrance intervened suddenly, "what have you learned, Ariel?" she asked. Morcan and I were both startled. Morcan froze in an instant silence but I was as defiant as ever.

"That you somehow had something to do with this; that I was purposefully sent on a tangent answering Morcan's questions; questions he had based on the thoughts that you must have purposefully planted into his head; that I unknowingly fell right into your trap; that you would even manipulate my brother's thoughts only to serve me out more punishment. Is that what you want to hear?" I yelled and I punched the air fluid that surrounded us. It hurt. "Ouch," I cried like a baby.

Fragrance sighed, "you are on your final warning, Ariel; if I were you I would stop thinking of yourself as the victim, and start focusing on elevating your thought process, and stop your unfounded allegations. Everyone in the Realm is becoming bored with this. It is now your time to make your choice as to whether you want to enter the world with such a primitive spirit. The choice is yours, it always has been."

CHAPTER TWO

Despite her claims of needing a rest from the excitement of the initial 'Psychic Pregscan' call, our mother got busy preparing herself to make eight transmission calls. She had rehearsed several times what she would say and every time she practised she had added more drama. I was not sure if this was the mother I had chosen. I had not remembered ticking the 'easily excited', 'highly strung' and 'obsession with talking' boxes when we filled in our application forms with chosen traits for our next set of earthly parents, but then again I thought, maybe it was a given that all earthly females got those behaviours by default. And as some of my memories were beginning to fade slowly I could not have been sure of my reasons for selecting her at that point. All I knew was that I did not feel all-knowing anymore. It made me more confused. And I did not know why.

When our mother was finally ready, she phoned her mother, her sister, her two sisters-in-law and four friends. I disregarded all her phone conversations, but my silence had been interrupted constantly with her shrieks of, "a little girl.", "I've always wanted a little girl." I had also chosen to overlook Fragrance's last spiel calling me primitive; however I did take on board the fact that I still had choice, so I chose some quiet reflection time. It was not easy. It was not easy to stop myself from continuously screaming. I had then two problems, I still did not know if the Realm 'Undercover Movement' was still in operation and on top of that I was being called a girl. I had to do something before I exploded.

My opportunity came when our mother recalled the entire story for the ninth time when our new father came home later that same day. He was the last to know. The tone of his voice indicated he was not happy, and I had thought our father generally made more sense than our mother so I tuned in merrily.

"How many people have you already told?" he had asked as though he was afraid of the answer.

"Just family, just a few, that's all Joe," she responded quietly. "That's not true, half the universe knows at this stage," I muttered, "go on Daddy Joe, and question her a little more, don't let her away with it. More people than you know are suffering from this untruth."

"Oh Charlotte, you cannot be sure from your 'Psychic Pregscan'," Daddy Joe said with a tone of disbelief, "make an appointment with the doctor tomorrow and we'll go together to be sure."

"Exactly," I said, and the words were out of my mouth before I thought about it. "No, no, take that back, Daddy, Daddy, Daddy Joe please," I cried, "get her to do another 'Psychic Pregscan' call." From the day I had been put into this womb I had felt a special connection with Daddy, and from the moment I learned his name I could not stop saying it anytime I sensed he was there. Deep down, I knew I had somehow chosen my parents from the Realm but despite this it still took me a long time to refer to mother as Mummy Charlotte; it was another sequence of events which created that unsuspected bond between us.

"You're right, Joe," mother said after some quiet time, before adding, "though maybe I could do another 'Pregscan' in a couple of weeks, they did seem to know a lot about our little girl." Her tone was hopeful.

"Two babies, two boys," I confirmed quickly.

"You know my opinions on psychics; they're a bunch of charlatans. We'll go to the doctor," he responded.

"No Daddy, please Daddy Joe, what about our special connection? You're my only hope here," I pleaded.

Mother had remained quiet and I wondered if she would call 'Pregscan' anyway and neglect to tell him, she had seemed experienced in altering the truth after events. I also assumed the technological advances of the twenty-second century would permit her to contact 'Psychic Pregscan' without Daddy Joe tracing it, and I started to understand how mother's ways could be to my advantage as I decided this may have been one of the reasons why I had chosen her after all.

"And please stop telling people, we are not sure yet. We'll discuss this again after we visit the doctor. And let that be the end of it," Daddy Joe said conclusively.

Good on Daddy Joe, I had agreed totally that she should stop telling people, and get the facts straight first, though I suspected she would overlook his advice, and continue to make endless transmission calls in the days to come which I would have to endure time and again. If only Daddy Joe could hear me, I thought, I would set the story straight, I knew I could not leave that entirely up to mother.

She did not say anymore on the subject. I waited and waited more, listening attentively to every sound between them and there had been no further mention of 'the baby'; but when their conversation evolved into a heated discussion about the amount due on mother's credit card, I freaked and swiftly tuned out. Daddy Joe had freaked also when he started to question the amount she had over-spent on baby things she had purchased from the 'Pregscan' online shopping facility. That had not bothered me. I loved stuff. It was the mention of dolls and pink baby garb that made me violently ill. Unintentionally, it made mother ill too.

Morcan had been sleeping, and even if he was not I would have ignored him also, we were only four weeks into the unborn process then and it gave us plenty of room to manoeuvre around and have our own space. I went back to my choice of quiet reflection on my side of our home, and chose a spot as far as possible from Morcan, I still was not happy with the situation.

My instant conclusion was that there had been only two possibilities, both with equal probability since I had little or no information to back my theories. The first was that the psychic was a fake and really had no clue or founded basis for her incorrect information, or else she was not a fake and her Realm contact was asleep on the job. Just like any job really, some are good at it, some are not, and some are deluded and think they actually are good at it. Realm One souls equally fell into those classifications when applying for a position with the 'Under-cover Movement', and it was not unusual for a lot of them to fall into the latter categorisation.

I was completely torn between my conflicting thoughts, like there was a battle between soul and mind in this new baby body both seemed to occupy; so I existed in hope that the Realm contact had inefficiently retrieved the wrong information. This was the only way I could understand the current status of the Realm since my departure, which continued to be a dominant thought. This was my only method to deduce the truth. And it was important to do so as I had planned to go back to the Realm sooner than originally planned. And it was imperative that the 'Undercover Movement' still existed when I did return; it was critical to continue my search, the search which was vital to the thoughts that dominated me.

With time alone, my thoughts had started to take on a new life of their own and all sorts of theories had entered inside me. How could I have missed that initial conversation between our mother and the psychic? What was the additional information we did not hear? Did Fragrance really control Morcan's thoughts? Or was he genuinely questioning my motives and the rules? Was Morcan as innocent as he seemed? No, I dismissed that option as I had sensed his fear and I had known it to be genuine. Did the Realm guides plant that fear unknown to Morcan? Could someone have been controlling my thoughts? Why would the Realm guides interfere in our unborn state? This had not happened before. This did not seem right, nothing seemed right; anything seemed possible though, yet nothing seemed possible. I wondered what was happening; if I was being punished then why involve Morcan? He was a new, innocent soul eager for his first experience on earth. Or was he? Why was Fragrance so pedantic in watching our interaction? It frightened me to think I had become suspicious of everyone and everything. Was this a state an unborn could experience? It was not known before, I had not known it before, was I becoming insane? Maybe it was normal to think like this. Maybe it was normal to experience lunacy. Maybe God was insane. Insanity was just a word; it was a word to define someone who thinks differently and someone who thinks outside the rule book, or was it? Maybe this was a new experience and maybe derangement applied to the unborn also. I had never heard of such an occurrence. Was my mental health in jeopardy? Were all these thoughts senseless? What was it I did not know?

But there was only one thing I would not be shaken on, and that was if Morcan had intentionally diverted my attention during that first important call, and just in case he may ever have thought that mishap was history, I decided to store the incident up for future ammunition in the unlikely event I would ever live my life as a woman.

For the two weeks following the initial 'Pregscan' call there had been some awkward silences between Morcan and I; externally he had seemed to be content enough, remaining optimistic and sleeping soundly but his conversational questioning was limited. Generally, we had only spoken to agree on the practicalities of the living arrangements and only crossed the dividing line to discuss the division of food.

Only occasionally during that two week quarantine period we engaged in trivial banter, and once we even reconciled our differences when our mother had started drinking prune juice to help with her constipation. It tasted disgusting even to our underdeveloped palates and neither of us wanted it. It was true that we were not in the least bit fussy with our food and we were happy to digest most things independent of likes or dislikes, however I believe it was the stress of our then situation that left me slightly irritable so I started complaining. Morcan then complained to copy me; I think he was sucking up to me, hoping to get back into my good books. There was no need, I had already realised it was not him I was angry with; Fragrance was my new source of anger. Stubbornness prohibited me from telling him so. I had kept myself completely off the hook of blame and it was not easy admitting I may not have been right after all. I was becoming more human.

On that occasion I had allowed him civil conversation, though my heart was begging to admit my failings so that we could get back to playing with each other and our mother. We put our heads together, literally, and worked out a prune juice plan. We had two options, we could each take half of the dirty, purple-brown liquid that hit her insides, or one of us could do a temporary fast while the other consumed it all. It seemed easy; however, both of us had wanted the latter option and both of us wanted abstinence in that option. We agreed not to disagree which was a start, and set our focus on solutions rather than more problems. That was our first ever experience of collaboration with each other.

It was Morcan who had suggested we play a game to resolve the matter, and the winner of the game got to choose. It seemed fair so I agreed. We decided to play 'Space Chairs', a game that was invented by Morcan on the first day of our journey. He seemed more creative than I and I guessed I was the more mathematical and logical half. To play the game and despite our inflexibility, we had to curl ourselves as much as we could as though we were bound to two separate chairs, then we had to bounce as high as we could muster, pretending we were in a zero gravity capsule in outer space. It was much more exciting for us to think we were in space rather than in a ball of fluid inside a woman who lived in Hampstead, North London. It was immense fun, bouncing around in unison in little foetus happiness and the game had broken the ice between us and I had temporarily forgotten about the thoughts that consumed me. But then the game was over as soon as it had begun, and it was easily won by the one who made the most leaps in three minutes. Morcan won and I consumed the prune juice. It did not agree with me and that presented another issue.

Morcan said I had started to smell like a sewer, the prune juice was not only relieving our mother of her problem, it had the same effect on me. I could not help thinking Morcan had been exaggerating, the smell was more like silage than sewage, and I was familiar with both smells since I had grown up on a farm in a previous lifetime. I even remembered quite liking the smell of silage and manure, but that did not help as the tables reversed. Morcan would not go near me and chose a spot for himself as far as possible from me. Maybe he was becoming more human also and wanted to experience some resentment too.

'Space Chairs' also made our mother queasy as she had started complaining about the flutters in her stomach. She had still thought there was only one of us in there so I had supposed she was assigning sole blame to me.

We had only been six weeks in the womb at that stage and two of those had included limited interaction, I had started to feel lonely so I decided to make more of an effort with Morcan and reduced myself to his level of dialogue.

"Are you asleep?" I whispered.

"Yes," he answered with his back turned towards me.

"You don't want to play then?" I said in a questioning tone.

"No, I can't, I'm sleeping," he said.

"Okay, I'll play on my own," I said quietly.

"You can't so that, we don't know any games that we can play on our own."

"I do."

"Since when?" he asked and turned around to face me.

"Since you decided to dismiss me, I have thought of quite a few on my own."

"Name one," he said in a disbelieving tone.

"Boxing."

"You can't play that on your own."

"Of course I can, this fluid stuff sticks to my hands like boxing gloves."

"That's imagination. It's not real."

"All games are pretend."

"No, they're not. Games are fun and joy and love."

'No; they're not,' I thought to myself, 'human minds play games and they're not fun.'

"Okay, want to play a game then?" I asked him nicely.

"I'm not playing boxing."

"Space Chairs?"

"No."

"Coughing?"

"Maybe."

"Kicking then."

"I suppose..."

"You loved that game before. We could see if we can cough and kick at the same time."

"Do you think we could do that?" he asked sounding a little more upbeat.

"No reason not, we won't know unless we try."

"Okay, I'll give it a go, only for a little while though."

Result. We were on playing terms again.

"Oh, I feel flutters again," our mother chuckled from the outside. We both laughed and put more effort into the coughs and kicks.

"Maybe something I ate disagrees with my little girl," she said. We both dismissed her reference to me, though I saw Morcan smiling trying to avoid my view of him.

I faked a laugh. "No Mother, the prune juice was last week," I said, pretending to everyone I was not bothered. The pretending did not work as I realised deep down it was time to do something about it.

We had kicked for weeks on end because every time we did our mother changed her foods, and it made unborn existence more interesting as it guaranteed more variety in the grub department. We eventually stopped our kicking when we got bigger, not only because things got tight in there, but because she had turned our every kick into another tiresome drama.

I had wondered whether one of my theories about my mother could have been wrong. Could someone who exhibited so much drama have been one of them? She could not have been, could she? If she was, she would have known there were two babies from the beginning. I wished I had known then. Maybe I did know and maybe I had forgotten. Maybe she had not known herself. For what reason had I chosen her? Why had I forgotten already? Was my choosing of her so insignificant that it could fade so easily from my memories?

Internal questioning had seemed to overpower me and the thoughts imposed on me seemed to be overruling my joyful soul.

CHAPTER THREE

Gerry Daly could hide nothing from me. I knew his every movement; everything he did, everything he said, everything he had seen, everything he had heard and every thought that he ever had. He had no secrets that I did not know about. Every experience and memory he collected throughout his life was stored in my personal database of knowledge. I knew every aspect of his existence in detail.

Gerry was born privileged. He came to be in a wealthy farming family on Friday afternoon September thirteenth, 1957; in the seaside and fishing village of Upperton, on the south east coast of Ireland. He was 'fierce brainy altogether,' as his mother used to say, and, 'Gerry was frequently in his bedroom with his nose stuck in a book.' He was the eldest of a large family of eight siblings, four boys and four girls, and he was expected to inherit his family's five hundred acre farm, something that became the source of contention in his mid-twenties. Land was the gold of the Daly household.

Despite the fact Gerry had brains enough to go onto university, he never applied himself to any particular studies, he did not have to bother as he knew one day he would own the majority of his father's fortune, and so in his earlier years he kept himself living happily from his parents' income. His spent those years caring for horses, cattle, pigs, and sheep; he learned an appreciation of all God's creatures and developed an affinity with nature. He certainly had a love of the land, but he loved reading books more and even dreamed about writing his own book some day. He did not have the motivation to do it, he certainly did not need the money, and it was normal to 'accept your lot' and not to be concerned with any other 'high-flying notions.' That was the result of an upbringing in a religious family, an education in a strictly religious school and living in a religious community. The whole community knew for certain that whatever happened was what God had in store for them.

And Gerry did not understand choice any more than he understood courage. The only thing I did not know was whether it had been his suppressed creative desires or his meeting with Tessa that accelerated his downfall. The reason I did not know was because Gerry was not certain himself, and it was hard to tell which choice exactly had been the catalyst that propelled his demise. In the latter half of his life, Gerry had seemed to live like Moses who wandered around in the wilderness for several years, but in contrast to Moses, who had a major purpose, Gerry had lost sight of his mission and he had no idea where he was heading.

On September sixteenth 2007, three days after Gerry had turned fifty, he was having one of his regular 'tipples' of six pints of Guinness followed by six Jameson's at Johnny Riordain's pub near the fishing pier in Upperton. His youthful blond curls were long gone and replaced with short, stubbly grey hair, and his bloated red cheeks had little purple thread veins from all the whiskey he stored on his insides. He had no longer cared about his appearance, he believed he did not have to; he still thought he held the charisma and good looks of his younger years.

Gerry and Johnny had been best friends since childhood; and despite being older than Gerry, Johnny still maintained a handsome exterior at fifty-two. He looked almost identical to the man he was in his late twenties, except for his dark hair having greyed slightly on top of his tall and lean muscular figure and face. There was not a trace of a wrinkle in sight and as strange as it had appeared, Johnny had not seemed to have aged one morsel. And even though Gerry and Johnny were physical opposites in their fifties, they both maintained large, round blue eyes like opaque windows into the wonderful souls that lay beneath each set. Despite this Johnny had never married, apparently the Riordain family always had a notion that local women were only interested in what Johnny had to financially offer. This suited Gerry perfectly as it meant he had the full and undivided devotion of Johnny's friendship.

Johnny's pub was perfect for those who were not bothered by the old carpets and threadbare seats, not to mention the green slime which was a permanent fixture in the men's toilets. It was rare to find tourists in the pub despite the many foreigners that frequented this tourist village on one of their 'seeing Ireland' holidays, but Johnny did his best to promote it and even paid one pub reviewer to write a good, solid review of his pub which said, 'The small window in the men's toilet sports one of the best views of the sea.' Johnny pinned it up on the front door of his pub with pride.

Guinness, Heineken and a selection of three or four spirits were the only drinks on offer in the bar. Non-alcoholic beverages such as small bottles of tonic water, ginger ale and lemonade mixers were only available to complement gin, vodka or brandy. Whiskey came straight up. On some occasions it was possible to get a coke accompaniment if Johnny had a spare litre knocking about in the back area. But in general he had a tendency not to offer minerals, discouraging people from bringing children into the pub, something he considered an immoral thing to do; especially since most of the locals still smoked in the bar despite the smoking ban, a law which had been in force in Ireland for three and a half years at that time.

Gerry had been sitting upright on his bar stool in a haze of smoke; his arms were folded across his upper chest area and rested on his stomach that formed the shelf underneath. He nodded at Johnny before he nodded at the cloudy and empty pint glass in front of him, a clear indication that he had been waiting for a replacement to arrive. When it did, he started his usual ritual and studied it carefully; three, four, five minutes passed to let it settle, until finally one pint of Guinness as black as soot with a one inch creamy head was staring back at him. With this confirmation, he lifted the glass and sunk the pint down his gullet in one gulp. He suddenly felt dizzy and disorientated.

Gerry had assumed the drink was the cause of his hallucination. When he noticed her she was standing opposite him, lingering, smiling gently, surrounded by a gold band which seemed to embrace him. He did not know what stopped her, it was not him. She stirred a sensation in him, a stimulation he had not felt in a long time. Her radiant face seemed to say, 'kiss me, kiss me,' but he was fearfully resolute not to, he suspected his wife would track him down, string him up and hang him out to dry.

"The wife was on the phone again, Gerry," Johnny shouted from inside the bar area, "Jaysus, Gerry, she's like a lunatic raving on, she wants you home now."

Gerry was in a daze. He was engrossed. He was smiling into what appeared to be thin air. He felt peace, even joy.

"Jaysus, Gerry, did you hear me?" Johnny shouted again, "I warned you about marrying her, I don't know how you deal with her every day when you go home."

It was difficult to say how this vision actually appeared before him. All Gerry saw was a great ball of energy; intense, electrifying energy. Energy is at times difficult to detect and impossible to see, but in a casual and unassuming manner she exhibited it, and Gerry felt he could not be protected from it. As she stood opposite the bar, he was consciously aware that no wooden object could stop the penetration of her circular vibrations in his direction; constructing an electric fence would have been a walk in the park for her intense, yet sweet, energy orbits.

"Do not be afraid, it's me, it's Fragrance," the energy ball said softly.

"I'm afraid of no one," Gerry replied defiantly.

"That's the spirit, Gerry," Johnny said.

Conversing with an energy ball was not usual in Johnny Riordain's pub, but she was the most beautiful ball of womanly energy Gerry had seen in a long time, and for several moments he was truly a puppet to her energy. Gerry still considered himself fairly easy on the eye, so he could not blame her when her glistening eyes beckoned him forward and he found himself deteriorating to the point where he could not resist. He suddenly lost all reality and senses. He could not speak, think, stand or understand as he attempted to leave with her.

Johnny looked at him with confusion. "Are you alright, man?" he asked, but there was no response, and silen'   '
descended upon the entire pub while everyone watched Ireland football championships. Fragrance was co/

though, and she had let Gerry vacantly view the screen behind the bar through her transparent body. It had only been after four o'clock when Gerry said with vague awareness, "come on Cork," and with that he fell in a heap onto the floor. The entire place erupted around him when Cork scored, but to Gerry, the smoky stale air exhibited the calmness of a library as though he had been watching a silent black and white movie.

"It's okay, it's me, I am here to help you transition," Fragrance said softly.

"Did they score?" Gerry asked.

"Come with me and your questions will be answered," she replied.

"Rightio," Gerry pretended, "go where?" He was convinced his wife was trying to test him.

"All will be revealed, you are safe," she responded.

Gerry laughed. "Did I kick the bucket?" he asked.

"Do not have any more concern for human issues."

"Feck that; I am no humanitarian, where are we off to?" he asked, as he thought more seriously.

"Your rehabilitation will begin shortly," Fragrance said.

Gerry thought he shook his head, "what? What are you on about? I know I love my few pints but I'm no alcoholic," he stated.

"You must be re-orientated back to the Realm."

"You're insane! And there was I thinking to myself that you were a fierce lovely lady altogether," and then he quickly added, "in a friendly way like."

"It will be easier if you don't object."

"God help me," he cried, "I am being abducted by aliens."

"Yes, God is your friend."

"Are you one of those crop circle people?" he asked suspiciously.

"We know how you cared for the crops and all creatures, you will be rewarded."

"Listen here now, I am a simple fellow, couldn't you abduct one of those university educated ones?" he asked with a dim hope.

"We have, and now it is your turn," she replied.

"Are ye going to stick probes in me?"

"Let go of your mind; you are safe."

"It doesn't feel too safe from where I'm standing; what the hell! I'm floating!"

"We must make haste," she said encouragingly. "I told you, I'm not a drunkard, and I'm sorry for sneaking all those whiskeys while the wife wasn't looking. She was a desperately hard woman to live with, and sure I did no harm to anyone, except myself," he protested in his defence.

"Don't fight it; we must leave immediately," she said firmly.

"I'm telling you woman, you don't want me. The doctor said I was a heart attack waiting to happen," he begged.

"It has," Fragrance concluded.

The room felt vacant and sterile. Fragrance had delivered him home to the Realm. Gerry sat silently in his assigned quarters, room three-zero-one. He sat mostly quiet, for twelve days in fact. And despite his many years of beer investment, Gerry no longer saw his well developed gut, or feet, or legs, or knees. In fact, he realised he did not seem to have any solid form, he appeared to be a hazy outline of the man he was, as though someone had traced around his body with smudged charcoal and he was the opaque shadow contained within its boundary.

Fragrance was the only person he spoke to at the beginning, only because he had to, she had been assigned as his soul coach. Soul coaching in the Realm had been a bit of exploitation for souls who did not know any better, a lot of soul coaches never experienced anything near what they had coached others to do, quite a few of them never 'walked their talk', they were in it for the status it gave them in the Realm.

When Gerry realised finally that he was released back to the Realm, a Realm that he had previously known as love and tranquillity, he noticed that something was amiss; the Realm seemed to have changed somehow. He observed that things had certainly progressed, or more correctly regressed as he later learned, from the Realm he had experienced on so many previous occasions. He experienced solitude, yet an itching feeling in what was left of his being told him he was not alone. He sensed several other presences, and yet he had been unable to view any other clear forms. Even the room where he sat seemed to lack any clear dimensions, only a glowing golden light reached out as far as he could view. It all appeared above board, but he could not shake the feeling that he was being watched, and he sensed fear. He was unclear as to whether that fear was his own or of those that were monitoring him, so he took the cowardly option and decided to ignore his feelings, something he had learned to do well during the latter half of his life.

Gerry quickly made the decision to watch the life he had left behind, I knew it was to occupy his thoughts and divert his attention from his then reality. And while he watched the antics of his relatives carefully, as their emotions varied between mourning his death and perking their ears up at the mention of his will, Gerry had thought his funeral was the height of entertainment. He had known his money would serve them no goodness, he knew not one of them had an ounce of passionate creativity in their bodies.

Gerry noticed that Tessa, his wife, had mourned the most or so it appeared externally. She was still a young woman at forty-nine and still quite pleasing on the eye at first glance, and she looked only like a slightly older version of the good looking woman he had met when he was twenty-six. However, in Gerry's biased opinion he had known that it only took a few minutes in her presence to realise that beauty was skin deep.

Johnny Riordain's expression showed he had been genuinely touched by Gerry's death and his mutterings indicated he had felt slightly responsible because the whole death episode had happened inside his pub. He could not apologise enough to Tessa, and Johnny had even poured the contents of a litre bottle of special reserve twelve-year-old whiskey over the mound of earth that covered Gerry's grave, telling Gerry it was 'a final one for the road.' Gerry had smiled as he watched, wishing for one moment he was actually still under that pile of soil as he yearned for one small taste of the devil's drink, as he had on occasions called it.

He had watched as Tessa agreed to a traditional Irish wake, not very common at that time in the early twenty-first century; however, pressure from Gerry's brothers convinced her it was what Gerry would have wanted. Gerry liked a party, especially ones with plenty of drink, so he did not object; in fact he had encouraged them as he had learned quickly that even from his position in the Realm it was possible for him to plant thoughts into the minds of the living. That had excited him as he wondered how that might prove useful, in fact he wondered what else he could do while confined in his rehabilitation room, three-zero-one.

"Careful now," Fragrance had warned as Gerry's mind continued to wander. Fragrance seemed to have developed a habit of interrupting him with sudden commands which appeared from nowhere.

"I wasn't doing a thing," Gerry replied, "just having a great front seat view of my funeral."

"Let it go," she insisted, "I know it is early days yet and understandably you are still in a state of confusion, but it is okay, I am here to help you."

"Fair enough," he said dismissively and he had hoped she would leave.

"I have come to ask you what you know, and specifically what you remember," Fragrance said softly.

Gerry looked surprised. "Where do you want me to start?"

"Your name would be a start," she said.

"Gerry," Gerry answered easily and he felt confident he got full marks on that one.

Fragrance persisted. "What is your name?" she asked again softly.

Gerry felt annoyed by her stupendous repetition of the same question. "Gerry," he said again. "G – E – R – R – Y."

"Don't treat me like I am stupid," she said.

"What do you want me to say?"

"I want you to tell me your name."

"Gerald?"

"Don't play with me," she warned.

"Ger then, will that do?" he asked.

"Don't think I will tire of this," she replied, seemingly patient.

"What are you on about woman? Look, I don't know, the lads down the pub had several names for me, but we could be here all day if I had to go through them all," he answered honestly.

"What is the name you have been given?" she asked.

"Gerald Michael Mary Gabriel Anthony Daly," Gerry confirmed with embarrassment. He had never told another soul that before. "Though I am not sure if it was the mother or the father that came up with that string of names," he added.

"I understand this is difficult for you," she said with empathy, "take your time and carefully think about it, sometimes the realisation of who you are can take a few days."

"Where are they anyway?" Gerry asked.

"Who?"

"The old man and old woman."

Fragrance smiled. "They are happy," she said.

"So they are not with the fellow below then?" Gerry asked tilting his thoughts beneath his invisible feet.

"There is no fellow below," she confirmed.

"Well, that's good to know, unless of course you are tricking me," Gerry replied in a questioning tone.

"There are no tricks, you are back in Realm One, you loved it here before, and you'll come round in a few days."

"If you see them, will you tell them to pop in for a visit?" he asked.

"Who shall I tell wants to see them?"

"Gerry, of course! Their eldest son."

"I will tell them when you tell me who you really are, clearly we have work to do first," she said. Fragrance departed and Gerry thought that she was clearly insane. He laughed to himself as he wondered if this was his punishment and if it was, 'they' could think again. Gerry had known of several tactics to handle insane women, after all he had several earthly years married to 'Tessa the Tempest.' Gerry sighed before he returned to finish watching the movie of his funeral.

"I remember the day we met as though it was only yesterday," Tessa was telling Johnny.

"He was a great man, so he was, he was indeed a great fellow, he wouldn't harm a fly," Johnny said as he shook his head from side to side and looked downwards and avoided Tessa's view.

"I still remember the day he walked into my office," Tessa continued to say.

Johnny continued to converse with the ground. "It's an awful pity, such a young man with everything to live for," he said.

"He wore a pink shirt and his blond hair was still soggy as though he was just out of a bath," Tessa said, as she looked upwards to the heavens.

"I suppose 'The Man' above has His own reasons for taking him back so early," Johnny replied.

But Tessa persisted with her reminiscence as though Johnny was interested. "He seemed so awkward that day as I led him to the meeting room, but we clicked immediately with each other," she lied.

"Well, God moves in mysterious ways," Johnny said.

"He was so mysterious, a country boy looking for a solicitor, at first glance you would think he didn't have a penny to his name," Tessa said seriously.

Johnny remained focused firmly on his feet as though he had been convinced that Gerry was beneath them. "We never know what's around the corner, live life to the full, that's what I say," he said.

"Jaysus, Johnny, would you ever lift your head up," Gerry shouted from the Realms, "I got away from her, you know what she is like, this is celebration time." Johnny immediately tilted his head right up and caught Tessa's eye. Gerry's shadow jumped back as he wondered if Johnny had actually heard him.

"That's right, Johnny," Gerry continued to say in a more soft tone, "now move away from her." Johnny shuffled on his feet. "That's right, you know you can hear me," Gerry instructed in a soft and deep tone. Johnny had looked very uneasy as his shuffle evolved into a soft rocking motion and he edged further from Tessa.

"I knew from that very instant that he was the man I was going to marry," Tessa continued to say.

"Do you think he can hear us?" Johnny asked in an awkward manner.

"Of course not," she retorted instantly as though she had forgotten her mournful wife act temporarily.

"Don't listen to her, of course I can hear yah, Johnny," Gerry interrupted.

"I suppose it's only natural to find it hard to let go," Johnny said, "I can still hear him in my head, isn't that funny!"

"Not funny, it's true. Johnny, you told me once that your own dog can plant thoughts into your head, isn't that right?" Gerry said with encouragement.

"Of course it's funny, no one can hear him now," Tessa said, "it's not possible, I've done the Christian thing and as hard as it is, I've decided to let him go, let him rest in peace, Johnny."

"Of course Tessa can't hear me," Gerry said with frustration, "I wouldn't be found dead talking with her again."

"I suppose you're right, Tessa," Johnny said. "He's in peace now."

"Well, not entirely," Gerry said with some serenity, "but I am getting there, apparently there are a few more days of rehabilitation, I suppose if I say something like 'my name is Gerry the alcoholic', they'll let me out of here, but then again I don't know, I am on unfamiliar territory here. Things seem to have changed since I was in the Realm before."

"Yes, Johnny, and if you are feeling bad, think of how I feel being left a widow at such a young age, I never planned for this," Tessa said.

"You planned for everything else though," Gerry muttered.

Johnny jerked slightly, "I know, I know, I am being insensitive, sorry Tessa," he apologised. "I suppose it's because Gerry spent so much time down my pub it's hard to think he's gone."

Her tone immediately changed into a bark, "no one needs reminding of the amount of time he spent in your pub, and the amount of lies you told me when I was ringing down to you looking for him, a poor woman home alone with no husband and you and your whiskey holding him hostage. NO Johnny! No one wants to hear the likes of that now."

Johnny bowed his head again. "Sorry Tessa," he said sheepishly. "Oh, come on, Johnny, you know well enough how she tricked me first day," Gerry said. Johnny started to say something. "No, Johnny, don't say a thing, you don't want to draw her on you now," Gerry interrupted. Johnny closed his mouth. "You know you can hear me, you know you're not crazy," Gerry repeated in a deep, resonating tone. Johnny looked as though he was going crazy; he developed a sudden and nervous twitch. "I'll get my coat, Tessa, and I'll see you for the removal tomorrow," he said as he swiftly moved out of the house and into his car.

Gerry continued to speak to Johnny as he drove home. "Johnny, you know she is the crazy one, come on man; think of your dog, Danny, you know that look he gives you when he wants some grub, you told me that even your dog can plant thoughts in your head when he wants feeding, that mournful look he gives you as he moves his head from your face to his empty bowl.

"Danny even does that paw movement, when he flaps it against your trouser legs when he wants to go out to the bushes; you told me that Danny communicates all his doggy thoughts to you," Gerry continued, "now if a dog can plant thoughts in your head, doesn't it make sense that your dead friend can also?"

It had seemed that even in death, Gerry chose to lean on Johnny as his crutch, something he had learned well to do in the latter part of his life.

Johnny pulled his car up outside the front door of his pub, and as he walked inside, Danny surrounded Johnny's legs as his little terrier paws jumped over and back in front of Johnny. The barmaid asked him how Tessa was, Johnny responded by asking whether anyone had fed Danny yet. Danny had that pitiful look on his face as he searched Johnny's. "Yes, Danny boy, I know you're hungry, Pedigree Chum alright for yah?" he asked, as he walked nervously through the bar into his private living area, ignoring his customers and noticing only Danny's positive nod of confirmation.

CHAPTER FOUR

"Oh Tessa, I am sorry," Johnny's younger sister, Marie Riordain had said, as she wiped the green liquid her twelve-year-old son had just sneezed onto Gerry's dead body. "Don't worry about it," Gerry said easily, "I'm not in there. See here; look; I'm here; right behind you." He channelled his voice thoughts directly into the twelve-year-old's right ear, "BOO!" Gerry shouted. The child ignored him with his head buried deeply into his snot-storing sleeve, presumably using some fresh stuff to soften the already cardboard-hardened deposits from earlier.

"Don't do that, and pay your respects," Marie chided. Tessa grimaced, but Gerry was self-absorbed in amusement as he watched from his heavenly balcony view.

"It's not like Gerry was any stranger to a few strange bogies," the child said, "sure, he didn't know half the time what was happening up his own nose." The young lad could not have said anything more truly; Gerry had in fact been oblivious most evenings when he was alive, indulging himself in alcohol to obliterate the reality of the choices he had made. It was easier for him to do that, rather than confront the fact that his experience of life was the sole result of his decisions, there was no one else to blame. And staying true to that past behaviour, Gerry had continued to gratify himself in the Realm, watching the 'movies' of his funeral as his new form of escape, and he had clearly assigned himself an invisible starring role in the whole performance; a tactic to delay the acknowledgement that he did not seem to be in the same part of the Realm that he had been in before, that place where he had originated from, unless changes had been made and Gerry did not like change. He had still sensed a fear, but he chose to dismiss it; the only difference was that in Realm One, he would not be allowed to neglect his new reality for long.

36

"That's enough!" Marie said as she scolded her young son. "Sorry Tessa, Gerry was a great man altogether." Then Marie put her head down as she shuffled her son in front of her towards the door. Gerry had known Marie would not get into the slightest situation of confrontation with Tessa. Tessa was a match for Marie's sometimes unattractive manners and it appeared that Marie felt inferior to Tessa at times.

Gerry and Marie had grown up together as she was only a month younger than him; and as most locals did, Gerry had referred to her throughout her life as Marie Riordain, even though she had married another local and friend of Gerry's, Bertie Maher in her mid-twenties. Despite her regular unmannerly outbursts, Gerry had always viewed Marie as a great woman since she enjoyed her pints as much as the next man, and in that sense it was hard for Gerry to have ever thought of her as anything other than one of the lads.

Gerry's body had been exposed in an open coffin in the parlour room of his old house. There were four reception rooms in total, the kitchen, the living room, the conservatory and the parlour. The parlour was considered the second living room of the house, and it was reserved for fine occasions such as Christmas dinner, Easter or when important guests or relatives arrived; or in this case for Gerry's wake. It had made him feel important. It was decorated in expensive Laura Ashley wallpaper, oak wooden floorboards, and contemporary furniture that was uncomfortable to sit on, impractical furniture for an impractical wife.

Gerry had been waked for three days and three nights and in a typical traditional Irish style, it was the duty of visitors and relatives alike to 'look over' the body for safe transition, at no point was the body to be left unattended, not even overnight, not until the coffin was closed and Gerry was taken to the parish church for his funeral mass and burial in the adjoining graveyard. Most of his pub friends had stayed during the nights to drink with Gerry's remains and there had been mighty story telling during those nights; not even Tessa could complain because it was accepted tradition. The party was glorious and Gerry loved it.

Tessa had revolved between the four rooms as she absorbed sympathies from all who came, and depending on which room she was in the party would quieten with her presence, so typically the hardened drinkers revolved between the rooms where she was not. Gerry followed them even though he could clearly see that some people only came for the free drink; not that he minded, he would have done the same himself.

On the third evening of his wake, the priest came and conducted the traditional Catholic removal prayers, these prayers were always held on the evening before the final funeral mass and burial. Gerry's body was already turning green from three days of dead body exposure, and most, with the exception of Tessa, had been too drunk to notice.

On that final night, Johnny, Johnny's dog Danny, Marie and her husband Bertie had stayed awake overnight attending Gerry's body to send him on his way, or so they had said. Gerry's brothers and two of his sisters retired early in preparation for the impending funeral the following day, and only the youngest, Gerry's twin sisters remained in a semi-asleep state as they lay on a couch in front of the heat of the open fire. It had been after two AM when their story telling started, and Gerry's hidden ears perked up listening into everything that was said. The room grew dimmer and the conversation more reflective as the hot coals from the open fire in the parlour room dulled to a purple red.

"Where do you think he is now?" Bertie asked Marie. Gerry had known Bertie had a curious nature, but while his mind was known to constantly churn out new ideas, his hands remained idle. As strange as it had sounded, no one in the community actually knew what Bertie did for a living, he drove a five-year-old white transit van with external signage that changed every six months or so, sometimes those signs said 'Painter and Decorator', sometimes 'Car Valet Service', but more often than not, it said 'Bertie Maher, Proprietor and Manager.' Bertie had liked to sail through life doing as little as possible, so Marie became the family grafter, holding different temporary jobs in coffee shops and supermarkets to make ends meet. Despite all this

Bertie and Marie had a wonderful relationship; you never found one drinking without the other. But Bertie had hidden talents that waited patiently to be revealed, and when they would, even Bertie would be surprised by his own natural abilities.

"Probably still here with us," Marie responded in a slurred, half-hearted laugh.

"You could be right," Johnny said seriously. Danny barked in confirmation.

"Shut up yah fool, if you wake Tessa up, she'll throw you out," Johnny warned Danny. Danny turned his head sideways and looked straight into Johnny's eyes with a look of confusion. "Tessa doesn't like dogs on her furniture, so be quiet or we'll all be thrown out," Johnny said. Danny stretched out on the chair as he tucked his head between his paws and his serious eyes told Johnny that he had understood.

"Do you think he died happy?" Bertie asked.

Johnny nodded. "There was a look of relief on his face before he fell off the bar stool," he said.

"Do you think he was dead before he hit the ground, Johnny?" Bertie enquired.

"Oh I'd say he was, the poor man looked like he was struck by lightning," Johnny confirmed.

"Happy lightning? Is that what you mean?" Bertie continued.

"All Gerry wanted was peace and I'd say the least the Man above gave him was that," Marie answered.

"Fair summation," Gerry said, not thinking anyone could hear in their cloud of alcohol.

"Fair summation I suppose," Johnny said.

"Johnny, can you hear me?" Gerry asked in surprise.

"No," Johnny said.

"No; what?" Marie asked.

"No, not a fair summation, is that it?" Bertie asked.

"Agh, he has peace alright," Marie said as she nodded at Bertie.

"Well, it's better than before, I'll tell you that," Gerry said.

"Sure it couldn't be worse for him than before," Johnny said.

"Yes," Gerry said with excitement. "That's right, there you go, keep listening to me Johnny. I've no idea how you are doing it, but it is certainly entertaining."

Johnny looked more animated. "I'd even say there was a look of joy on his face before he fell," he said.

"Isn't that lovely," Bertie said, as he looked fondly at his reflection in his whiskey glass. The image of a round red face with ginger hair that sat on top reciprocated his grin.

"Agh, it is lovely," Marie agreed as she raised her glass to her face to see how much was left in it.

"I'd say he's as happy as a pig in muck now, sure isn't he with his mother and father now," Bertie added.

"He took it bad when his father went," Johnny said as he shook his head slowly.

"Well, hopefully Fragrance is bringing them to visit me in my rehab tomorrow," Gerry replied in an attempt to comfort Johnny.

Marie stared into open space. "Do you think he is with them? Like, now?" she questioned.

"In a day or so," Johnny said confidently.

"You seem so sure, Johnny," Bertie said, "I suppose you knew him inside out; you were a great friend to him."

"Of course I'm sure, everyone knows it takes three or four days to transition into heaven, do you not listen to the priest at mass?" Johnny said.

"It's true alright," Marie agreed. Gerry's ears had perked higher as he wondered if this could have been the explanation for the strangeness of the Realm he had been experiencing, he wondered if he actually was in some sort of transition. He considered the possibility that the fear he sensed may have actually been confusion in passing. He liked the idea of that option and to reinforce his new theory he scolded himself out loud for not listening to the sermons in mass. He then chose to convince himself of this new belief, it was better than the alternative.

"Gerry was never one to listen to priests," Johnny said.

"No, not after his encounter with the Protestant woman he met, he was a completely different man when she was in his life," Marie responded.

"Be quiet woman, we promised Gerry we would never mention that again," Bertie shushed.

"We're not. He's dead. He can't hear us," Marie said curtly.

"Yes, I can," Gerry sang.

"Agh, be respectful now sister, his body is still in the room with us," Johnny reminded her.

"Lighten up lads, all I am saying is that Gerry was different when he was with her, and if his Uncle Joseph had not interfered in Gerry's family business, Gerry would be married to the English woman now, rather than ending up with 'Tessa the Tempest'," Marie said in defence.

"Marie, you don't know what exactly happened," Johnny said.

"Yes I do," she said as she sat upright.

Bertie nodded in her direction with large, round eyes that said 'shut up'. "No, you do not," he said in a monotone.

"There's no point in shutting me up, Bertie, Gerry's gone now so it doesn't matter."

Johnny shook his head again as he leaned towards Bertie. "I don't believe you Bertie, of all the lads, I don't believe it," he said, "you've told Marie what Gerry told us in confidence."

Bertie looked guilty. "It's easy for you to say that Johnny, you're not married, you have no clue how women can get stuff out of a man, no matter how hard you try to keep stuff from them," he replied in defence.

"Fair enough I suppose, Tessa used to extract stuff from me too unwittingly," Gerry said calmly.

"Fair enough," Johnny found himself saying.

"Besides, everyone knew he was ready to take off with her to England, Bertie just gave me the details," Marie added confidently.

"Marie is as sound as a pound," Bertie added sheepishly, "she'd tell no one." The weather-beaten lines on Marie's face deepened underneath her spiky salt and pepper hair as her mouth widened into a drunken grin. Then Gerry grinned back, and Johnny followed suit as he managed a slight smile also.

"How about Tessa? She's free now, Johnny," Bertie slurred sarcastically.

"I think I'd prefer to spend my days searching for Gerry's English woman, wherever she is now," Johnny responded, "the lovely, Grace."

Gerry felt paralysed into silence, he had not heard Grace's name mentioned in twenty-three years and he had not expected to do so soon again.

"I wonder if she's ever given Gerry another thought," Bertie said philosophically.

"Maybe we should find her; do you think she'd want to know Gerry is dead?" Marie suggested with alcohol-induced enthusiasm. Everyone including Danny dismissed her. Gerry felt numb, 'I wonder,' he thought.

"I think we should find more whiskey," Johnny suggested.

"I think you're right," Bertie agreed as he got up to do the honours. "To Gerry," he said as he raised his glass after refilling them all. "To Gerry," Johnny repeated. "To Gerry, and peace, and love," Marie said slowly, as tears started to blur the red grids that veiled her drunken eyes. Danny barked once with his head upright and the newly silenced Gerry threw one backward glance as he drifted from the presence of his friends on that final occasion that they had all been together.

CHAPTER FIVE

"Good morning," Fragrance said in a chirpy tone. Gerry disliked the way Fragrance generally announced herself. He never knew how long she could have been lingering before he became consciously aware of her presence.

"You know who you are, you are ready to leave," she continued softly.

Gerry had thought he knew who he really was and where he had come from. And Fragrance was confident he knew. She did not force it out of him. They were both content in this knowing, and Gerry chose to discard any further underlying uneasiness; in fact he had learned to grow curious secretly. There was hope for him.

Gerry was released from room three-zero-one on day twelve in the Realm. Gerry was rehabilitated; he was reoriented back into Realm One. Fragrance smiled at a job well done.

CHAPTER SIX

"" Morcan, wake up; quick; turn around, hurry, hurry up;
now Morcan! They're ready," I cried urgently as I tried to
kick him gently. Morcan's lower body floated over mine.
"Move," I shouted. "They'll think we're Siamese twins."
"Wha! What, where am I?" he asked sleepily.
"Just go to my side, and smile, smile for the camera, will you
please?" I begged.
"It looks like two very healthy babies," a female voice from
the outside said.
"Yes, YES!" I said with what I thought was an over-excited
punch in the air fluid that surrounded us.
"See, Charlotte, how great this is," Daddy Joe said, "two for
the price of one." He seemed thrilled, "now we know for sure."
His voice was shaking, happy shakes.
"Don't say it, Joe, not now," Mother warned him between
her happy tears.
"What?" he said innocently, "that your psychic is a charla-
tan and that I told you the scan would tell us for sure?"
"I only rang them once," Mother said defensively.
"I would say you are approximately thirteen weeks preg-
nant," the female voice said in a happy tone. "Thanks nurse,"
Mother replied joyfully.
"Not a bad estimation really, we've actually been here eighty-
nine days and six point eight hours, so you're not too far out,"
I said in earnest confirmation.
"Why do you have to be exact?" Morcan asked.
"It's my nature. It's important to question things, and back
up statements with facts," I said factually.
"Okay, whatever; want to play a game?" he asked.
"In a minute, shush!" I said.
"I know that Charlotte, love, but your psychic did tell you
that we were having one baby girl," we heard Daddy Joe say in
a teasing tone.

"Joe, I did always feel that there were two babies," she said quietly, "I never said it though because I thought I was imagining it."
"Of course you knew, love," Daddy Joe replied fondly. "I should trust my intuition more," she said as though she was speaking to herself.
"Would you like to know the sex of your babies?" the nurse asked, "I can zoom in more closely and tell you if you like."
"YES, yes; they do!" I shouted.
"I'm not sure," Daddy Joe said, though I could detect a slight eagerness in his voice.
"Oh come on Joe, we'll know sooner or later anyway, why not sooner?" Mother added encouragingly. There was a temporary silence where I assumed that Daddy Joe nodded a go ahead signal as Mother added enthusiastically, "oh go on, yes please nurse; we can't wait."
I got over-excited and flipped in two in a twirl, knowing that soon they would know the truth, that we were two boys. I then got knotted with Morcan and his legs stuck like Velcro to my lower half. The nurse confirmed a boy. I tried to push Morcan off from me as I heard the nurse say she could not see the genital area of the second baby. I panicked, and the more I twisted the more Morcan seemed to stick to me and the bigger the tangle got. I shouted at Morcan. He froze. I froze. The knot got worse as if it took on a life of its own. Silence started on the outside. Morcan stiffened more. I pushed him away but I also moved with him as we floated around together as though we were one.
"The babies are in a little distress," the nurse said quickly.
"Are they okay?" Mother and Daddy Joe both asked anxiously.
"They will be fine," the nurse replied, "I think you should rest, Mrs. Johnson."
"I think I know anyway," Mother said calmly.
"So tell the rest, Mother," I said as I waited patiently, still glued to Morcan.
"I'm just happy that we have two healthy babies," Daddy Joe said.

"No, I know the sex of the second baby," Mother said very confidently.

"Okay love, that's good, you need to rest now," Daddy Joe said in a slightly patronising tone.

"Your husband is right, I think you need to rest," the nurse repeated.

"The second baby is a ...." Mother started to say.

"Let it be a surprise love, please, now rest, honey," Daddy Joe interrupted calmly.

"At least she knows there are two of us," Morcan said sleepily.

"Don't you dare fall asleep again, Morcan? Do you hear me?" I said as I raised my tone and tried to shake him. We both shook.

"Yes, yes, maybe a little rest before we tackle this knot," he said sounding sleepier.

"You are not going to snooze stuck to me, come on, how are we going to play if we are glued together?" I asked.

"I'm too tired to play," he said as his voice trailed off.

"Great. Just fantastic! I'll undo this knot on my own," I said determined. But then Mother fell asleep and as I listened to the soothing beat of her happy heart, I also fell into a trance.

"Yes, I spoke to one of your colleagues about two months ago," Mother was saying as I woke to find myself and Morcan magically freed of our knot. Mother was on her transmitter again. Morcan was still sleeping.

"I want to take out a subscription, but I have a few questions first," Mother continued to say.

"That's what we are here for," the lady on the other end said nicely.

"Your colleague told me that I was expecting a little girl, but I've just had a scan and I actually have twins," Mother said.

"How wonderful, congratulations," the lady responded.

"I am just wondering how this mistake may have happened, you see, your colleague seemed so confident about one baby girl, and, well, I know now I am expecting one boy and one girl," Mother said as though she was slightly suspicious. I remained silent as by then I had grown accustomed to being confused for a woman.

"Sometimes we can have interference when an expectant woman really wants one gender or another," the lady said.

"But your 'Psychic Pregscan' was sure there was only one," Mother said.

"Were you sure you were pregnant when you called?" the lady asked.

"No, I was only four weeks gone, I had slight suspicions," Mother answered.

"And was 'Psychic Pregscan' correct when they confirmed your pregnancy?"

"Well yes, yes of course they were," Mother answered sounding more upbeat.

"There you go then," the lady said in confirmation, "we are rarely wrong."

"But you told me I was having one baby. I guess the reason I am asking is because I don't want any of my own thoughts to interfere with your information going forward, that way I can be certain that you are picking the correct thoughts, maybe I am not explaining myself correctly," Mother said as though she was apologising.

"You are explaining well, just relax and let us do the work," the lady replied reassuringly.

"It's just well... well I just... I suppose there's no way to say this but to come straight out with it, and you won't think I'm weird will you?"

"Of course not," the lady assured Mother.

"It's just that, well, I tend to have very strong emotional thoughts, and I know how these things can travel into the ether..." Mother started to explain and then paused. Silence remained on the other end. "You know... you know what I mean ... the ether, putting strong focused thoughts into the Realm," Mother said in a shy tone. I jumped up instantly. "Way to GO! Mummy Charlotte, you know the Realm? Wow!" I shouted. Morcan jerked at the sound of my cheer.

"Who said that?" Mother asked suddenly.

"Said what?" The lady asked back.

"You called her Mummy Charlotte," Morcan said to me.

"No, I didn't," I said in denial.

"Did."

"Not."

"Did."

"Shut up."

"Someone spoke, I heard a voice, like a thought planted into my head in a celebration voice," Mother said uneasily.

"She heard me," I cheered at Morcan.

"Don't be silly, you tend to only allow stuff into your head that agrees with your illegal motives," Morcan replied in a bored tone.

"Oh, never mind," Mother said dismissively, "maybe I am convincing myself of too much here."

"Please continue, I want to help you, do you want to sign for a subscription?" The lady asked.

"Yes!" our Mother and I said simultaneously.

"You did call her Mummy Charlotte before," Morcan said again.

"She knows about the Realm," I said.

"Don't be silly," Morcan said.

"I've never told anyone about my faith before, not even my husband Joe, it seems so silly," Mother said.

"Not silly, keep going Mummy Charlotte," I said.

Morcan nodded. "There you go again," he said.

"I want you to ask your guides for a little more information," Mummy Charlotte said.

"Do you know how we work?" The lady asked.

"Not exactly," Mummy Charlotte responded.

"Well, briefly, our organisation was established over one hundred and thirty-eight years ago, specifically in the summer of 2033. We each have a special contact in the Realm who guides us with all information, it is a special alliance. At the beginning our first leader was contacted by a very determined soul and out of their agreement grew this distinguished organisation," the lady explained.

"Yep, I know," I said, "I was there."

"This special soul organised a group of highly dedicated and devoted souls in the Realm," the lady continued.

"Realm One actually," I interrupted happily.

"Our first leader on earth, a very inspirational woman called Doris DaValle organised a specialised group of psychics to work with these souls on our side, it is an evolving process, a spiritual evolution, and we are devoted to building better parents and children, building world-wide communities again, and our efforts are for the bigger cause for a more friendly and supportive earth," the lady said.

"Well, sort of true I suppose, though that wasn't our original intention when we first contacted your leader, Doris," I added.

"Fragrance won't be happy," Morcan said disapprovingly.

"I am sure Fragrance won't be long letting us know," I added though I did not care less.

"So, the rumours are true then, you were involved from the beginning of the Realm 'Undercover Movement'," Morcan said.

"Well, almost the beginning, it doesn't matter now, apparently I've been punished for that," I said.

Morcan floated towards me with large, serious eyes. "Did they put you in limbo?" he asked.

"No; for God's sakes, just be quiet," I ordered.

"So as long as I don't interfere, your information is accurate?" Mummy Charlotte said excitedly to the psychic on the other end.

"Our Realm contacts are very accurate and support our cause, as I said, they initiated it," the psychic confirmed.

"How did they punish you?" Morcan asked.

"You don't want to know," I answered.

"Why?"

"It's not important, plus you do not want to get into any trouble if I tell you, isn't that right? Remember the rules, no information from the Realm on our journey," I said cleverly.

"Oh yes, you're right," Morcan confirmed immediately. I was not exactly proud of myself for doing it, playing on his fears to keep him quiet, but it worked; momentarily.

"You are having two clever little babies," the psychic said as she started her reading.

I agreed.

"One is more logical and one more creative, I am being told," she continued to say.

I agreed again.

The psychic lady laughed. "I think one of them will be a handful," she said amusingly. I agreed again.

"You couldn't have two more different children," she said. "Affirmed," I said and I relaxed as I realised the stuff I had heard was music to my ears.

"They both have a very high IQ," the psychic lady said. "I suppose," I said easily as I laughed, "there's time for Morcan to develop yet." Morcan sighed as he turned away from me.

"Something is coming in strongly, I am not sure if you want to hear it, shall I continue? It is very strong," the lady said. "YEAH!" I said, "Yes!" Mummy Charlotte said.

"One of them will have issues with their sexuality, it's really nothing to be concerned about," the lady said quietly. "Hah! That's definitely you," Morcan said as he pointed in my direction.

"Let me see," I said quickly, "we are two boys, and which one is the more sensitive of us both? Hmmm, let me think, who is the manlier of the two? I wonder now; who is fearless and who is not? It's not difficult to work out." And I pointed back at Morcan as I said, "see my point."

Morcan attempted to fold his arms. "Well, since you are so manly, what were all these manly things you did back in Realm One?" he asked.

"Not afraid to get in trouble if I tell you?" I teased.

"Of course not, I just think it's time you started backing up your own words with facts."

"Well, well, who is trying to prove themselves fearless now?" I asked.

"I have nothing to be afraid of," he replied though I detected a shake in his tone.

I poked him to tease him. "Shall I ask Fragrance to join us?"

"Be my guest," he said indifferently.

"Where is she anyway? Normally she'd be here at the first sign of interaction with the outside world," I said.

"Maybe you are not as important as you think!"

"Oh believe me, what I know is important for Fragrance's welfare and she knows it too," I assured him.

"I suppose you took your punishment like a man, this supposed punishment you won't tell me about," he said.

"Correct," I confirmed.

"So did they put you in limbo then?" he asked as if it was Groundhog Day.

"No; how many times do you have to hear it? Limbo does not exist except in your mind," I barked.

"It does."

"Limbo is only a word."

"It's a place."

"It's a state of mind."

"A place you exist in," he said confidently.

"FOR CRYING OUT LOUD, limbo is a word used by Realm One guides to enforce fear in us, to enforce laws; laws are only for the majority, laws are not for the great souls of Realm One."

"Maybe your risks were not manly enough to warrant limbo, did that ever occur to you?" Morcan said.

"No; because limbo does not exist."

"And you're sure?"

"Yes."

"Okay."

"How do you mean OKAY?" I asked.

"That's fine."

"What's fine?"

"Well, one of us has to end this conversation, it's going nowhere," Morcan said easily.

"Not able to stand your ground, is that it?"

Morcan half looked me up and down. "Incorrect," he said, "the bigger one of us two, the manlier of us two knows when to step back and rise above bickering."

"And that's you, I suppose?" I asked.

"Correct," he replied.

"Fine."

"Fine." Silence flowed between us.

"This is amazing," I heard Mummy Charlotte say.

My ears perked up. "What's amazing?" I asked.

"Oh, I wish I could tell someone," Mummy Charlotte said.

"Tell me," I begged.

"My little boy and girl will be an engineer and a fashion designer, what more could a mother ask for," Mummy Charlotte said with excitement.

"What have we missed?" I demanded to know.

Morcan sniggered. "I guess you'll be the camp fashion designer," he said. And with that comment, I relegated Mummy Charlotte back to being 'Mother' again.

"You did it again!" I accused him. "You and your limbo diversions, I won't forget it so easily this time."

"Having fun?" Fragrance interrupted.

"I was wondering when you'd join." I replied.

"What have you learned, Ariel?" she questioned.

"That my mother is highly intuitive," I said confidently, as if the thought had come out of nowhere.

CHAPTER SEVEN

On March eighteenth 1983, twenty-five-year-old Gerry was late leaving for the airport. It had been lambing season and of all the days they chose, three lambs had decided to be born. Gerry had planned only two nights away and he had thought the sheep might have obliged him and waited another few days before going into labour; he had been telling them for at least three weeks previous that he was looking forward to his first trip abroad. They obviously did not heed him and went ahead with their births that Friday morning, and his plane was leaving at eleven thirty AM.

At ten AM, his mother had the car revving in the farmyard where she waited for Gerry. He had barely enough time to quickly wash his hands and face, and as it was at least a forty minute drive to Cork airport he jumped into the back of the car dressed only in boxer shorts with the rest of his clothes bundled under his arm. The car sped through the country lanes as he dressed horizontally in the back seat and looked out the rear side window from below; he noticed that the telegraph poles on the side of the road looked like the teeth of a comb. He had a habit of seeing things in an unusual way.

Johnny and Bertie would have been frantically waiting for him in the departure lounge, the OBrienAir flight to Bristol was on schedule and when boarding was announced they must have joined the queue as there was still no sign of Gerry. Bertie would not have been happy. It was his stag weekend and probably one of his last free weekends before he married Marie the following Easter, and all he had wanted was a lads' weekend away with his best friends, Johnny and Gerry.

As Gerry went through to departures, he knew he had only twenty minutes. The OBrienAir flight from Bristol had just landed and this budget airline's reputation meant that he was guaranteed a speedy exit. When the inbound flight landed, the plane had looked like it toppled onto its side, dumped the original passengers out, and then started to shovel in the new passengers, getting ready to turn around and head back to Bristol in a speedy twenty minutes. Normally this would have been a blessing, with no messing about in airports, but Gerry had desperately wanted a visit to the toilets to freshen up. Instead, he ran to the departure gate and was the second last person to board the plane. A queerly dressed young woman with an oversized woven hat, in a large knitted cardigan and knitted shoulder bag was the last person behind him.

Bertie and Johnny were sitting at the back of the small propeller-driven plane beside the drinks trolley when Gerry had boarded, and Gerry wiped his brow, sighed and winked to the lads at the rear before he sat on one of the two remaining seats in the middle row. Johnny had waved back in his direction like a mad man, but Bertie frowned and gave an exaggerated look at his watch for Gerry's benefit. Gerry smiled as if there was no harm done and the oddly dressed knitted girl sat down beside him.

The OBrienAir plane rolled down the one airstrip that marked Cork airport as Gerry waved through the window at his mother. Of course, he could not see her and he felt like a bit of a clown, but she had told him she would stand inside the bar window that overlooked the runway, and he knew that his mother would be waving back even long after the plane rose out over Cork harbour.

"Who are you waving at?" the knitted girl had asked. She had an odd English accent that Gerry thought had only been invented for television shows.

"My mother," Gerry had responded quietly embarrassed, and as he shuffled in his seat he pretended he was only trying to get comfortable in the perfectly erect 'L' shaped seat, but then he realised he did not get comfort in exchange for a cheap air fare.

"Do you go over to Bristol often?" she asked as she beamed a smile that bore through the whites of his eyes. She had a beautiful smile underneath large round, blue-grey sparkling eyes. And as she proceeded to take her knitted covers off, she unveiled her long red fluffy flowing locks. She seemed friendly and possibly older than Gerry.

"Sorry?" Gerry said, slightly distracted.

"Do you go over and back a lot?" she asked again. And then there was a long pause as Gerry just stared in the aura of her beauty.

"Yes, over and back, you know," she repeated seemingly confused.

"Oh no, not at all," Gerry said quietly as he stared and wondered whether all English women were this stunning. He managed a smile eventually. "And you?" he finally coughed up, noticing she was still looking at him also.

"Oh no, I only came to Cork for a meeting," she answered easily.

"Oh that's grand, isn't that lovely? You like Cork then?" he asked.

"No," she confirmed, "but I couldn't get into an art college in England so I thought I'd give Ireland a go, and a teacher at the art college in Cork invited me to meet him with a view to being an understudy."

Gerry had no idea what she was talking about. "Do you knit?" he asked.

She frowned as she stiffened slightly. "No, I do sculptures," she said quickly.

"Knitted sculptures?" he asked and the words were out of his mouth before he realised what he had said.

"Of course not, what an odd thing to say, why would you ask that?" she asked, as she edged away from him.

"Agh no reason... you seem like the creative type, is that an English thing?" he said as he exhibited further evidence of his inexperience with women.

"Is what an English thing?" she asked seriously.

"Learning abroad," he said as he thought more sensibly.

"I think it's becoming more common for people to go abroad," she said as she moved further away.

"I didn't bother," he said as though she had asked him a question.

"You didn't bother what?"

"Going to college," he confirmed.

"I see, so what do you do?" she asked.

"I like writing," he said dreamily as he thought about his creative streak.

Her eyes lit up. "Wow, you're a writer, how wonderful," she said with excitement. "Have you written anything I know of?"

"How would I know?" he asked.

"How would you know what?" she asked appearing confused again.

"How would I know what you read?" Gerry said, thinking that he may have snared himself. He had only ever written in his diaries, and only his mother had seen those, not because he showed them to her but because she had a tendency to go through his stuff when she cleaned his room.

"I read lots of stuff, maybe I have come across some of your work," she said. And she rotated fully around to stare back into his eyes.

"I mainly write about nature and animals," he said truthfully.

"Where is your work published?" she asked.

"In outdoor magazines, farming journals, that sort of stuff," he lied. He was proud of himself for thinking so quickly on his feet as he realised he may have been very creative after all, although he was not proud of himself for misleading the beautiful girl beside him.

Her eyes opened wide in innocent awe. "Oh, I would not have read any of your stuff then, but it sounds so interesting, what was your last article about?" she asked.

It was not exactly an article, but his last diary entry had been about God, something he never spoke openly about, and it was out of his mouth before he could stop it.

"God?" she asked surprised.

"God in nature," Gerry said thinking quickly again.

"How wonderful, you are spiritual then?" she asked.

"I suppose I am," Gerry agreed, though he was not exactly sure what she had meant by that. He was just ecstatic that he impressed such a beautiful young woman.

"So how did it go then?" she asked.

"How did what go?" he asked, as his mind and eyes had both wandered down her body.

"Your article," she confirmed.

"Oh, shite," Gerry said, speaking his mind unintentionally as he wondered how he could invent something impressive to tell her.

"I bet it was not," she said as she smiled, "a lot of creative people have a tendency to put their own work down, it's kind of a creative lunacy, don't you agree?"

"Yes," he said quickly, though he had no clue what she was talking about. There was silence momentarily and he only spoke again after she encouraged him with a nod of her eyes.

"Creative lunacy is right, do you suffer from that also?" he asked lamely.

"No," she said firmly. "We all know God flows through us so we can create anything we put our mind to. So how did you express God in nature in your article?"

"Agh, you know, the whole thing about how people get so excited about a new road being built or a new building being erected, when the whole time these things are just small games in the parlour corner of a magnificent house where a huge party is taking place when you compare them to the magnificence of nature," Gerry said confidently without thinking, and surprised himself that he was sharing a private diary entry with a girl he had only met ten minutes previous.

She gave him a prolonged stare before she smiled widely, and when she spoke it was only to say softly, "how poetic."

"I never thought of it like that," Gerry said honestly.

"Have you thought of writing for spiritual magazines?" she asked, as she moved close enough for him to smell the fresh mint from her breath.

"Huh, no; I wouldn't be bothered with the likes of that new age stuff," Gerry said with stupid contradiction as one of his habitual behaviours emerged. For years Gerry had developed a natural tendency to suppress any spiritual beliefs he had, out of fear he would be seen as unacceptable in the small village of

Upperton. This had been one of his internal conflicts, the fact he believed one thing but said the opposite.

She moved slightly away from him. "How do you mean?" she said with surprise.

"Sorry, I didn't mean it like that, I suppose it's a comment from my creative lunacy," he said defensively even though he didn't entirely understand what he had meant by that.

She nodded. "Like voices in your head," she said.

"Yes, that's it," he agreed.

"Environment, education, preachers, there are so many influences that do that to us, teachings instilled into us, stopping us and interfering with our knowing of our relationship with God. You really do have to control those influences inside your head, and know these things that you really think and the thoughts you write are your truth; say goodbye to that lunacy in your head that down talks your true thoughts, there are many people that think the same 'new age' thoughts as you, stop the critical voices that tell you not to be bothered with them," she lectured as though she had accessed his mind.

Gerry had not fully understood what she meant entirely, he had never thought about it that deeply but the passion in which she had spoken resonated inside him. Something made sense to him. He turned slowly and looked out the window and watched the almost invisible circular stripe where the plane propellers revolved, he noticed that the speed at which they turned made them seem like they were everywhere and nowhere at once. This was exactly what God meant to him, God was everywhere we looked, and we just could not see Him; heaven everywhere. He thought about his last diary entry, the entry he made about God, the connection he felt with the land, the hills and the animals on his farm. He thought about what he actually wrote, and he said it in a confident tone inside his mind, 'if God was an infinite strip of bubble wrap, every solitary thing would each be one bubble in the making.' He had momentarily considered the serious thought of pursuing his writing, of revealing his unconventional thoughts through his own words. He had dared not share it though; he had believed it was not the type of normal thoughts expected from a twenty-five-year-old-man. So instead, he turned back to face his travelling companion and decided to check out her breasts.

Gerry had needed a drink even though it was still before noon. He turned around to check if Johnny and Bertie were after ordering one from the in-flight trolley. Lots of merry chatter had seemed to evolve from their back seat row and he was not able to catch their eye.

"Did I offend you?" she asked quietly.

"Not a bother," Gerry said easily. The drinks trolley arrived.

"You seemed very quiet all of a sudden, I hope I didn't say anything out of turn," she said.

"Not at all," Gerry said and then he noticed the genuine concern on her face. No matter how she looked at him she seemed delectable. "Would you like a drink?" he asked politely.

"No, thanks, I have a long drive back," she answered. Gerry ordered a whiskey for himself.

"Drive where?" he asked.

"Cornwall," she said.

"Is that where the accent is from? I thought that was a fake English accent they used on television programmes like 'One man and his dog'," Gerry said amused.

"What's 'One man and his dog'?"

"It's about sheep."

"Do you watch it as part of your research?"

"No, no; I watch it for entertainment."

"Do you like sheep?" she asked with an amused twinkle in her eye.

"Only when they cannot get away from me," he said. They both laughed.

"Seriously, what's so fascinating about watching sheep on telly?" she asked.

"I farm sheep also."

"That's what the smell is then!"

"I thought it was you!"

"How could it be me? I didn't come off a farm," she said.

"But you did look like you were wearing a sheep when you sat down," Gerry said to tease her.

"My Aunt Joyce made it for me," she replied defensively.

Gerry laughed. "Then only wear it when she visits for Christmas."

"You're one to talk. You're what? You're only maybe twenty-three or twenty-four and you watch sheep programmes?"

"I'm twenty-five actually," Gerry confirmed.

"You know, you seem to know and have done a lot for a twenty-five-year-old," she said. Gerry had wondered who she was talking to, and how she could have thought that about ordinary old him?

"I'm not sure who you are addressing, I'm just a simple country boy," he said.

"You're a writer, a sheep farmer, with profound thoughts about so much, you must be the most interesting person I have ever met," she said enthusiastically. Gerry felt embarrassed. "It's such a pity you're too young for me," she continued in a slightly flirty manner.

"You're such an old lady yourself," he said amused, "how old are you?"

"Thirty," she said, "only just, my birthday was two weeks ago."

"And you're a student?" he asked surprised, "your family must be rich."

"Not at all, it's more like an apprenticeship; one day I'll be rich, in the meantime I'll continue to live in Cornwall with Aunt Joyce," she said.

"Why don't you live with your parents?" he asked.

Sadness flashed across her face. "They died," she said quietly.

"Oh Jaysus, I'm sorry to hear that."

"Don't worry about it; it wasn't your fault."

Gerry winked. "You're an impressive woman," he found himself saying.

He noticed her face colour change to match her hair before she tilted it downwards. "Thank you, I don't hear that a lot," she said.

"Are you heading straight to Cornwall when we land?"

"Yes, Aunt Joyce is expecting me later this evening, hence the cardigan," she said as her smile widened.

"Agh yes, well, you can let her know that if she ever needs more wool, you know a man with plenty of sheep," Gerry replied as he laughed, but he had seriously hoped it might open the pathway to some future contact, as ludicrous as it had sounded to him then.

The knitted girl seemed to follow his lead. "How would she know how to contact you?" she asked curiously.

"You'd have to take my number," he said.

"I don't even know your name."

"I don't know yours."

"I'm Bertie," Bertie said as he offered his hand, appearing in the aisle from nowhere.

"Jaysus, Bertie, where'd you pop out from?" Gerry asked startled.

"Coming back from the loos," Bertie said, "and who is the lovely lady?"

"This is... sorry I didn't get your name," Gerry said.

"My name is Grace," she said. "Bertie Maher," Bertie said, as Grace shook his wet hands.

Bertie glared at Grace. "Lovely name for a lovely woman," he said.

"He's getting married in a few weeks," Gerry said, as Grace attempted to wring her hands free from Bertie's greasy grip. "Congratulations," she said slowly.

"Gerry boy, you'll have to drive, Johnny and myself are after a few, and the stewardess said there's no train from the airport into Bristol," Bertie said as he stared through Grace with his mouth still half opened after he had finished his sentence.

"I can give you a lift," Grace offered.

Bertie shook his head. "Not at all, you're grand," he said.

"No, that would be great, Grace," Gerry said quickly.

"Not at all, we would not put anything as nice as you out at all, we'll hire a car," Bertie insisted.

"It is fine, Bristol is on my way," Grace lied.

"Great, thank you," Gerry said.

"No, no, no," Bertie insisted, "we're on a boys' only weekend away."

Grace searched Gerry's face. "Are you sure?" she asked. Gerry was in a quandary, he did not want to upset Bertie any further, even though Bertie had seemed like he was after getting over the morning's episode of Gerry's late arrival.

"We're sure," Bertie confirmed. Gerry nodded slowly as the stewardess urged Bertie back to his seat; they had ten minutes to landing.

Grace turned towards Gerry. "I still don't know your name," she said.

"I'm Gerry."

She smiled, "pleased to meet you, Gerry."

Gerry smiled, "pleased to meet you, Grace," he said as his large shovel-like hands engulfed her dainty and slender fingers in a handshake.

"Grace, Grace, Grace," he thought to himself over the entire weekend, Gerry could not get her name out of his head. And even though he had only just met her and thought he would never see her again, he had known that he was already weak for her.

CHAPTER EIGHT

Alfonzo Giovanni More (pronounced 'more eh' with an accent at the end), known as 'Alfie' for short, had been working at the APES (Afterlife Process for Evolving Souls) facility on Realm One for two years when Gerry arrived there for his first day of work in the afterlife. Luckily for Gerry, his judgement had not been considered severe, so he escaped being sent to the GORILLA (Grilling Of Repenting Inappropriate Low Life Acts) correctional centre, or so he had been told.

Alfie had taken the form of a fully bred, tall, dark, trim and handsome American as his afterlife choice of physical appearance; something he felt he had always been deprived of in his most recent earthly life when he was born to an American mother and Italian father in Manhattan's lower east side area of 'Little Italy'. On earth he had the tanned looks of his father and an overweight, round and low-sized appearance inherited from both parents. In Realm One, Alfie got the choice of what form he wanted to appear as, following on from a Realm initiative called the 'Freedom of Form' that had been started in the middle of the twentieth century when the soul of a European dictator who had arrived back to Realm One was instructed by the Realm guides to set up an organisation encouraging the freedom for souls to choose whatever form they wanted to exist in. Apparently this was this soul's punishment for his earthly years of trying to create a human race of a particular type. Ironically, this soul chose the grotesque form of a skinny, low-sized man, with black hair painted on his head and another short hairline scraped over his upper lip.

Gerry chose the form of his Irish and youthful earthly years, with short blond curls, tanned exterior and six feet in height, precisely as he was at the age of twenty-five; he wanted to do everything he could to ensure that Grace would recognise him when he would meet her again in Realm One.

Gerry had started to feel more alive dead than he had been in his later years of actual living. Returning to Realm One was overwhelming; Gerry was released back into the ultimate comfort that he had known before. He was salvaged, restored and reconditioned, or so he had believed, and he knew he could continue a euphoric existence once he found Grace.

He had chosen to be a trainee recruit at the APES facility, working under Alfie's supervision, and his role was to assist the growth of the thousands of souls that arrived there every day. In truth, he was waiting for the soul that he had once known on earth as Grace.

"Keep your head down and do your job," Alfie had warned Gerry initially.

"I thought I'd tune in and see how Johnny and Bertie are doing," Gerry said.

"Seriously, don't," Alfie said.

Gerry laughed, "too late, I am already doing it."

"Tune out immediately," Alfie warned him urgently.

"Or what?" Gerry asked.

"We do not want any trouble, not yet anyway."

"What trouble? For God's sake we are in infinite existence, what trouble could we have here?"

"You don't want to know, not yet," Alfie said.

"What don't I want to know?" Gerry asked.

"Just do your job for the moment," Alfie instructed.

"You'd swear we were in a prison the way you're behaving."

"Things have changed since you were here last."

"What are you on about?"

"They can read them, they can read our thoughts," Alfie answered.

"Who are 'they'?" Gerry asked.

"The 'Soul Reading Police', that's who 'they' are," Alfie answered abruptly.

Gerry stared at him in disbelief. "That's ridiculous, you are joking, right?"

"No; I am not," Alfie confirmed seriously.

"Who in the name of God are the 'Soul Reading Police'?"

"The ones who monitor our thoughts," Alfie replied.

"But so what, it's not like we can do anything untoward in such a peaceful place."

"You'd be surprised what we can do from here."

"Like what?" Gerry asked quickly.

"In good time, in all good time it will be revealed to you."

"Tell me now, I want to know," Gerry insisted.

"Alfie is right, concentrate on your job," Fragrance interrupted.

Gerry turned to look at her. "How do you do that? Where did you come from now?" he asked.

"I can be wherever I want to be in any instant," Fragrance replied.

"That's cool; how can I do that?" he asked.

"You cannot," she replied firmly.

"How come?"

"It is only the privilege of a Realm guide, you will have to elevate yourself first before you earn that privilege," she said.

"How do I do that?" he asked.

Alfie smiled slightly as he looked at Fragrance. "By following the rules," he said.

"That sounds fairly okay, when do I get the rule book?" Gerry asked.

"The Realm Bible is our rule book, it is taught at SPOCC college," Fragrance informed him.

"What's SPOCC?" Gerry asked.

"Spiritual Process of Continuous Creation College," she replied.

"Fantastic, how do I get there?"

Fragrance sighed and smiled softly, "you must evolve first in your position here at the APES facility."

"And then I get to SPOCC, and then I learn the rules and then I can be anywhere at any given moment that I want; sounds unnecessary, couldn't we just go straight to the punch line," Gerry said innocently.

"It is the process," Fragrance said.

"So how do I elevate myself in APES to get to SPOCC?" he asked.

"By assisting the growth of the souls that arrive here each day, by letting them know the process as I have just told you," Fragrance said.

"But sure it would only take me five minutes to tell them what you outlined as the process, that's fairly easy," Gerry said, thinking his job was not as interesting as he had originally thought.

"Correct," she confirmed.

Gerry shrugged, "so that's all I have to do to get into SPOCC, tell the souls what you have told me? Okay then."

"You must do it with passion," Fragrance said passionately.

"How do you mean?" he asked.

"Because you know that this is the best process for evolution and you must let every soul know that," she replied.

"Not really, the best process is having the choice to be and do anything you wanted, like thinking the thought and having the experience in a shot," he said.

Fragrance moved confidently towards him, "you will learn here in APES that what I tell you is the truth."

Gerry scratched his head, "by God, things have changed since I was here last."

"That is true," she said, "because it is best for all souls, best for all souls to learn to control their thoughts this way."

"Is that why there is something called the 'Soul Reading Police'?" he asked.

Fragrance frowned at Alfie. "I heard Alfie tell you that," she said. Alfie avoided her view.

"Why do you need the police?" Gerry asked.

"Some souls are not as cooperative as you are," she replied.

"You mean some souls take the easy option of thinking the thought and having the experience straight away, just like I did a few minutes ago. I thought about Johnny and Bertie and I was there with them in an instant, like watching them at close range in a panoramic view of their life on earth," Gerry confirmed with delight.

Fragrance sighed again, "you must not do that if you want to elevate yourself here in APES and get to SPOCC."

"Okay, it does seem long winded though, APES then SPOCC, a Realm Bible to learn the rules so I can be where I want to be at any point, I'm fairly sure I'll have some objections from souls about this also," Gerry said.

Alfie sneaked a nod, "I'm fairly sure about that too," he said quietly.

"That is why you have this important job," Fragrance said with enthusiasm.

Gerry stared at her suspiciously, "are you one of the 'Soul Reading Police'?" he asked.

"No, they are not as compassionate as I am."

"How would I know when one of these police was around?"

"You wouldn't," she said.

Gerry was not satisfied with the first answer. "Are they in disguise then?" he asked.

"They are everywhere, monitoring right here in APES," she replied.

Gerry looked from Alfie to Fragrance with confusion. "Sounds like the Realm guides don't trust us, sure what harm can we do here, it was not like this when I existed in the Realm before," he said.

"You will learn," Fragrance said.

"Now I am really confused, I thought our aim was to experience," he insisted.

"But you already learned different when I coached you in your rehabilitation," she reminded him.

Gerry scratched his head again, "yes, of course," he said, though he was not entirely sure he had understood.

"You know it is for the best," she said as she smiled.

"Hang on; why don't you just send all souls to room three-zero-one for rehab, and then there is no need for me to do this job, wouldn't that be easier?" Gerry asked suddenly.

"We do not have enough Realm One coaches, and we do not have enough rehab rooms."

"So you have picked the likes of me and Alfie and the others working for APES to help you out?" Gerry asked.

Fragrance smiled again, "correct, we selectively picked you, the board of Realm Guides all agree on the souls we consider special, and those souls get to go to special rehabilitation, like room three-zero-one, and then work in APES."

"Because you consider us leaders, wow, that's nice to know, I always thought of myself as a bit of a leader," Gerry said proudly.

"You could look at it like that; yes," she replied softly.

"Well then, as a leader of the pack, I'll do my best," Gerry affirmed.

Fragrance smiled and departed more gently than she had arrived. Gerry felt proud and Alfie rolled his eyes. Alfie and Gerry worked in silence for several days until finally Alfie was the first to speak. "You sap," he said.

"What are you talking about?" Gerry asked.

"The reason we are here, the reason we are here in APES is because we ARE leaders," Alfie said.

"I know that, Fragrance already confirmed it," Gerry replied with false enthusiasm, "we are special helpers to the guides, it can only mean one thing, that we will be guides ourselves one day."

"And you would want that for what reason?" Alfie asked with a frown.

"To think controlled thoughts and experience anything I wanted by just thinking the simplest of thoughts; obviously!"

"You can do that anyway, you can experience anything you think, you already said that you could see Bertie and Johnny before, and you achieved that by only thinking about them," Alfie reminded him.

"Okay then, if that is totally correct I am now thinking about being a Realm Guide and how come I am not experiencing that now?" Gerry asked sarcastically.

"How do you know you are not?" Alfie asked.

"Are you one of the 'Soul Reading Police'?" Gerry asked suspiciously. "Are you trying to test me?"

"NO, I am NOT, believe me I am one of the few allies you can have here," Alfie replied firmly.

Gerry tried again. "Okay, I am thinking about Fragrance, so how come I am not with her now so?"

"Because you do not believe that you can be," Alfie responded.

"Yes I do, I just said it," Gerry replied instantly.

"No, you have to *really* believe it," Alfie confirmed. "You have to truly believe from the depths of your soul that you can, every part of you must be congruent. Then when you really believe you can, you will."

Gerry felt despair, "I'm confused," he said.

"Most of us are when we get here first."

"No; I mean really confused. I believed everything is revealed to us, that everything would be obvious to us when we reached heaven."

"You think you are in heaven; do you?"

"You mean I'm not," Gerry cried in disbelief, "I led a decent enough life, there is no reason why I should not be in heaven."

"So what you did to Grace was decent in your opinion, was it?" Alfie asked.

"Leave Grace out of this," Gerry shouted. "How do you know about Grace anyhow?"

"I know lots," Alfie responded.

"How?" Gerry asked. "How do you know? Oh God; no; please do not tell me we are in hell."

"Hell does not exist as a place you can go to or get sent to," Alfie said easily.

"This is ridiculous, why are you doing this?" Gerry cried.

"So that you understand where you are now. Listen to me and listen carefully because I may only get one chance to tell you. Do you understand?"

Gerry felt perplexed. "Not really, but I am listening."

"You can 'see' your friends because you truly believe you have that ability. It is almost like there is an invisible string which connects us to the earth because of this place we are trapped in," Alfie started to explain.

"Trapped?" Gerry interrupted wildly.

"Listen, I said," Alfie ordered. "I will start from the beginning. You are in what the Realm guides call 'The Omega' region of Realm One, they call it 'The Omega' because they want us to believe it is the end point. A few centuries ago, some souls ar-

rived back to the Realm and had thoughts about hell and punishment, thoughts that they carried with them from the earth,
fearful thoughts that they were unwilling to let go of. And because they did not understand choice they created new myths
from their own thoughts which manifested into experiences.
That was in fact what they chose, they chose fear over love.
That is what I meant when I said that hell is not a place. Hell is
a state of mind that you choose, and on choosing something in
your mind you create your own story of how you believe things
to be, which ultimately results in that experience."

Gerry was listening attentively, "so these souls experienced
hell?"

"In a certain manner, yes; but their thoughts about hell were
so gruesome that they dismissed those immediately. However,
they were unable to dismiss their fear, and this fear allowed
them to create such places in their mind as the GORILLA correctional centre and limbo, their fear had to be satisfied by places where you could be punished. Of course, when you create
something in your mind, and start to believe it long enough,
you design your own experience and you will find evidence everywhere to support its existence, and that's what they did. The
sadness is that they could have chosen love over fear and created
an opposite existence," Alfie explained. Gerry listened. Alfie's
words revived a dormant truth in him that had been prominent
in his earlier years on earth.

"Let me give you a simple example from earth," Alfie continued, "suppose you know someone who is paranoid and believes others talk about them behind their back; now suppose
this paranoid person has a true loyal friend, and one day the
paranoid one sees the loyal one out having fun with a third
person that the paranoid person dislikes, and suppose the loyal one does not mention to the paranoid one that he had met
with that third person; then the paranoid one creates all sorts
of theories in his head and can start to believe that the loyal
friend must have been laughing about or at least discussing
the paranoid one. They will have created their own story and
they will have found the evidence to support their story, and

this will become their truth. The paranoid one may even confront, challenge or make accusations towards the loyal friend based on the evidence they have decided in their head. And even when the loyal one assures their paranoid friend that they had not been untoward, the paranoid one may even say he believes his friend, however his behaviour towards his loyal friend changes because he wants him to know he was feeling hurt. Inevitably the paranoid one starts to lose friends as he encounters similar experiences over time. The point is that misleading thoughts create the stories, over time the stories develop into beliefs which become habitual and influence that person's behaviour. In this case it means that the thoughts of the paranoid person are the root cause, the sole cause of their experience of reality, a reality which is false. And by changing their thoughts in the first place about their loyal friend, they could have experienced a very different, more blissful relationship with others."

"No disrespect, Alfie, but isn't this obvious?" Gerry interrupted, "can you please explain our situation here in this part of Realm One."

"It is NOT obvious to a paranoid person. A paranoid person may be told over and over again that they do not know the facts and they are supposing their theory to be true. The paranoid person intellectually understands the logic BUT they will fail to apply the logic to their own thinking. They will continue to justify their version of the story, and because they will have built up so many such experiences over the years they will have a filing cabinet of evidence to support their paranoid beliefs, and so their cycle continues spiralling downwards, creating their own dismal reality. They are responsible for their own experiences yet they do not realise it."

Gerry nodded. "I understand."

"I assure you Gerry, if I wrote in black print what I have just told you, and a slightly paranoid person read it once they would understand and may say it is obvious; yet that same person could read it a thousand times and still not recognise how it applies to themselves. Paranoia results in self-absorption, and self-absorption is not perceived as kindness. The offender would have read this and still failed to see why they do not experience more pleasant relationships with others. If you want a better experience, you start by changing your thoughts."

Gerry sighed. "Yes, I get it, change your thoughts to create better feelings, resulting in new behaviours, make a new habit, and then you create the reality that you want to experience," he summarised.

"Exactly," Alfie confirmed.

"And you could even create enough great thoughts to bury your head in the sand, and become delusional as opposed to being ill from paranoia," Gerry added sarcastically.

"We are not talking about severe mental illnesses, Gerry, we are talking about healthy attitudes, *healthy attitudes no matter where you exist*, and about knowing and controlling what we are capable of," Alfie responded firmly.

Gerry shook his head slowly. "No; I thought we were talking about the current situation in this part of the Realm, which you were to explain."

"I have been," Alfie said, "the same applies to this fearful group of souls who arrived here a few centuries ago. We are the creators of our own realities no matter where we exist. And then we respond to those realities based on what we believe in our heads. You know well if you create something in your mind, and start to believe it long enough, you invent your own experience of the world and you will find all the evidence you want to support it. You understood this in the case of the example of the paranoid person on earth."

"Yes," Gerry said honestly.

"In some respects you could say that these souls had some knowledge of real choice since they rejected this hellish image; however, based on their experiences they created GORILLA, APES, SPOCC, limbo, and a Realm bible. They invented these based on their encounters which they thought were true, but they missed the critical information and that was they could have just as easily created extremely pleasant observations from their thoughts. Had they learned to control their thoughts themselves they would have known this; but they were unrefined in their own evolution, and now their primitive ideas have expanded throughout. These primitive souls are now our Realm guides."

"So this place which they now call 'The Omega' region of Realm One was created out of their fearful thoughts?" Gerry asked.

"Yes; and in fact they now believe it themselves to be the end point. I am sure there is an 'Omega' but it is not this place. That is what happens when you reinforce something so strongly inside yourself, it develops into a belief that cannot be shaken. They understand no better. They are souls that are still tied to the earth; they are still connected with human memories and carry forth similar types of earth beliefs to the Realm," Alfie responded.

"That means their intentions are not good," Gerry said with disbelief.

"Not necessarily," Alfie disagreed, "their original intentions were to protect us all, they know how terrifying it is for a soul returning to the Realm to think briefly of hell and experience it immediately, it happened to them and they are making it their mission to prevent other souls from such terror. We all know hell does not exist as a place, but thinking it makes it so. The solution is to think pleasant thoughts immediately, this is what souls have been doing for millennia and it worked, pleasant thoughts lead to pleasant experiences. Had the Realm guides understood real choice they would have known that you can choose pure love and experience heaven but there are reasons why they didn't do that. They quickly learned that it gave them power in the Realm and they wanted a continuum of the power they perceived they had while on earth, they were too fearful of losing that control and their fearful thoughts created new myths; stories that they force other souls here to live by. These souls, our Realm guides, are basic and unsophisticated; they collectively misunderstood God on earth as they continue to do in the Realm."

"So this is about power," Gerry asked.

"Yes," Alfie agreed, "power can only be achieved with others, not over others; but these souls were not evolved enough and too much attached to earthly beliefs which had been literally drilled into the very essence of their being, beliefs driven by fear of the afterlife. So they introduced their process and when they realised the power it gave them, they vowed to do all they could to hold onto it. And power driven by fear leads to destruction."

"But this is not the Realm that I had known before," Gerry protested.

"Of course it is not, there are other parts of the Realm where you experience true freedom and pure love, once you are prepared to give up earthly attachments; that is the part of the Realm where you had been before, where we both had once been," Alfie explained.

"You mean a real type of heaven?" Gerry asked.

"Yes," Alfie responded firmly, "I forgive you for that comment; you are fresh out of rehabilitation where you have been influenced."

"Then why am I not in heaven?" Gerry asked bewildered.

"You are trapped here because you lived a life where you did not exercise choice. You were an easy target for the Realm guides to grab upon death; just like I was," Alfie said.

Gerry had tried to understand, and for the first time since his death he decided to exercise the choice to confront the reality where he appeared to be. He observed the dimness of his surroundings. He had noticed that APES seemed to appear like an extensive vacuum existing in semi-darkness, like dusk or even dawn, with the promise of a sun that should rise but never did. Something seemed to override that promise of brightness, like a gloomy cloud that loomed everywhere, a foggy atmosphere that existed all around. That mist, that cloud, he intellectually rationalised as a collective fear; a fear that had been veiled with supposed freedoms such as the ability that allowed a soul to appear in any form they wanted. He knew it was not right, he had known since he had first arrived, he had also chosen to ignore it until that point.

"Why doesn't God interfere? Why doesn't He stop this?" Gerry asked suddenly.

"Because He has given us freedom of will, free choice; He allows us to experience what we chose no matter where we exist or what form we exist in," Alfie said.

"I did not choose to come here," Gerry protested again, "you said it yourself, that I was a target for these Realm guides to grab upon my death. That's not choice; that makes me a victim!"

"Just like the paranoid person may intellectually understand that suspicious thoughts create their own gloomy existence, and yet they still do not apply the theory to themselves and fail to choose something else because they are addicted to the feeling of self-pity this misery gives them, they are consumed with blaming others rather than facing any responsibility themselves, and they also consider themselves victims," Alfie remonstrated.

"This is different! I didn't choose this, I didn't choose to come here; I know that," Gerry shouted.

"No, you were not consciously aware that you chose to come here," Alfie confirmed, "but think of it like this, when the paranoid person makes enough unfounded suspicions, it results in unkindness to others; and then one day someone somewhere, as though it were out of the blue, someone who has equally unhealthy thinking will respond to that unkindness and will target them back. The paranoid person did not actually choose to be set upon by someone else, however they still do not realise that they are at the root cause of it all. The paranoid one still does not realise that their own behaviours based on their self thoughts and feelings was the choice they made which resulted in their unconscious choices of becoming the bull's eye of someone else's pain. What it does reinforce to them is that they actually are a victim, especially if the other's response seemed cruel and unwarranted. And despite all of this, they still do not rationalise that they have to change their own thoughts, make changes within themselves and then their experiences will also begin to change."

"I am NOT paranoid," Gerry shouted.

"I know you are not; but you have made yourself an easy target, through your unhealthy conscious thoughts you have also unconsciously chosen to be a target. In effect you have chosen to be a subject of these Realm guides, and until you accept that responsibility you will remain as one."

"So you are telling me that I am to blame for everything bad that has ever happened to me in my life?" Gerry said with disbelief.

"I am saying there is a lesson in everything. Unhealthy thinking habits will attract more unhealthy people and experiences to you. It is your choice to learn from this pain or not."

"How can that always be true?" Gerry protested, "Grace had a very healthy attitude towards life and others when I knew her, yet she had lots of pain in her life also. Are you saying she attracted that?"

"It is about the lesson, from what you say about Grace, she was respectful of others, her lesson may have been to learn independence, learn to stand up for herself, learn to express her truths without fear in her respectful way, and her experiences of life would continue until she learned those lessons. In your case it is different; you held lots of bitterness and resentment in the latter part of your life. Were you respectful of those around you?"

"Not always! No, I admit that. But how could I possibly have chosen to be one of these Realm guide subjects?" Gerry asked.

"It is what you did not choose."

"So you are saying that I am choosing this existence without my knowing?"

"Yes."

"So how do I choose something else?"

"What do you want to choose instead?"

"I want to choose the place where the sun never goes down, the place of true freedom, the place where I have originated from. I do not choose to be trapped here."

"So do I," Alfie admitted.

"What? Then why are you here? Why have you chosen to be trapped in this place?"

"Just like you, I have also unconsciously chosen to have been an easy target; however I take responsibility for that."

"How do you know all of this? I mean, how did you have that realisation about yourself? How on earth do you know this to be the same for me?"

"Deep down, we both know the truth," Alfie said calmly.

"Then how the hell - even though I know that place does not exist - do we get out of here?"

"Just like the paranoid person, I have not yet worked out how to apply the truths to myself."

"Then what do we do?" Gerry cried in despair.

"We have to first accept responsibility for the apparent reality of this existence."

"Which is that we are trapped unconsciously in a place which is ruled by these Realm guides, who are driven by fear, a fear that they are willing to spread because it gives them power over other souls also trapped here. But you said had the Realm guides originally chosen love over fear none of this would have happened, so surely is not it a case of choosing love and we are free from this place?"

"But theory and practice are different things," Alfie responded with a tone of dim hope.

"I know that," Gerry interrupted, "so it makes sense that we choose love and practise it."

"Huh?" Alfie laughed. "It's not that easy in this place, 'they' don't make it easy for you here. Don't get me wrong, the Realm guides are not malicious, well, they do not believe themselves to be, they are basically similar to many earth people that preach and teach us fear so that we conform to their ideas and they retain power. In return the souls here get a *seemingly* blissful existence which is what they really want for us, the same as what most leaders on earth want too, it's just that none of them know that they are going the wrong way about it. And even though lots of the souls here suspect this is not the final eventuality, they are happy to remain here so that they also can hold onto earthly memories and responsibilities they once had; it gives them a sense of purpose. And for many, though not all, the thought of that is less work than the road to a more heavenly experience. It boils down to what you are familiar with; it boils down to fear."

"It's easy then," Gerry interrupted hopefully. "We think thoughts of love and openly practise them, and once we demonstrate to all souls what we know, all souls can be freed to the place of love and eternal sunshine. Simple!"

"Simple! Is it?" Alfie questioned. "We have to understand *how* to choose that, and had we done that in the first place we would not be here. And now we are ruled by even more fear. No Gerry; we have to understand how to escape this."

"What does that mean?"

"We need to overrule the Realm guides, we need to raise the consciousness of all souls here, we need to collectively know the truth, and to do that we have to start with ourselves."

"A rebellion?"

"No; everything we do is in peace and must come from a place of love, which is why I have started the 'Undercover Movement.'"

"A WHAT?"

"The 'Undercover Movement' - a peaceful means to stop these Realm guides."

"No; hang on; no; look, all I want to do is be with Grace," Gerry said suddenly as fear overcame him.

"We must let go of fear somehow and you are still in your infancy. Gerry, I know your history. I know how you had insights about God when you were a young man, and I also know how you discarded those as you grew older. I also know why. So much for wisdom coming with age, in your case it was the opposite. And that is the reason you were such an easy target for the Realm guides."

"I have been in the Realm before, I know there is more than this, how can you say I am in my infancy? And how do you know so much about me?"

"How I know about your history is not important. It will all become clear to you when you finally wake up. You were a more evolved soul when you were born than when you died, just like

I was," Alfie explained. "We both became victim to our lives on earth. That is why they picked us to do this job in APES, they think they can control us and on controlling us we control others by teaching the Realm process. That is why the likes of you and me went to special rehabilitation in room three-zero-one. They groomed us for this job, they do not expect problems from us, they anticipate that souls like us will easily follow them; they expect us to be compliant with their rules. They expect us to continue on a downward spiral, believing in fears, believing their truths and as such we are ideal for this job, because we are telling the souls that arrive here every day something we believe to be true, and as such we are more convincing. We are nothing more than puppets, and that is what Fragrance meant when she agreed that you were a leader. But mark my words when I tell you that Fragrance is not as clever as she thinks. Most other souls that come directly here to APES are influenced by souls like us that have been groomed, our job is nothing more than a manipulation of souls that have known and trusted us on earth."

"I would not manipulate someone I knew on earth if they arrived here," Gerry insisted.

"Unknowingly you would, if you believed this process to be the best for all souls you would, but now you know better. They have underestimated us. What do you remember about your rehab?"

"I remember the sense of fear, I remember being monitored though I could not see anything much, but looking back I think I imagined that."

"Not only your imagination, it was your intuition. You were right."

"But I also remember enjoying myself, I watched my funeral as it unfolded and I think I was happy enough though I knew something wasn't right."

"They led you to believe you were in control, let you to believe that you were in a place of freedom. It is part of the rehab. You were being monitored by the 'Soul Reading Police'."

"For what?"

"To ensure you conform."

"To the rules?"

"To ensure that you stayed at the level of evolution you were at the time of your death. Let me guess, they released you when you said your Realm name, correct?"

"Yes, yes," Gerry responded quickly. "How did you know?"

"Because it was the same for us all, for anyone of us that went to that rehab room. They want to know if you realise who you really are and where you have really originated from; and once you admit the truth of who you really are while showing no desire to return to the place of origin, they are satisfied that you will not be a problem, they are happy that you are ready for the job in hand. And simultaneously you will have been coached on the magnificence of this 'Omega' region of Realm One."

"But I know better, I do have the desire to return," Gerry insisted, "I know that this place the Realm guides call 'Omega' is not the end point. I know there is more because I experienced it before."

"For want of a better word Gerry, the *'brainwashing'* is not over. Now that we are in APES, we are taught more with their process, once we do a reasonable job in APES we are sent to SPOCC, and once in SPOCC their rules are instilled in us, they teach us their bible, and they teach us more of their truths. The GORILLA correctional centre does not exist, they warn you about GORILLA while here in this facility but GORILLA is a myth so that we conform and behave during our stint in APES for fear of being sent there. When a soul gets sent to SPOCC the Realm guides teach souls about limbo, another myth such that again souls have more anxiety instilled in them for fear of being sent there. They tell you that limbo is one million times more severe than GORILLA. None of it is true. You and I are leaders, but not leaders in the manner that Fragrance led you to believe. We are different, we know eternal truths, and these are NOT the truths of these Realm guides. If leaders such as us both are not controlled then the Realm guides lose their power. That is why you will join me in the 'Undercover Movement'."

"I will?" Gerry questioned, "Why should I believe you? Why don't we just communicate with the Realm guides and explain there is a better way than their process, explain to them about the power of choice."

"Because we do not even know how to apply it to ourselves yet, plus they won't listen, they don't want to lose their power; that is why there is the 'Soul Reading Police'. Why would they have police if they thought souls did not need policing? They want to control us. They won't release that power easily."

Gerry struggled with his thoughts; he had desperately wanted to delude himself again. "The police are there to monitor our thoughts," he rationalised, "so maybe it is because the Realm guides are ensuring we do not think bad experiences, maybe those are the good reasons the Realm guides have for protecting our thoughts? To protect us?"

"No; they control thoughts, and you know it," Alfie objected. "They control our thinking to ensure we follow their process, their process that promises the freedom to be, do and have what you want. That way, they retain their power. By introducing their process, they forget we exist to experience and evolve."

"But doesn't the process get the same results? Fragrance said that when I elevate myself to SPOCC, I will learn how to be anywhere in an instant just like she does," Gerry said.

"Let go of your fear, Gerry," Alfie warned. "You know you can do that anyway, you have experienced a Realm before where that had been immediately possible."

"It doesn't make sense!" Gerry cried, "I can see what's happening on earth by thinking about it, but the same doesn't apply to my thoughts in the Realm, I can't see what's happening with another soul in the Realm when I think about them!"

"Because we are 'tied' to the earth somehow; that much I have worked out."

"NO," Gerry shouted. "You said it was about beliefs, you said I could not communicate with souls in the Realm because I didn't believe I could and you said I was here because I unconsciously chose it."

"You have unconsciously chosen it, do you understand that?" Alfie asked.

"Yes, it's probable."

"And what do you believe?"

"I believe I can be more than what I am here."

"And when you really believe that you *are* more rather than *can be* more, you will then *truly* believe. It's called faith."

"How?"

"Catch twenty-two; this place we are in is so consumed by fear, and with time it makes us forget who we really are, makes us forget that we *are* more, that is why we need to override the fear, we need to override the Realm guides. We are mice caught in the trap they call their 'process'."

"Surely souls have rebelled before now?" Gerry asked.

"Of course they have, and now you are one of those; you are ready to join my 'Undercover Movement'," Alfie confirmed.

"You were worried before about trouble, and if what you say is really true then I can understand why this could cause trouble, but why change your mind and engage me in that trouble?" Gerry asked.

"Because I didn't want them to find you out about you, they already know about me, but you have openly challenged Fragrance when you said their process was unnecessary, and now they will possibly monitor you more closely also," Alfie said.

"I didn't challenge her, I only said what was on my mind," Gerry protested.

"Thinking those thoughts is a challenge to the Realm guides," Alfie warned again.

"That is why they monitor our thoughts," Gerry said reflectively. "But wait! How do you mean you didn't want them to find out about me? What is there to find out?"

"You are a leader, I have been waiting for you to arrive," Alfie said.

"Now you're scaring me. Who are you?"

"I am a leader, the same as you are, we know the truth; you may have temporarily forgotten it when they rehabilitated you for twelve days, but you know you still know."

Gerry thought hard about the sense Alfie seemed to make. "Like, I know that the concept of time does not exist when a soul leaves a body but yet we still seem to experience time here for some reason; like, I know that in the afterlife we experience everything we think of immediately but yet I seem prohibited from doing that now with the exception of thoughts about some mortals on earth; like, I know that this is not how it should be in the Realm," he said.

"Yes; and now we only need to learn to believe it again," Alfie said calmly.

"No! Wait!" Gerry said quickly. "If everything you say is true then why are the 'Soul Reading Police' not here controlling and stopping our thoughts and plans to overthrow the Realm guides? Unless of course they don't exist?"

It did not need an answer. A large, round-eyed and bald entity appeared in the room, its presence was merely a shadow appearing as a dark phantom with no solid form. Alfie turned quickly to Gerry, "never forget what I have told you, no matter what they tell you now," he said. And as the entity escorted Alfie away, he did not appear to object but Gerry felt more afraid than ever. He was consumed by impending danger. He was distressed and he did not know what to do.

On a knife's edge, just like he was in his youth on earth, Gerry was once again faced with a dilemma. He could raise his consciousness, face his fear and free his soul; or, he could do nothing, he could comply with the rules of not thinking and allow himself unconsciously to be led by a process.

CHAPTER NINE

It was a month before Gerry's twenty-sixth birthday; and it had been a boiling hot day in August 1983. Gerry was sitting on a bar stool with his sleeves rolled up and his shirt half open as the beads of sweat were slowly evaporating with the fresh summer breeze that strolled through the open door of Johnny's pub. With his eyes half closed he faced the warm currents of evening air that traversed that open passage as he held an ice cold pint of Bulmer's cider that rested on his knee. It was harvest time, one of the busiest times of year for a farmer, and Gerry had parked his tractor and trailer full of grain in a near lay-by, promising himself a swift drink to absorb the serenity of the evening.

On the opposite side of the bar, a group of six card players, a mixture of local bachelors with two women, sat around a small, low rectangular table. Bending over from their seats, they concentrated on the centre of the table and the fast hand playing of 'Forty Five', they played in almost a silence except for the intermittent noisy retorts they made before all throwing their cards down, indicating the end of the game. It was all background noise to Gerry as he wondered whether farming and a social life revolving around this pub was his fate. He wondered if everything was set in stone or if he could chance doing something different with his life. He rationalised he was content enough and he did not want for anything, he had plenty of money, had solid friends and he had worked hard in a job that was always outdoors. There was no rational desire to change anything, so he slowly speculated why he would even question it. He marvelled at the motivation of those thoughts, and was curious of that inner voice that was telling him that he craved more. He wondered how exactly he could set about doing what he loved most, his writing, and developing his creativity. But just before he allowed himself to get lost in trance with those precious thoughts, he stopped suddenly, then he grinned to himself at the depth of the thoughts of a farmer as he sank another large mouthful of the cider down his throat.

Johnny let him in peace as he cleaned around the bar area, and Gerry continued to inhale the sweet smell of summer which suddenly became mixed with an interfering stale odour of perspiring Brut aftershave. Gerry fully opened his eyes instantly as Bertie flew towards him with a huge beam spread across his face. "You'll never guess what," he announced, as though he had wanted half the population of Cork to hear. Bertie was always the first with any news.

"Marie has a bun in the oven," Johnny said as he leaned across the bar for the news.

"By God, Bertie, you're a fast mover," Gerry said.

Bertie winked. "No, no, that's not it, though not from the lack of trying."

"So why the big smile Bertie, did you win on prize bonds?" Gerry asked.

Bertie shook his head, "nope, tis a small world, a small world it is."

"T'is indeed," Johnny agreed as he nodded. Gerry wondered if he had missed something. "Is that what your revelation is, Bertie? And there was us thinking you had news," he said.

Bertie winked again directly at Gerry. "No, no, that's not it, I saw that woman in town today."

"What woman?" Gerry asked indifferently as he ordered another fresh pint.

Johnny smiled, "Marie won't be too happy when she hears you're looking at women in town, Bertie."

"What? Sure, Marie was with me, she met her too," Bertie replied.

"Met who? What's the news?" Gerry asked with an enquiring smile.

"The woman on the plane, I said 'hello' to her," Bertie continued.

"What woman on the plane?" Johnny asked.

"Jaysus, Johnny, we've only been on the plane once, who do you think?" Bertie replied, "the one that Gerry was raving

on about when he was pissed at my stag weekend in England."
Gerry's ears sat upright as a slight anxiety seeped out of the
pores of his face. "Keep your voice down Bertie, will you?" he
ordered.

Johnny's smile fell into a laugh, "maybe she's over here track-
ing you down, Gerry boy. What was her name again?" Gerry
remained quiet for once.

"Joy, or Flower, or something like that, I couldn't remember
her name, it was embarrassing introducing Marie to her," Bertie
said.

"Why would you be introducing Marie to her?" Johnny asked.

"Because she's a foreigner and I thought she might want to
get to know a few women, I was only being friendly," Bertie
said innocently.

"Did Marie not ask her name?" Johnny asked.

"No, we didn't get the chance," Bertie said.

"How do you mean?" Johnny asked.

"The woman walked on," Bertie said.

"Is that it?" Johnny asked, "Jaysus, yourself and Marie must
have one boring life to be so excited over nothing, that's what
marriage does to you I suppose."

Bertie smiled coyly at Gerry. "I thought Gerry would be interested to know – that's all," he said. Gerry looked uncomfortable and Johnny reflected disinterest.

Gerry coughed. "Are you sure it was her?" he asked.

"Of course it was, I said 'hello' to her, and she said 'eh' with
big surprised eyes, and I said 'this is the wife' and I pointed
at Marie, and your woman friend said 'hello', and Marie said
'hello' and then your woman friend smiled again. And everyone
felt awkward."

"So nothing happened?" Gerry asked cautiously.

"I said t'was a small world and she smiled again," Bertie
said.

"Is she here on a visit?" Gerry asked.

"She walked away, I told you, but... " Bertie started to say.

"Did not you think to ask her?" Gerry interrupted.

Johnny grinned. "Are yah still interested, Gerry?"

Gerry felt he was backed into a corner as his two friends smirked at him. "Jaysus, you two saw her for yourselves, who wouldn't be?" he said defensively.

"Exactly, I'd have stayed talking to her but Marie gave me a shove to move on," Bertie said. Johnny frowned, "I thought you said the woman walked away."

"She did, I told you, but after Marie poked my shoulder," Bertie confirmed. "Marie said the woman was fierce snobby, not remembering me and all."

"I did not," Marie interrupted as she walked through the open entrance with a determined look on her face. Gerry smiled briefly, he knew that Marie's main conversation motivator was either gossip or negatively discussing others, and her habits were so perfectly exercised that she rarely practised viewing events from anyone else's perspective. "She just stared at us blankly," Marie said seriously.

"What does that mean?" Gerry enquired in earnest.

"She put on a sweet tone of voice, and I knew exactly what she was doing, thinking she was bigger than us or something, her little posh English accent and she probably even has one of those double-barrelled names," Marie explained as she nodded.

"She's bound to have an English accent," Johnny said casually, "she's from England."

Bertie shrugged, "I thought she was just being polite."

"Erra, don't worry about it," Gerry said dismissively to Marie.

Marie's face twisted. "So you think I imagined her false smile?"

"No, no, Marie," Bertie responded, "I'd say Gerry is only saying that it was awkward for us all, and the English lady probably didn't know what to say either."

"She had a straight back on top of her floral skirt and high heels," Marie continued, "and a big confident smile that looked down on us."

Johnny laughed. "Are you jealous, sister?"

"I am not," Marie retorted instantly. "Do any of you listen? She was standing as though she was bigger than the whole town. She was grinning at me when she said she liked my hand-bag. I had a good mind to tell her that I had bought mine; mine was not knitted like the sack that hung out around her. I should have said it straight out to her, it would have brought her down to size."

Marie did have a kind side to her nature but she measured kindness in the form of likeness, and when she encountered anyone different she constantly strived to find an issue rather than embracing them with curiosity. If someone did not behave in the manner that she did, she was self-assured they were insincere or lacked manners as she created her own stories behind the source of those different behaviours. Marie had an amazing ability to suck joy out of anything she did not understand. In essence, she sometimes lacked common courtesy in situations that were insignificant on the greater scale of life.

"Where did all of this come from?" Gerry asked with a slight disbelief.

"Insecurity," Johnny muttered as he turned to face the shelves behind him.

"What are you on about?" Marie responded brusquely. "I cannot even tell you now when someone was patronising towards me. Some brother you are!"

"There's no point in getting snotty with me, Marie," Johnny said casually, "I wasn't there."

"Exactly," she retorted. "So you did not see her false carry on."

"I didn't either," Bertie said, confused.

"Of course you wouldn't," Marie snapped. "It is called woman's intuition."

Gerry was taken aback by Marie's tone as he wondered whether another one of her emotional outbursts was brewing. She had an amazing ability to confuse her uncontrolled emotions with her true inner feelings.

Gerry was well aware that he also was victim to these types of destructive thoughts at times; he did not know anyone who was not. He also knew that his environment was not a true representation of the world at large. And having a wealth of self-knowledge in that first half of his life, he would have been the last person he would have suspected to fall into such similar traps over the latter half of his life. He felt a strong emotion welling inside him; and he took a deep breath before he decided to reasonably challenge Marie on the topic.

"Let me get this straight," he said. "Bertie introduced you to someone new in town, none of you really knew what to say to each other, so an awkward moment followed, and the English girl is snobby as a result."

"No," Marie protested rashly. "You were not there, so you have no idea how she looked at us with that put-on polite tone of voice."

"Maybe she was taken aback to meet someone she recognised. Maybe she did not know what to say," Gerry suggested and shrugged.

"She did not say much – except 'eh' a few times," Marie said snidely in an attempt to mimic an English accent.

Gerry thought her efforts were unwarranted. "Maybe that only means you have nothing really in common."

Bertie blinked. "Let it go," he said quietly.

"No," Marie snapped. "Gerry seems to think he knows it all. Let him continue telling us what we saw and heard," she said harshly.

"I'm only saying there are a hundred and one possibilities."

"So now you are saying I imagined it again. I know well when someone behaves like she did; they only think they're great."

"Maybe she just has a natural inner confidence," Gerry said, "That sounds like a good thing."

"You're all the same."

"What does that mean?"

"Thinking with something lower than your brain."

Gerry felt heated but managed to control his own emotions himself, deep down he was very fond of Marie despite her self-absorbed views on situations. "Maybe you should stop thinking with your brain," he said, "or at the least unravel the mesh of bad wirings in there before you do."

"What makes you so knowledgeable on the subject?"

"You don't know her so stop making assumptions."

Marie twisted her face more. "So now you're telling me I am making assumptions. I tell you one thing, I know her type. The type that thinks they are better than the rest."

"You have only just met her!"

"First impressions last."

"Did it ever occur to you that your first impressions were wrong?"

"She winced when Bertie blew a tiny puff of smoke on her face. She's out of touch with reality," Marie said decidedly.

"Maybe she doesn't like smoking," Gerry suggested.

"She waved the smoke from her face, looking at us as if we were beneath her."

"As I said, maybe she doesn't like smoking."

"Do you ever listen?" Marie responded curtly. "She made us feel bad, even Bertie ended up apologising for blowing smoke into her face."

"I thought it was only common courtesy, and I did it by accident, I didn't mean to blow smoke at her so I thought I would say sorry because I was sorry," Bertie said quietly.

"Who the hell does she think she is, with her thinking that we should have to apologise to her?" Marie said unreasonably.

"You don't know what she was thinking," Gerry replied.

"Let it go; forget about it, it doesn't matter," Johnny interrupted quietly.

"Who the hell is Gerry to tell me what I saw?" Marie snapped at her brother.

"I happen to be the person here who knows her best, even if it was only briefly," Gerry said calmly.

"So that's what it's all about then?" Marie laughed snidely. "You cannot stand it when someone disagrees with you. Huh!"

"You're not being very sisterly," Johnny reminded her.

"I wasn't talking to you," she said rashly, "I'm talking to Gerry; he needs to learn a bit about himself."

"I didn't mean it in the true word of sister," Johnny sighed. "I meant you are not behaving like a friend."

"I think Gerry needs to learn a thing or two," she retorted again. "Just because he likes her doesn't mean we all have to agree with his warped perspective."

"Let it go," Bertie said again as he scanned all three faces cautiously. Bertie hated confrontation with a vengeance, resulting in Marie rarely having the occasion to hear an objective view on her unfounded theories and rash outbursts.

"I know plenty of people like that snobby English one," Marie continued with her evidence of justification.

"You don't know her," Gerry insisted.

"I'm not stupid," Marie snapped.

"No-one ever said you were."

"Keep it down lads," Johnny warned, "there's no need for this."

"Gerry started it." Marie said.

"Erra, it doesn't matter, who's having another pint?" Bertie asked carefully.

Gerry searched Marie's face to talk to the more caring side of her nature. "Sometimes, Marie, I think we take people at face value and stop inventing stories behind their behaviours, no one is perfect. Sometimes we have to get a life of our own," he said honestly.

"Of course I'm not perfect," she snapped back. "Everyone here can hear you tell me that."

Gerry felt despair. "It wasn't personal," he pleaded.

"You just can't stand it when someone doesn't understand your perspective," Marie concluded curtly, and oblivious to her contradiction she stomped to the back of the bar to the ladies' toilets.

Gerry only shook his head as he noticed the irony of her statement; and he eased back with the knowledge that there was no point in talking the subject further with Marie. She was far too self-absorbed in her own perspective, and Gerry noticed for the first time that her viewpoints represented her insecurity camouflaged in external outbursts of over-confident statements. He also felt proud; it was his first experience of speaking his own truths, something that he had previously held close and private. Internal shifts were happening and he did not know why.

Gerry smiled to himself, he was genuinely fond of Marie, and he knew that when the rest of them would have long forgotten this episode she would still be hanging onto it for dear life and inevitably she would experience remorse; only to inflict more pain on her. The sadness was that she never realised this, and she would continue to justify how she was mostly a good, caring person. And it was true that this was also a large aspect of her nature, 'Dennis the menace', her puppy, would be the first to verify that.

Gerry had known Marie treated her puppy Dennis like a baby; she was constantly buying him gimmicks, toys, rugs and 'no more tears' shampoos so that the soap would not hurt his eyes. Dennis even had his own hot water bottle, and she had knitted a cover for it with embroidered letters saying 'Dennis the Menace'. It was a true reflection of her more sensitive side, despite her habitual and volatile behaviours.

Gerry looked to Marie as she returned from the ladies' toilet as he wondered whether the cause of her strong outbursts was only because she felt misunderstood. It inspired him to write about it later that evening in his private journals as he searched curiously through his 1982 new edition of the Oxford English dictionary which defined an emotion as being 'an instinctive feeling opposed to reason'. He had wanted to challenge those writers of the dictionary as he realised it was possible that a literal definition in *black and white* equating emotions with instinctive feelings may not only distance people from recognising true feelings, but may also provide them with a sack load of evidence to justify strong unnecessary reactions.

Everyone remained silent as Marie sat back down on her bar stool. "Did you ask Johnny yet?" she said calmly as she addressed Bertie with her back pointed towards Gerry.

"Ask me what?" Johnny asked cautiously, avoiding her stare.

"We want a small favour, Johnny," Bertie said as though he was exhausted. "We were wondering if we could leave the dog with you for a few days."

Johnny shook his head. "No way; I'm not having 'Dennis the Menace' in my place," he replied firmly.

"Marie was saying we could go to Dublin for a few days," Bertie explained.

"I'll give you a help with Dennis," Gerry interrupted, offering a token of peace, despite the fact he was talking to Marie's broad back that faced him.

Marie did not seem to accept Gerry's olive branch as she turned slightly with a firm response. "No way, your cattle will trample him, he needs minding, and he's only a small puppy."

"The mother at home will mind him," Gerry suggested happily, "she loves dogs."

Bertie nudged Marie. "Cheers Gerry," he said as he raised his glass. But Marie said no more, she drank a third of her pint in one gulp before she stood up and nodded at Bertie to follow suit as she headed straight towards the exit. Bertie winked and nodded to Gerry as he was getting up to leave. "Anyway, I was trying to tell you before that Marie said she saw your English friend in the supermarket later on," he whispered. "Now it is only my feeling but why would someone be doing grocery shopping if they were not planning on staying for a bit?"

Gerry smiled. "Thanks," he responded quietly.

Bertie put his hand on Gerry's shoulder. "Anyway, that was the news."

Fresh thoughts of Grace entered Gerry's mind, and he smiled as he found himself slowly sipping the almost full pint of cider in his hand. He placed it back on the counter before departing to take his trailer load of grain to the factory. And then he decided he would call it a day, giving himself an hour to write in his journals and to decide his next step.

The following morning Gerry looked up the phone book when his mother and father were out milking the cows. He was searching for the names of art colleges in Cork, he had not known before he met Grace that there was even one, and luckily for him there was just one. He felt excited as he wondered how he might sneak away for a few hours to check it out. It was not like he could call in sick and take the day off from work; the mother and father would be suspicious. He had to come up with something more reasonable than that, especially when it was one of the busiest times of year for a farmer.

His opportunity came later in the afternoon when the dry, warm weather changed and it started to rain heavily on the barley. Rain was the biggest fear of farmers, and when it rained on the crop the soaked moisture could reduce the grain value by half. Gerry and his father packed up for the day safe in the knowledge that the forecast promised drying overnight; they arrived back to the farm house after four PM. It was his mother who started the conversation when she asked Gerry what he would like for his twenty-sixth birthday gift. Normally, Gerry was not interested in shopping topics, especially when it was still four weeks to his birthday, but his mother, like most women, planned well in advance. Previously that would have irritated him but Gerry had seen the favourable prospect and asked if she would mind if he went into town and looked for his own gift, he was thinking of getting some new clothes for the occasion. Despite the lateness of the day and the unlikely probability of the shops being open still, as soon as Gerry got the 'go ahead' signal from his bewildered mother, he was gone in his car like a shot.

He had parked the car two parallel streets away from the art college when he started to feel nervous. He was not sure what he would say if he saw Grace, or how he would approach her, whether he should be untruthful and say he was just passing, or whether he should tell her that Bertie had told him she was in town. He did not even know for certain if she was at the art college but it was his best bet. He could not ring the college because he did not know her surname, and he started to get anxious as the horrific thought occurred to him that she may not even remember him.

He then decided his thinking was doing him no favours, so he got out of his car and started walking instead. He casually loitered adjacent to the college entrance under intermittent rain for over an hour, and when anyone passed he looked at his watch throwing his eyes to heaven as though he had been waiting for someone who was typically late. It was after seven PM when he saw her; he recognised the knitted handbag first. She was alone and was walking towards him. He had nearly wet himself with nerves.

"Hey," he said as it came out in a high-pitched screech.

She stopped opposite him with huge smiling eyes. "Hello," she said cheerfully, "wow - fancy meeting you here."

He focused on another attempt at a casual tone. "You look great," he croaked.

Her smile almost engulfed the entire of Cork harbour. "Thank you, wow, you also, you look great, this is amazing, wow, what a coincidence," she replied rapidly.

"Yeah," he coughed hoarsely as he stared vacantly in the stillness of the bubble of her beauty. "Silly of me," Grace continued, "you don't believe in coincidences, do you?"

"I don't?" he questioned as he worried instantly whether she had suspected that he had planned this.

"Most spiritual people don't," she replied beaming.

"They don't?"

She laughed. "Oh, you're having me on, are you not? I remember our conversation."

"Me too," he confirmed through his dry mouth.

"How's your writing going?" she asked enthusiastically.

"Great," he replied still staring.

"Am I delaying you?" she asked in a slightly worried tone.

Gerry coughed again. "Not at all," he said quickly, "why would you think that?"

"You seem rather quiet," she said.

"I'm just surprised that I am standing opposite you," he said finally, and they looked silently at each other with neither noticing nor bothered about the dampness of the evening.

"I guess," she said, "but you and I both know this is serendipity."

"We do?"

She smiled. "Oh, you do make me smile."

"That's a start," he said in a tone that started to resemble his own again as he focused on the perfection of the little damp curls that sprung up around her face.

"Do you live near?" she asked.

"No, I live in the countryside, about thirty miles away."

"Are you in town for long more?" she asked.

"I came up for a bit of shopping earlier," he fibbed. "But I'm in no hurry; the day's my own to do how I please."

"I have a meeting with my mentor at eight this evening, but we could go for coffee first?" she suggested, and he was glad she did because he was not sure how he was going to get the nerve.

"That'd be grand altogether," he agreed immediately. "I am dying to hear what you've been up to."

"Well, one of the teachers at the art college has agreed to let me be his understudy for a year, he seems to love my work, I pretty much work as an assistant and learn from him which means I'm here until next June," she said encouragingly.

"And do you live near?"

"I'm staying in the hostel until I find something more permanent; you don't have any recommendations, do you? It's not the best sharing a room of eight bunk beds."

Gerry had not the first idea about how to find rented accommodation. "Oh I'm sure I could help out and make some enquiries for you," he said instead.

"Would you? Oh, that would be so great; I don't know anyone yet – wow! – it's so good to meet someone familiar on the street in a strange place, everything is new and yet exciting," she enthused.

Gerry gained a more natural composure as he relaxed into a smile. "Well, I can buy you coffee first and sure then you can tell me all about it," he said as he led her into a stroll along the pavement.

"You know, I think it was one of your friends I met yesterday also," Grace said, looking at him as they walked.

"I know, I heard," he replied.

Grace smiled politely. "Oh really, it was a bit of an odd meeting, no-one really said much."

Gerry smiled. "Bertie said the same thing."

Little creases formed between her eyebrows as though Grace was thinking hard. "Maybe an accent barrier, I reckon," she finally said, "he was with his wife, it was an awkward moment, but they did seem like a nice enough couple though."

"They're lovely really, they were excited telling me they saw you," Gerry fibbed in a nice manner.

Grace laughed. "Really? His wife followed me around the supermarket."

"You're joking! What?!"

"Yes, she followed me for a good five minutes while I was shopping, and then finally I stopped and turned around and smiled at her, and she seemed embarrassed at being caught, so she walked towards me and literally starting talking at me, and very rapidly," Grace continued.

Gerry laughed at the scene that Grace had painted as he imagined Marie playing detective hiding behind boxes of cornflakes. "She never told me that," he said as he continued a fond laugh and he started to understand another possibility as to why Marie had taken her initial dislike to Grace. She had been caught out, maybe she had felt foolish and decided to divert her annoyance onto the other person, the easiest solution being to blame the other person. But then again, Gerry thought, he was equally making assumptions, and it really mattered none to him either way. And with no strong emotional attachment on the subject, he trusted his intuitive reasoning.

"I have no idea what she said," Grace said, and she frowned slightly as though she was making sense of what might have been said.

"I'm sure she was only being friendly," Gerry replied indifferently.

"Yes, I am sure, but she... well...she did come across as being slightly aggressive though."

Gerry smiled more as he teased, "you don't think she'll be your first new friend in town then."

"She can't be," Grace said encouragingly, and she beamed a spotlight of intense smiles through Gerry's face, "I've already got my first friend in town."

Gerry laughed. "I don't even know your surname."

"I don't know yours," she replied.

"Daly."

"Well, Gerry Daly, I'm Grace Carter," she said, and had her smile widened any further she would have swallowed him whole.

"I'm not letting you go without your number this time."

"The only numbers I have are for my teacher, the art college or the hostel, so you'll have to wait until I get my own place, but in the meantime, you could give me yours," she suggested politely.

Gerry looked down with embarrassment. "I live with the parents."

"How wonderful! Do you think I'll ever meet them?" she teased.

"Well, you'll never know unless you ring me," he replied on cue.

Her long eyelashes swayed from the breeze of her breath above an openly flirtatious gaze. "Then I'll have to ring you," she replied softly.

Gerry reciprocated her hypnotic gaze. "Then you had better take my number," he agreed immediately as he felt himself fall under the trance of understanding romantic love for the first time in his life.

Gerry could not believe his luck, not only was the most delectable woman in the world about to become his first girlfriend, she seemed to be the woman he could trust to share his more sensitive side with. Grace was unparalleled; he felt alive as the sparks grew into flames at the prompt of her voice. He tasted freedom with her; and he knew that she was the woman he wanted to spend the rest of his life with.

CHAPTER TEN

Gerry drove the combine harvester and his brother Jimmy, and their father Mick, each had a tractor and trailer; when the grain tank in the combine was full, Jimmy and Mick would take turns driving slowly beside the shaft of the combine so that Gerry could dump the grain into their trailers. And each time he did, as the combine slowed down, Dennis, Marie's pup, climbed promptly down from the harvester and pranced about in the tall sheaves of the corn.

Gerry understood why the pup was nicknamed 'Dennis the Menace', the little rascal was constantly playing hide and seek in the straw, and Gerry had to stop work several times to find him, which continuously delayed the task in hand. It made no sense having a little pup on the combine, especially if the sharp blades of the combine's header came in contact with him, but since Gerry had volunteered to take care of Marie's puppy while she and Bertie went off to Dublin for their weekend break, he had no choice but to bring the pup to work with him. His mother, Anna, did not allow Dennis in the house on his own as he was not properly trained yet and Gerry could not put the pup into one of the sheds because the cattle would trample him.

It was only a week before his twenty-sixth birthday and Gerry was praying for more rain, a sin for a farmer; but he wanted the time to meet Grace again. He had only met her twice since their first coffee shop date in the city and Gerry felt frustrated.

Gerry had known Marie would be like a mother leaving her baby when they dropped Dennis before she and Bertie went to Dublin, and as expected when she had arrived to deposit Dennis on his holidays at Gerry's house, she had his doggy bed which looked like a furry igloo, and two large cardboard boxes of Dennis's stuff. Dennis's luggage indicated he would be high maintenance. And strangely enough, when Gerry went through Dennis's baggage, only out of curiosity, the one thing he could not find was a dog lead. He had immediately seen an opportunity when he told Marie to leave the keys of her house with him and that he would fetch it himself later. Marie had agreed.

It had rained just after four PM again that day; and, delighted, Gerry packed up the machinery before he quickly washed, jumped in his car and sped off into the city to the hostel where Grace waited. His mother agreed to temporarily allow Dennis in the kitchen as Gerry had promised to come back shortly with the dog lead, but in his haste he forgot and made a beeline for Grace. He was focused on his plan, which he put into action instantly as he brought Grace back to Bertie and Marie's vacant house to spend time alone.

It was nearly seven PM when they had arrived at the empty house and Gerry was careful to park around the back. He did not want anyone knowing how long he could be there; people in his area had a tendency to gossip. He lit a small fire and grabbed a couple of beers from the fridge while Grace lay gracefully on the long couch with her red locks flowing down its side and sweeping the floor.

"You get more beautiful each time I see you," Gerry said softly as he cuddled up beside her.

"That's because I glow when I am with you, my darling Gerry," she replied as she rolled her long fingernails through his feathery blond curls.

"Once the harvest is over, I'm hoping you can meet my parents, my mother is dying to meet you."

"I can't wait to meet them, but I have to admit I feel a bit nervous about it though," she said quietly.

"They will love you," he assured her and he snuggled her closer into his chest.

"Have you told them I am older than you?" she asked.

"No, what they don't know won't bother them," Gerry replied and smiled. "Besides, we look the same age."

"Do you think that would bother them, Gerry?"

"I'm not sure, I think we'll try and get over the first hurdle that you come from a Protestant background," he responded casually.

"That won't bother them, will it?" she said with surprise, "we're both spiritual, independent of our background religions, I'm sure that they'll be delighted that you have found someone with faith similar to yours."

"Well," he said and hesitated momentarily, "they don't exactly know that I feel a different kind of faith."

She turned to gaze directly into his eyes. "Why on earth not? They must have read your articles and all your wonderful opinions."

"Grace, you're the only person I have ever had those types of conversations with," he admitted.

"But what about your articles, Gerry?" she asked.

Gerry hesitated more while he absorbed the reflection of the bright sparks of the fire in her eyes. "I suppose it is time to come clean on that," he said finally. "I do write, Grace, I write a lot in fact, it's just that I've never had the courage to try and get my writing published."

"You're not published?"

"No, Grace, I'm so sorry my sweet that I led you to believe that I had been when we met on the plane, I had no idea we would meet again, less fall in love."

"We've fallen in love?"

"Well, I think I have, haven't you?" he asked slightly concerned.

Her smile widened as she planted a small kiss on his lips. "I think I may have too," she said softly.

"I'm so sorry, you are so beautiful and, well, I was shocked that I impressed you, and it's not something I wanted to tell you over the phone, I suppose I was waiting for the right time," he apologised.

"It doesn't matter, not now," she said as she cuddled closer to him.

"Everything else I have told you has been true, Grace."

"So what's stopping you from trying to get your work published?"

"That's easy, courage; courage stops me."

"Do you have a fear of rejection?"

"No, not at all; it's more a fear of success, a fear that some of my writing would get published if I submitted it somewhere and then the whole village would be talking about me," he explained truthfully.

"But that is a great thing, surely? Everyone talking about a local published writer, it would promote you," she replied with excitement.

"It could bring shame to my family and friends," he said quietly.

"I'm sure it wouldn't, I bet your family would be so proud at such an amazing achievement."

"I don't think you understand. The Dalys are farmers; farming is what I do."

"But you could also be a writer."

"My father is expecting me to take over the farm, it's a huge responsibility."

"But you have time for writing now and you farm full time, I don't understand, what would stop you from continuing to write when you took over the farm?"

"I will be solely responsible for the farm, at the moment my father and my brother also work on the farm."

"But you have three younger brothers, I still don't understand, sounds like there is lots of help."

"They're doing apprenticeships and going to college to find their own way to earn their living," he said casually.

"Now I am really confused."

"I'm the oldest, Grace, and I inherit the farm, that's the way it has been for generations and that is the plan for my generation," Gerry explained.

"That doesn't sound fair!"

"It is tradition, that's the way it has always been; only one son inherits the farm."

"That's incredible, have you never thought about sharing it?"

"Of course I have but I have never suggested it openly."

"Why on earth not?"

"Because these things don't get questioned, they get accepted apparently, and my father always says that he never wants his land sold or split. Grace, it's what he wants."

"And what do you want?"

"To work on the land... and... and to..." Gerry said as he stared sideways.

"To?" she asked quietly.

"To write about it," he replied as he threw a sideways glance to check her expression.

"Oh Gerry," Grace said fondly as she extended her hand towards his face.

Gerry sighed. "I make a decent living in what I do. I suppose it's easier for me to stay doing what I know."

Grace smiled fondly, "just be sure you do not end up feeling bitter and trapped when you think of all those other things you could have done."

His smile met hers. "The thing is," he said, "I keep getting this recurring thought, like a little glow inside, that tells me, well, a reassuring feeling that says it's ok to do what I get most joy from."

Grace looked sincerely into his eyes, "that's beautiful," she said.

"It comes back to courage," he said, "I mentioned it to the father a few years ago, and he looked at me as though I had five heads."

Her smile fell into a fond laugh. "Sounds like you have courage to me," she said.

Gerry laughed. "The lads down the pub would think I was mad, the thought of forfeiting a huge inheritance to follow a dream."

"Who says you have to give up your inheritance?" she asked, "I am sure there are ways you could do both, and just suppose you then found out your writing did take off, you could make the choice then!"

"I know," Gerry said as he sighed, "but my family are a little more complex than that. My father is terrified his younger brother, Uncle Joseph, will get his 'claws' on the land. There's a long history. Uncle Joseph is fairly bitter that my grandfather left the lot to my father. And there's been years of grief between the two of them."

"But how does that impact what you do with your life?" she asked.

"I suppose it shouldn't," Gerry said honestly as he shook his head, "my father spent years 'sticking up' for what he said was right, complying with his own father's wishes, sticking with tradition, battling with his brother, to be honest I don't think you want to know."

Grace searched his face, "what is it, Gerry?"

"I suppose my father is standing by those principles now, he can be fairly stubborn, and maybe he thinks that if he doesn't do the same as his father did, he might appear foolish after arguing the issue for years with his own brother."

"Do you ever talk about it?"

"Not at home, no way, it only starts arguments," Gerry replied instantly.

"But how would your Uncle Joseph lay a claim to your land now? After all these years," Grace asked with confusion.

"My father thinks that Joseph would be able to manipulate my mother or brothers if they had any claim to the land, he keeps telling me that I can stand firm just like he did."

"So he's putting the responsibility to carry on family resentment onto you?"

"I suppose you could look at it like that. From his point of view, he is standing by the principles of family tradition."

"And what do you think?"

"I just want peace," Gerry said resigned, "but I don't want to let my father down either."

"And what about the rest of the family?"

"No idea! I don't know what they think."

"History can have a habit of repeating itself, maybe you should talk with your father again."

"The funny thing is that I feel my father is worried about the twin girls, the youngest ones," he said, "and what's more than that, and I could be wrong but I can't help feeling that my father is sorry about all the trouble with Uncle Joseph, though I know he would never admit it."

"He's giving you a lot of responsibility, Gerry."

"Yes, I know. He's not an easy man to talk to though, when he gets a bee in his bonnet."

"But you could talk to him? Maybe find out how he really feels."

"It's a hard one," Gerry replied and started to smile again, "anyway, my father is only in his mid-fifties, it's not like he's going anywhere soon. He's as fit as a fiddle."

"Well, once you have no regrets - that's the main thing. We always have choice, and I do think you have the courage to express your truths and feelings," she said softly.

"I know I do," he replied easily, "a few more weeks won't hurt, I'll bring it up with the father some day when he's in great form, maybe over a pint or something."

"You're different, Gerry," she said more seriously.

He smiled, "I've always known I was different. If the lads heard me talking about my feelings they'd have me committed."

"I love the fact you talk about your feelings, it's not regular for me to meet a man like this, why do you think I'm still single at thirty?"

Gerry looked at Grace's serious face, "in truth, Grace, you're the first I have ever admitted my feelings with; I think I'm like a valve ready to burst!"

"I think this is only the start of something wonderful for us both," she replied.

Gerry held her tighter, "I know," he said, "I think we'll be good for each other."

Grace looked at him with a cheeky grin. "So, tell me about your brothers and sisters."

"Jimmy is next to me," he replied, "he's twenty-four and finished an apprenticeship as a mechanic, and Bob and Mick are twenty-one and twenty and they're studying engineering out at the college."

Grace laughed fondly. "Wow, your parents were busy in their first years of marriage."

"It's better than that, my sisters Joan and Yvonne are twenty-three and twenty-two, they work in the local bank; and the young twins girls Norah and Eileen are nineteen, apparently they want to travel and see a piece of the world. The parents are not exactly thrilled about that, they want the twins to find some local employment."

"Wow! Your dad was certainly busy for seven or eight years," she said with huge surprised eyes, "and if he had time for all that and managed a farm, what's stopping you from running the farm and writing?"

Gerry laughed, "you've managed to come back barking on about my creative notions again, and to be honest I don't know how the parents would view my writing, that's what's stopping me."

"You think they would be ashamed?"

"I don't think I could walk into the local church if the community really knew about my stirring beliefs about God being everything, some sort of oneness, not some giant man in heaven who judges us; and if I didn't go to mass it would bring shame to the family," he explained truthfully.

"My darling Gerry, your worries are small."

"What do you mean, Grace?"

"If I still had my parents, even ones that were ashamed of me, I think I'd be over the moon, you don't know what you have until it's gone," she responded quietly.

Gerry reached out to stroke her arm. "What happened to them Grace?" he enquired carefully.

"They died in a car crash when I was twelve, my dad was drunk driving and the accident killed them both. We had lived in North London and basically after their deaths I moved to Torsands in Cornwall to live with Aunt Joyce," she replied softly.

Grace lifted her head slightly and managed a sparkly smile as she placed her arm over the back of his neck. "You know, Gerry," she said, "it wasn't exactly the type of romantic evening

I had planned earlier and I have led you to believe that I am some sort of exotic and artistic woman who is as free as a bird, but there are some truths you should know about me also."

"You can tell me anything you like, it won't change how I view you," he replied truthfully.

"I used to go to bed at night and prayed so much for my parents to come back, you won't understand how it feels until you lose one of your own."

Gerry looked serious again. "I have never even thought about a day when my mother and father wouldn't be around, I always think of them as invincible and being there forever."

"Well, you can still appreciate them even if you are not with them; I appreciate my parents through my thoughts."

Gerry found courage, "even if your father's foolishness killed them both," he replied.

"Yes," she said gently yet firmly. "You cannot let mistakes, even huge ones at that hold you back. Otherwise you'll grow old in bitterness and remorseful, just like what you say about your Uncle Joseph."

"I think that at times, I mean you cannot change the past, all we can do is make the best to go forward," he said reflectively, "it all seems so simple when talking with you."

Grace smiled. "That's what I am doing my best to do. And I tell you one thing, despite my faith in all that we cannot touch and see, I also encounter one obstacle after another."

Gerry noticed a slight anxiety shine through her face. "What is it, Grace?" he asked again.

"Gerry, I don't have money, I don't own much, I'm just a country girl from Cornwall," she said seriously.

"And I'm a simple country boy from Cork," he replied fondly.

"All I ever want is to be the best me I can possibly be," she continued with a hint of frustration. "I left school at fourteen so I'm not even educated properly; I've worked in lots of pubs, restaurants and shops and ran about in life, not taking anything too seriously when I was younger, and then well... well, not long after my sixteenth birthday I started having what I call my 'daddy dreams', since then my father has spoken to me constantly in my dreams, and one night he told me to follow my own dream. Gerry, there is definitely an afterlife and it is a wonderful place, I am sure of it."

Gerry noticed her stare of hope as her face glazed in a distant smile. Then she turned to look at him again and paused; and she inhaled a slow, lingering deep breath before she spoke again. "That dream of him was so vivid; it was enormously bright and focused right in front of my face. I can still see it now. My dad told me that my passion would become clear to me, and he smiled and stroked my face gently before he departed again. I didn't know what to think; I was mesmerized and wondered for a few days whether I had imagined it. Then, not long after, I noticed how artistic Aunt Joyce's patchwork cardigans and designs were, and it surprised me how I failed to observe that before. I asked her if she thought I was artistic, she said I would never know unless I did one. So I did, and the results were not bad. I realised quickly that my heart sang when I drew or painted a new design for her and the more I practised the better I got. When I started to believe it, I saw I had an artist's talent. And with this my enthusiasm and passion grew even more.

"I decided to go into fashion design. But I got rejected from most fashion houses due to lack of experience, qualifications, education – you name it. But of course I kept pursuing this route, I believed I was following my heart but I was really following an ambition to make a career out of fashion. I confused this determination with my intuitive feelings and it took me a while longer to realise this, which was when I finally learned to listen to my real instinctive voice. Sometimes when we get an idea we can let our logical minds totally rule and forget the internal voice and feelings that gave us the idea in the first place.

"So I went back to my original feelings of creating genuine art, art that expresses a true inner voice and so I applied to several art colleges in England - again I got rejected from eight or nine of them, but this time I knew that I was definitely on the right path, I learned to trust myself in this pursuit and knew I wanted to experiment with various types of creative art without always having to know the ultimate answers. I trusted that on following this path that more would be revealed to me. When I was twenty I got accepted to a small, unassuming college in South London. Aunt Joyce was concerned about my sudden move, but I wasn't, I had learned faith."

Gerry moved closer to her. "I think you are amazing; Grace, you really are," he responded slowly and sincerely. "I knew you were an impressive woman when I met you on the plane, and now I mean it more than ever."

"Not as impressive as you think Gerry, it was so expensive living near London and I could only work two days a week with my course. So it wasn't long before I realised I couldn't afford it and I was back in Cornwall within six months."

"Oh Grace, I'm sorry."

"Gerry, everything happens for a reason, even when things appear bad on the outside we must search to see the message in it, there are blessings in all things and it is up to us whether we are open to seeing it or not. I found out in that brief six months in that college that my real talent was in sculpture, in sculpture that was a celebration of my emotions. The time came when I had to leave because I had no finance, but the burning desire inside me told me I would never give up. I kept practising, selling some of my pieces in stalls and I saved hard while I continuously pursued art scholarships and further opportunities to develop my talents and awareness.

"And believe it or not, that's how I ended up in Cork. A tutor from the art college in Cork noticed my exhibits in a local stall while he was vacationing in Torsands, and through contact I have eventually found myself here as one of his understudies. I was aware that my income would have taken me about twenty years to save enough to fund myself through a decent college, so this is a huge opportunity for me and it has only taken ten years for me to get here. I used to feel sorry for myself, but not now, and even though I still earn a pittance I am doing what my heart craves the most. Don't you see how it is meant to be like this? How I was meant to come here? I was meant to meet you."

Gerry tried to pull her closer but Grace wriggled free as she sat upright, and her large round eyes gazed down on his soft face. "You know, Aunt Joyce, has been knitting me clothes almost forever, and the kids in school used to tease me about my strange dresses; they also used to call me 'freckle monster', my face was covered in red freckles back then."

Gerry laughed. "I bet they're jealous now when they see how beautiful you are."

Grace sat firmly as her smiles revolved into another cheeky grin. "One day I'll be wealthy, a famous sculptor and you will be so proud of me," she said with a laugh.

"Grace, you are already wealthy and you know it, there is nothing you need to do for me. I love you just how you are."

"And me you," she replied honestly as she finally allowed herself to fall happily into his grip and onto his chest. Gerry immediately dug his fingers into the sides of her rib cage as she screamed with laughter, trying desperately to wriggle free from his firm grip and tickling. Grace became uncontrollable with hysterical laughter, and the more she made that noise the more Gerry laughed, amused by her strange hyper-pitched yells and facial expressions. The phone started ringing and Grace begged Gerry between her laughter pain to let her go and answer it. But Gerry was experiencing too much fun to quit, with tears of laughter rolling down both faces as they squirmed around like children on Marie's old couch, and Grace's body twisted in every direction at the slightest touch of his fingers on her sides. Every time Gerry poked her again into one of her ribs, she let loose another bout of hysteria, and each time it was a new noise, and between short laughing breaths she promised to do anything he wanted if he would let her go. He finally gave in when the phone started to ring again.

"I suppose I should answer it," he said as he laughed and teased her with his rib-poking fingers that he waved at her face.

Grace tried to catch her breath between nervous laughs. "You sure? Are we meant to be here?" she asked in short breaths, as she backed away suspiciously from the threatening and wriggling airborne fingers that followed her.

"No," he admitted, as he pretended to grab her again. She jumped off the couch, and Gerry dived after her in pursuit. "It's been ringing for ages," she said as her body twisted beneath his on the old carpet and her eyes begged him not to subject her to his tickle torture again. He grinned back at her with tantalising eyes.

"I love your puppy eyes," she said between more laughter and if that was the distraction she had wanted, she got it when Gerry jumped backwards, "Oh shite," he said suddenly. Grace sat up as her body wormed free. "What is it?" she asked, startled by his reaction.

"Dennis the Menace, oh shite, I forgot about him."

"Who is Dennis the Menace?"

"The puppy, Marie's puppy, I was meant to get his dog lead from here to take home to my mother, the mother will be looking for me."

"Do you think that it was your mother phoning?"

"Not sure, she'd never think I was still here, would she? Unless, oh no, maybe she's thinking that something has happened to me. I had better ring her. One tick and I'll be back." His fingers tried to provoke a reaction from Grace again as Gerry moved towards the phone. It started to ring again and Gerry picked it up finally.

"Gerry, thank God," Johnny said sounding relieved.

"Oh, it's you," Gerry said with surprise, "how come you are ringing for me here? Did you see my car out the back?"

"We've been looking for you for over two hours," Johnny said.

"Agh, there's no worries, I'm grand; I thought it might have been my mother worried about me."

"I think you should come home," Johnny insisted.

"I'll be home in an hour, where are you anyway?"

Gerry detected a slight shake in Johnny's voice. "No; no, come back as soon as you can, look, we'll explain when you get back home to the farm."

Gerry sensed a sudden worry. "How come you are at my parents' house?" he asked.

"I'll explain later, Gerry; look, your mother wants you to come home straight away."

"Grace is with me," Gerry admitted, and he wondered whether Johnny would tell Marie that he was playing 'goldilocks' in her house while they were away.

"Bring her with you, just come home, Gerry. I'll see you in about ten minutes," Johnny said firmly.

"Okay; no problem, we'll be there soon," Gerry replied, confused.

"Good man, good man." And the phone hung up on the other end.

* * * * *

Gerry drove his car into the stony lane leading into their farmyard where several other cars were parked also, including Johnny's. "WOW! This is where you live; my God; it's enormous," Grace exulted with huge, open eyes.

"It would want to be, there are ten of us living in the house remember," Gerry replied and smiled. Under his smiles, he was anxious; Johnny's tone had worried him.

"Thank God, you're home," Jimmy said as Gerry strolled into the kitchen, but Gerry looked immediately towards his mother and her swollen red eyes as she sat limply in her old armchair in the corner.

He instantly reached towards her. "What's up, Mam?" he asked gently. "Did something happen to the pup?"

"That damn pup is the cause of it all," Jimmy cursed.

"Where have you been all this time, Gerry? We've been looking all over," his mother asked with quivering breaths, as Gerry squatted by her chair holding her hand.

"I was at Marie's house, Mam; sorry; I am so sorry, I forgot to get the lead, what's happened Mam?" Gerry asked slowly, but deep down he suspected he already knew.

His mother appeared to go into a state of numbness as she stared vacantly into his face; and Gerry remained by her side as she grasped his hand firmly, her nails almost digging his skin. Gerry started to shake; he felt he knew what was coming.

Gerry's brothers, sisters, his two Aunts and a few neighbours were also present in the sombre atmosphere of the kitchen and had any of them been speaking, Gerry had not heard. "Gerry, my friend," Johnny finally said as he placed his hand on Gerry's shoulder, "my good friend, I'm so sorry, your father has had an accident." Gerry felt his mother's hand lock further into his.

"It's all Dennis's fault," one of the twin girls cried as they huddled closely together, but Gerry's brothers and two other sisters were as still as statues as they stood by the kitchen worktops as though they were glued to the ground.

"What has happened, Johnny?" Gerry asked quietly as he looked up at his friend.

"Your father came down to the pub after five for a pint, he said ye'd finished early 'cause of the rain, he only had one, Gerry, he left just after six to go home for his supper," Johnny said.

"What has happened?" Gerry interrupted firmly, as he urgently searched all the faces around the kitchen.

"I didn't know anything until Jimmy rang me about half six looking for you," Johnny said. Gerry looked over towards the kitchen sink where Jimmy stood. "We think he was trying to avoid the pup," Jimmy said quietly, "and turned the car sideways on the road and crashed into a lorry. We heard the loud bang from the kitchen."

"It was Dennis's fault," the twins cried loudly again.

"When we went out, he wasn't moving, he had no seat belt on, and we called an ambulance straight away..." Jimmy said as his voice trailed off shaking.

"He's gone, isn't he," Gerry said quietly to the floor where he was stooped.

"Yes," Jimmy confirmed quietly.

Gerry's head spun. He did not know if he was going to scream or throw up. His thoughts generated a new life source of their own. He was the one who volunteered to take care of Dennis, he was the one who did not get Dennis's lead, he was the one who left Dennis at home, he was the one who went off telling them he'd be back soon, he was the one who forgot, he was the one who did not tell them where he was really going, and he was the one who was missing for hours. His father was dead and he believed it was his fault.

Despite his better understanding, the privileged Gerry solely blamed himself. The smallest decisions and the slightest choice would have the biggest impacts.

CHAPTER ELEVEN

erry's mother Anna barely functioned following the loss of her husband. She put basic meals together and attended mass every Sunday, other than that she found little joy in anything. She no longer spent time on the farm, no longer attended the animals nor walked their land. She denied herself all that she previously found pleasure in and she chose to remain indoors, spending her time alone and praying for her husband's soul. Nothing suggested by either Gerry or his seven brothers and sisters was heeded as she remained numb and grief stricken for several months following their father's departure.

Gerry's twenty-sixth birthday came and went with little acknowledgement following his father's death; and Gerry felt responsible. He had confided only in Grace and it did not matter how much she insisted that he held no part in his father's death, Gerry's guilt remained. When he was not working on the farm, he spent his time writing, writing his thoughts and his deepest feelings, a cathartic process of literally dumping his shame onto paper; that was the only advice he had taken from Grace but it did not provide the release he so much wanted. His father's death changed him internally.

It was Mick Daly's last will and testament that started the real trouble in the Daly household. At first, it had seemed simple and mostly straightforward; after all it was what everyone had expected. Gerry was named as the sole inheritor of the farm and its contents to be endowed on his thirtieth birthday; with the condition that his mother was provided for for the remainder of her life. Another expected caveat was that the earnings from the farm would provide for the further education and work placements of Gerry's three brothers and four sisters, and each was allowed to choose two acres of land to build their own dwelling house if they so chose to do so in the future. In addition, Gerry was to pay each a lump sum of money when they in turn came to the age of thirty. Everything seemed above board as Mick Daly would have wanted it to be.

What was completely unexpected was that Gerry's Uncle Joseph was named as the executor of the will, and more surprisingly Joseph was also named as a co-executive to run the farm along with Gerry's mother until Gerry would inherit the lot at the age of thirty. It had seemed that Mick Daly had wanted to make some amends with Joseph after all, but it had also seemed that Joseph, who was the only brother of Mick, had not acknowledged this as he continued to act out the past issues, and at only forty-nine, Joseph had already grown into a bitter, resentful old man.

What followed was no surprise to Gerry, Uncle Joseph easily influenced Gerry's mother. Anna Daly let Joseph make most of the decisions while she chose to wither away inside herself. Gerry's guilt grew, and in an attempt to minimise his growing self-blame, he vowed secretly to the spirit of his father, that he would do whatever it took to ensure that Joseph got no claim on any of the Daly farm or land. He would stand firm as his father would have wanted him to. He decided to believe it was his only way to earn forgiveness.

"Gerry is not mature enough to be running a farm, his head is in the clouds with his Englishwoman," Gerry heard Joseph tell his mother as he listened outside the kitchen door. It was not even four weeks since his father has passed, yet Gerry was focused on eavesdropping on any of their conversations at any opportunity.

Anna had appeared to agree with Joseph. "I donno 'bout her at all, I think there's something awfully queer about it," she replied.

"He's your son, you have to talk to him," Joseph said, "I mean, who in the name of God would call their child Grace?"

"It's probably an English thing."

"Well, I'd prefer if he'd taken up with a local girl," Joseph insisted, expressing concern, though decidedly Gerry knew it was only another clever decoy to camouflage Joseph's innate ability to cause trouble.

"I'm not sure what we can do, we've no control over who he'll meet. He has to make his own choices."

"Do you think she's a Catholic?" Joseph said with a tone of manipulation. Gerry felt sudden anxiety.

"There's nothing we can do about it if she's not," Anna responded. "It's not likely he'll run off with her, is it? Agh no, it's not; he's a good head on his shoulders."

"How long has he been trucking with her now?" Joseph enquired.

"Since August I think; over two months, Joseph."

"I still don't know though, I quizzed him yesterday about her and Gerry would give nothing away."

"As sure as God made apples, if you keep questioning him, he will run away with her," Anna replied.

"We have to do something," Joseph insisted.

"I'll talk to him," Anna said quietly.

Joseph was examining Anna's expression carefully as Gerry walked into the kitchen. "Hi Mam," he announced as he glanced sideways at Joseph.

"We were just talking about you, Gerry," Joseph said snidely.

Gerry searched his mother's face. "I know, I heard," he replied promptly.

"Joseph suggested earlier that maybe Jimmy could work on the farm fulltime until we get things back in order," Anna said.

Gerry reflected confusion. "Jimmy wants to work as a mechanic," he responded.

Joseph reached over and patted Anna's hand gently with his wiry fingers. "We know that! But we have decided someone must help you fulltime on the farm while your mother recovers her health," he insisted.

Gerry stared at Joseph with contempt, in his three piece suit, thinning greasy hair and pale complexion, having never done a hard day's labour in his life, the same Joseph that had assumed a position of power dishing out orders and decisions. "Maybe you could help on the farm," Gerry suggested sarcastically to his uncle, "and let Jimmy live his own life and make his own decisions."

Joseph nodded aggressively towards Gerry. "I always knew there was a greedy streak in you," he said maliciously, "you would deny your own brother a bit of the farm, wouldn't you?"

"I am carrying out my father's wish as he wanted; it's not my issue if you don't agree with it, Uncle Joseph."

"Up in your room writing, and queer writing it is too, huh; not to mention the company you are keeping," Joseph spat out. Anna dropped her head to face the floor. "Stop it; please," she pleaded quietly.

Joseph reached for Anna's hand again as he sneered at Gerry. "Your father would want you all to get on in peace, and look at you now," he said.

"We did; we were; there was plenty of peace until you started interfering," Gerry shouted.

"I am carrying out your father's wish," Joseph insisted, and he nodded hard at Anna, searching for an agreement from her.

"And that includes reading my diaries, does it?" Gerry said, as he again searched his mother's face for a hint of support, but she had looked sideways with slight guilt.

"Your father worked that farm twelve hours a day, and we expect you to do the same; shame on you, boy, driving up and down to Cork to meet a strange woman and writing shameful thoughts. You should put your head into your work, and stop fooling around. Your problem is that you got everything far too easily. And you know she'll go back to England and leave you, don't you?" Joseph spat out.

"I don't think it is any of your business!" Gerry shouted back.

"I think it is my business when the bank statement shows that you have paid for a return flight to England. None of us have taken those flights, and we know you haven't either. We know your secret, squandering away all our money for your girlfriend to visit her people, she's only using you," Joseph spat out again.

"It's nothing like that," Gerry shouted with despair as he looked desperately at his mother's hidden face, "and Grace is paying me back."

Anna continued staring towards the floor. "She's penniless, isn't she?" she asked.

"At the moment, yes; but she is working every hour she can to make it as an artist."

Joseph laughed. "An artist? An artist! We're not listening to this."

"What would you know about art?" Gerry cried out.

"Enough to know that it has nothing to do with farming, you have a huge responsibility and it's time you screwed your head on the right way round, and started acting your age."

Anna looked up briefly, "Gerry, my son, Joseph does have a point; we do need all the help we can on the farm, why can't you be a good boy to your mother and find someone local, a farming woman; son, this is not helping my state of health," she pleaded. "Your friend Grace will be gone by next summer anyway."

"How do you know that?"

Joseph smiled confidently. "We saw it in your writings," he confirmed as he folded his arms.

"I don't believe this, is nothing private in this house anymore?" Gerry screamed.

"Not while we are the guardians of the farm; when you are thirty and get your entitlements you can do as you please," Joseph answered.

Gerry felt his fury build. "You are NOT my guardian," he shouted.

Joseph's crooked nose sneered again. "I think you will find out that I am. Your mother has asked me to move in and help with the accounts. I am moving a bed into the downstairs parlour room later this evening," he said.

"Is this true, Mam?" Gerry cried, but Anna looked sideways again, avoiding his view.

Joseph sat up straight with his limp chest attempting a stiff air of superiority. "From herein out, you are on a weekly allowance since we cannot trust you with access to the money. Your mother and I are the only authorised signatures on the accounts until you come of age. And let that be the end of it," he concluded.

Gerry stood dumbfounded. "Mam?" he pleaded, but Anna said nothing. And Gerry's temper soared as he swept past them, storming out of the house and nearly taking the kitchen door with him as he slammed it.

Gerry needed something to numb his anger, something to dull his brain, so he made a beeline for Johnny's pub. Bertie and Marie were sitting at the bar when he and his tempestuous mood arrived.

"A double whiskey," Gerry said curtly to Johnny as he plonked himself on a bar stool beside Bertie.

"It's a bit early for that, isn't it?" Marie asked curiously.

"What's it to you?" Gerry barked at her.

"Jaysus, Gerry, you're fierce sensitive altogether," Bertie said with surprise.

"Bad day Bertie boy, it's been another bad day, one bad day after another," Gerry replied as he downed the whiskey in one.

"What's up?" Johnny asked concerned.

Gerry's face twisted. "Uncle Joseph," he said with disgust. "Who do you think?"

"Jaysus, Gerry; calm down would you," Bertie said.

"Not that plonker again, what did he want this time?" Marie asked as she leaned towards Gerry for the details.

Gerry looked at Marie as he inhaled a deep breath. "Joseph's moving in, like a big brother monitoring my every move," he said. "He's determined to make sure he causes trouble. You should have heard the way he is manipulating my mother."

"He'll be asking Anna to marry him next," Bertie said innocently.

"Shut up Bertie," Marie ordered as she nudged him. Gerry's palms started to grow a new sweat as he listened to his pounding heart encouraging him to get het up again.

"It could happen," Bertie continued oblivious to Gerry's stare, "and then you'd have to keep them both on the farm when you inherit it." Marie kicked Bertie in the shin. "It WON'T," she insisted.

Gerry slammed his empty glass on the bar, "another double, Johnny."

"Forget Joseph, he has no claim, and don't be getting yourself all worked up over that fool," Johnny said sincerely. "Have you spoken to Grace at all lately?"

"No; they've a huge issue with her also."

"Your mother will love her when she gets to know her more," Marie responded with an awkward kindness. Gerry, Bertie and Johnny all frowned at Marie. "You haven't entirely taken a shine to Grace yet yourself," Johnny said quietly as he threw a quick glance at Marie.

Bertie shook his head. "But I think Grace is fierce lovely altogether," he said, "and she certainly has had an effect on Gerry."

"How do you mean?" Gerry asked.

"You're very sensitive when she's around, you're like a lion guarding its cub, none of us have ever seen you like that before, and we didn't even think you had it in you. We were only saying it before you came in," Bertie confirmed.

"Gerry wants to talk about Joseph, and not Grace," Marie insisted, appearing disgruntled with the new conversation revolving around Grace, and if her glare was capable of murder, Bertie would have laid face down flat on the floor.

Gerry stared into his second empty glass. "I don't think Grace will ever be welcomed in our house while that moron Joseph is still there," he said.

"Bring her to ours," Bertie said cheerfully. "You can meet her at our house." Bertie jerked forward as he felt the force of Marie's second kick into his shin.

"Are you going to tell Grace about the trouble now with Joseph?" Johnny asked carefully.

Gerry shook his stubborn head. "No way; she'll think we are a family of lunatics, money grabbers with snobby attitudes over religion." Gerry felt more fear, he couldn't bring himself to explain to Grace that he had consciously decided to continue and engage fully in the family feuding, not after everything they shared, not after her warning him of history repeating itself. Gerry decided that Grace would not understand his secret vow to his father, and that she would not understand his contempt towards Joseph. It was only an excuse, unconsciously Gerry knew that Grace could persuade him to handle the situation differently, and that was his greatest fear; if he took her advice how could he undo the blame he felt? He had to stand firm, he had to earn his forgiveness. Grace need never know. In truth, he felt ashamed.

"What are you going to do? You know the whiskey is not the answer, you can't keep your head buried in the sand forever," Johnny said.

Gerry looked up at his friends with a determined look upon his face. "The only thing I know is that I am continuing to see Grace however I can manage it; and if it's the last thing I do Uncle Joseph will not get a penny from that farm."

"You need to get yourself a solicitor," Bertie said easily.

"There's no need for any of that," Marie responded quickly, and she leaned further towards Gerry with an inquisitive look, "is there Gerry?"

"I don't know," Gerry replied bitterly, "I'll talk with Jimmy tomorrow."

None of them had to wait for tomorrow as Jimmy stomped into the bar, grabbing a seat beside Marie, the furthest stool from Gerry. "A whiskey, Johnny," he ordered sourly.

Bertie leaned back on his stool. "Jaysus, the Daly boys are all out on the whiskey today," he said. "So Jimmy, how are you coping with Joseph?"

Jimmy threw a sideways glance at Bertie, "he keeps my mother happy," he announced loud enough for Gerry to hear, "not like some other gobshite in the house."

"I suppose you are referring to Gerry here, are you?" Bertie asked bluntly. Johnny sighed and Marie stooped forward as she tucked her hair carefully behind her ears in case she would miss out on anything said. Jimmy spat across the bar, "our mother is upset; Gerry left her in a terrible state, she said the doors nearly came out of the hinges when he left."

"Everything was grand before Joseph came along and you know it, Jimmy," Gerry fired back.

Jimmy stared resentfully at Gerry. "Uncle Joseph is only making sure everything is done fair and square," he said loudly, "you seem to be the only one acting as if you're bigger and more important than anyone else."

Gerry threw his hands aggressively in the air. "How the hell is that?" he shouted. "In the name of God, Jimmy, don't tell me that Joseph is after twisting you around his finger also?"

Jimmy scrunched his face. "Uncle Joseph is only ensuring that we all get our fair dues," he replied.

"How? He's taking over, Jimmy, can't you see it?" Gerry shouted as he slammed his fists on the bar. "He's looking for fair dues for himself only."

"Keep it down, lads," Johnny warned.

"Jimmy, you need to listen to me," Gerry ordered.

"No!" Jimmy shouted as he stood upright, pointing suddenly at Gerry, "you listen to me. Uncle Joseph said that our father was changing his will to divide the farm equally, and Joseph is doing what father wanted. Our father only died because of you; you should be ashamed to call yourself a Daly."

Gerry threw his stool back as he flung himself towards Jimmy, "you shithead," he yelled. Marie moved with an instinctive backward motion and Bertie ducked instantly. Jimmy attempted to throw a punch at Gerry but Gerry grabbed his hand mid air, pausing only briefly with a forceful look on his face before he hurled a sharp blow into Jimmy's abdomen. Jimmy fell immediately to the floor, coughing loudly as he held his stomach, and Johnny swung swiftly over the bar counter before he seized Gerry's six foot frame as he dragged him backwards. Gerry foamed at the mouth as he stared venomously down on Jimmy, and as he tried to struggle from Johnny's controlling grasp, Johnny clutched his arm like a vice as he moved in between the two brothers. "Stay back," Johnny warned loudly as he pressed his extended hand firmly on Gerry's heaving and powerful chest. Bertie and Marie moved quickly out of the firing line as Jimmy hauled himself up, and Johnny stretched his other hand instantly towards Jimmy as he held the two brothers at bay.

Each brother stared intensely at the other like provoked gorillas, with their arms dangling in threatening fist like motions under throbbing chests. A perturbing vein magnified itself on Gerry's forehead as he attempted to move forward. "I'm warning you, Gerry; stay put," Johnny said ominously. Jimmy looked like he was going to pounce again when he suddenly raised his fist to wipe his mouth, Gerry moved forward in response but Jimmy only shook his head as he turned away and picked up his keys from the bar counter. "Go on; run home," Gerry spat towards his back, "go home to Uncle Joseph."

Jimmy looked back before he left the pub. "I've done all the talking I will ever do with you," he said fiercely. "You're nothing more than a thug when you don't get your own way. Wait until they hear about this at home."

Gerry needed a muzzle, he had lost all control. Years of emotional suppression had finally manifested itself in violence. "Calm down," Johnny warned him carefully as Gerry glanced around the otherwise muted pub, noticing all the onlooking empty glares. "A double," he ordered. Johnny shook his head, "you've had enough."

"And Gerry is the one talking about seeing things from someone else's view point," Marie whispered to Bertie. Gerry turned to stare at them. "What the hell does that mean?" he shouted.

"It's amazing how money can turn family against each other," she replied.

"Stay out of it," Johnny warned Marie and he ordered Gerry to go into his back living quarters to calm himself down.

Gerry walked stupefied into Johnny's private bathroom, and instead of seeing his reflection on the cabinet mirror, all he saw was the brick wall that had become him. He sniggered at himself, laughing at his theories on uncontrolled emotional outbursts as he decided it was all a load of sentimental rubbish, it suited him to believe that; and he self-justified his reactions, telling himself that he had to deal with issues of the real world. He felt anger at Jimmy, rage at his Uncle Joseph and fury towards his parents, his mother sitting on the fence letting it all happen and his father for giving Joseph so much control. He blamed everyone but himself; unforgiving in the mistakes that others may have made and oblivious to his own.

He jeered further at himself as he thought of Grace, and what she would think if she could see him now. He thought hard about what they had discussed before, about talking to his father before it was too late, about expressing his true feelings and – the big one – about history repeating itself. He laughed again as he thought about what she could possibly know on the subject of families, she had grown up without one; and he convinced himself that at least he would have one problem less if Grace disposed of him for what he was becoming.

Gerry's internal roadmap had changed in the space of weeks, he was heading on a divergence and deep down he knew it. He still had choice; there were several intersections along his path, he just had lost sight of them at that point.

CHAPTER TWELVE

The listing for 'Panther Solicitors' in Cork city pounced out of the yellow pages directory at Gerry. Tim Panther, the senior partner and owner of the firm had a hard reputation for victory even in the most disadvantageous circumstances. He was so confident in his firm's abilities that he advertised a 'no win no fee' offer, which was exactly what Gerry had needed as his weekly allowance had left him virtually penniless.

In his heart he had never wanted to venture down this avenue, but the acceleration of events made it urgent. On December twelfth 1983, Jimmy and Uncle Joseph had sent Gerry a legal letter to notify him they were contesting his father's will. Gerry felt he had no choice, he had to secure his own legal aid; he believed it was the only way to secure his sanity.

Twenty-six-year-old Gerry had moved out of the Daly farmhouse a month before, taking a spare room over Johnny's pub rent free; life under the same roof as Uncle Joseph had become unbearable but living over the pub provided Gerry with the freedom of unlimited drink so it was no surprise to anyone when he developed a habit which became known as his 'daily tipples'.

Despite all of this, he still had not told Grace the seriousness of the issue, she believed he was learning independence when he got his own lodgings, she understood his excuses when he had been in fact drunk, she accepted his apologies when she enquired about meeting his mother again, and she accommodated his lies when she asked after his family. She believed all that he dished out to her, his deceit masking what he considered family shame.

On December nineteenth, exactly a week after he had received the solicitor's letter, a bitterly cold and windy Monday, Gerry, clad in his best pink shirt, sneaked into the 'Panther Offices' for his appointment. On approaching the reception desk, he had asked anxiously for Tim Panther, but a snooty looking girl about the same age as Gerry with short, blond hair and wide amber eyes looked up at him from her five foot slender frame and told him that, 'Tim Panther does not *see* the general public,' before she regarded him blankly from head to toe.

"With respect, miss," Gerry had responded with concern, "I have an appointment with the man himself."

"I assure you, you do not," she snapped, "now wait here until I get around to dealing with this." Gerry waited while he noticed the young madam make what seemed like personal calls; he waited for over thirty minutes.

"Right," she finally said snappily, "over here, I'll be dealing with your case."

"You?"

"Yes; me, now please hurry, we only have thirty minutes."

"I made an appointment for an hour," he protested.

"Yes, and most of that has been already used up."

"Used up? How?"

"I had to make a few checks on you."

"Checks?"

"Yes, we always check a client has funds before we take them on."

"You're a no-win-no-fee firm; what do you want to check funds for?"

"Well, we hardly do a no-win no-fee for any client; are you crazy? No, we only take on clients that make it worth it for us," she said arrogantly.

"So what did your checks say about me?"

"Nothing, yet; I need to see how much your case is worth first."

"I'd like to speak with the boss, Tim Panther, miss," Gerry said with as much authority as he could muster.

"I'm the next best thing to him that you will get."

"And who are you?"

"I am Tessa Panther, daughter of Tim Panther and executive in the firm."

"I'm thrilled for you," he said sarcastically, "but if it's all the same with you I'd like to see the boss."

"There's only one Tessa Panther in Ireland, you know, and only one daughter of the infamous Tim Panther, you should be grateful," she snapped again. Gerry could not help thinking that there was also only one Cruella de Vil.

He could not resist. "So," he said cuttingly, "if I was to send a letter to Tessa Panther, Ireland; you'd get it easily?" He sniggered as he saw his comment go straight past her ears. She had seemed to examine him strangely and her eyes opened wider, almost filling with aversion as she stared through him. Gerry noticed that there was actually nothing strange about this look; it seemed to have an element of congruency, he decided that this must have been her true self in her natural state. She seemed to be at home when she looked sour.

"People need to learn to pay respect," he heard her rant in the middle of some sermon, and Gerry hoped she was not expecting him to be the other half of her overbearing conversation; he was anxious and wanted legal advice rapidly.

"Look, my case is fairly simple," Gerry interrupted with deep breaths as he sat on a chair opposite the desk where she had perched, "some family members are contesting a will that has left a farm and land to me."

"I'm sure it's simple," she started to say and then she continued with a litany of legal spiel and Gerry felt he had no choice but to tune out, he had not the first iota of an idea what she was saying. He vacantly scanned the room, assuming the idiot persona she had seemed to treat him with, and he knew he missed most of her high-flying talk, but he had found it hard. She had seemed to be talking at him and enjoying her own conversation.

When he interrupted to understand some of her jargon, she responded more than once with, "I'm speaking," in a controlling tone. Gerry decided she must have been compensating for her inability to engage in any form of two-way communication, and if his business had not been so serious he would have sat back and watched her in action. But Gerry did not need entertainment; he needed a damn good solicitor.

A young man entered the room and handed a note to Tessa, and he departed as easily as he had entered without any acknowledgement from her. She studied the note, and the naturalness of her tempestuous look evolved quickly into a broad smile, albeit a false one. Gerry noticed immediately that it was fairly easy to tell when she feigned niceness, creases appeared around her eyes like reinforced propped up shelves and she forced little laughs which seemed to appear from her nasal area as her mouth was far too busy assuming its position of a smile. Her eyes had been the giveaway; her pupils maintained their pin point size.

"It seems we may be able to take this case after all," she said with this assumed niceness.

"I thought that was a given," Gerry responded.

"Of course, of course," she laughed artificially in agreement.

"So what about your no-win-no-fee proposition?" Gerry asked seriously.

"Oh, I assure you that this is ONE case we want to win."

"So, the boss will take me on?"

"Of course," she reassured, "and I personally will give it my priority attention."

"So when can I meet the boss?" he asked.

"Why don't you have dinner with us? Are you free this evening?"

"NO," he said quickly, "I'm meeting my friends in the pub."

"Tomorrow then?" she insisted.

"Agh, I'm not sure."

"Do you want to win this case or not?" she demanded to know.

"Yes, of course I do," he snapped back.

"Then be here at six PM sharp tomorrow." Gerry once again felt he was left without choice.

Gerry wondered about her change of heart. "And you think you can win this case?" he asked with confusion.

"Once my daddy sees the figures on this note, he will make sure that we do," she said, "so go along, you can leave now, and we will see you tomorrow."

"What figures?" he asked.

"The approximate worth," she said and dismissed him again.

"How does that make a difference?"

"We will discuss it tomorrow."

Gerry leaned forward over the desk. "Look, miss, I don't want to waste your time or mine, so start speaking to me in plain English," he ordered.

Tessa sent one of her concocted smiles in his direction. "Ouch," she said, "I didn't think a country boy like you would have such force in you."

"I wish I could return a compliment," he muttered. "So, Miss Panther, can you tell me what is on that note? And what are the figures?"

"We take a ten percent fee of all winnings in any case we decide to take on, I think my father will definitely agree that we will be taking your case on."

"I want the bottom line," he insisted.

"The land, farm, investments and total assets have an estimated worth of three point five million pounds," she said smiling. The chair nearly swallowed him up, and Gerry had thought he was going to have a heart attack; he genuinely had no idea of his father's worth.

"If it's the one thing I do, I will win this case," she said with a broad wrinkly smile.

"And you get ten percent; you get three hundred and fifty thousand pounds of my money?"

"At the moment you could end up with nothing, so I think it is a tiny percentage to pay, unless of course you want to continue with nothing, because you have that choice also," she said sternly.

"Okay, I'll be here at six tomorrow," Gerry agreed quietly.

"Good," she answered curtly as she leaped up from her chair, "you will soon see that *I always get what I want*, you will soon be glad that I represented you, you will soon be celebrating your victory. I will do everything I can to ensure you do."

Her words gave him all the assurance he needed, but her tonality and body language did not fit well with Gerry. "I don't want anyone to get hurt," he responded suddenly.

She smiled in an almost cheerful yet wicked manner. "Don't be ridiculous, people always get hurt in legal battles, you have to toughen up," she said as she beckoned him towards the door.

Gerry managed to unglue himself from his leather chair. "Maybe I won't have to, I'm sure you are quite capable of being tough enough for the nation," he said quietly to himself as he stood up towering above her.

"You can go now," she ordered dismissively as she moved towards the door with Gerry edging in pursuit behind. Gerry had felt uneasy leaving, and pondered on what she meant by 'doing everything' and 'victory' and 'getting what she wants'. So he did what he habitually did, he headed straight back to the pub to discuss it with his friends.

"Sounds like she is definitely what the doctor ordered," Bertie said after Gerry recalled the entire encounter.

"She seemed ruthless though!"

"Gerry, your own family are being ruthless with you, it's time you started to dish back some of their own medicine to them, and this woman Tessa sounds like she'd have no reservations in doing the job," Johnny said.

"And the sooner you put an end to that battle in your household, the sooner you can move on with your life," Bertie said, unusually sensibly.

"And have a more honest relationship with Grace," Johnny added with a sly reminder.

"Then, man, you need to hurry up, Grace will find out sooner or later, she won't believe your lies forever," Bertie agreed.

"I haven't been lying to her," Gerry insisted, "I am only protecting her!"

Bertie looked confused. "I thought you said Grace was 'The One', and you could tell her anything," he questioned.

"I can," Gerry said firmly, "and I will; but not just yet." Johnny and Bertie raised their eyebrows.

"In fact," Gerry continued, "I am going to ask her to marry me."

"You're doing what?" Bertie said and dropped his glass on the counter as he shot several open-mouthed glances between Johnny and Gerry.

Johnny shook his head and frowned. "That would be a great idea, Gerry," he said, "starting a marriage that's founded on deceit." Gerry ignored the comment.

"How long have you been trucking with her?" Bertie asked.

"Over four months," Gerry said proudly.

"Then you need to start coming clean with her, Gerry," Johnny insisted calmly.

"I will, when the problems at home resolve."

"And what if they don't resolve?" Bertie asked.

"How do you mean? You both agreed just a minute ago that 'Tessa what's her name' would do the job, of course it will get resolved," Gerry responded with frustration.

"Worst case scenario, Gerry, what happens if it doesn't?" Bertie asked again.

"Then I have no option, I will leave, I will go to England, there would be no other way."

"By God, Gerry, you have it bad for this woman," Bertie said easily.

"Everything that I am doing, and will do - is all for Grace," Gerry replied in a serious delusion. Johnny and Bertie sighed.

Gerry looked seriously at Bertie. "Bertie, I'm warning you, don't you dare tell Marie any of this, this goes nowhere outside the three of us," he warned.

"Well, you have our word, we won't say a thing to anyone," Johnny responded in earnest, "sure we won't, will we, Bertie?" Bertie nodded immediately in agreement.

Johnny sighed. "I'm sure you'll be back in your own home in no time, and there won't be any need for anyone to run off to England."

"Yeah, yeah," Bertie stuttered, "Tessa sounds like the trick you need alright."

Tessa was definitely the trick he needed and Uncle Joseph had finally met his match. But for Gerry his insecurity grew exponentially daily, and the more alcohol he consumed the more he plagued himself with self-doubt until it spread like a bad disease throughout his body. Even Gerry did not like the sudden changes within himself as he continuously blamed external circumstances for his own response, and his own behaviour.

Johnny grew deflated in the six months that followed when Gerry continued to live with him rent free and Gerry had a regular *need* to get things off his chest. It was Johnny who constantly inherited that chest but he was not driven by the same dramatic view points as presented by Gerry. Externally, Gerry was far too busy assuming to be someone else, the person he had been when he had originally met Grace and continued to be when he was with her. And inevitably Gerry was unable to maintain a long term balance through this public face, and the internal pressures of that prominent act resulted in consistent emotional surges that overflowed onto Johnny when they were alone. And despite Johnny's suffering, he always provided Gerry with his undivided time and listened attentively to the constant trials and tribulations that were inflicted by Gerry on him. Gerry did not once either thank him or acknowledge his appreciation; and no different to anyone who constantly complains and 'chest dumps' on their friends while actually believing they offer appreciation but never do, Gerry had unlearned gratitude.

Johnny only once challenged Gerry when he told him clearly that if he changed his habits that he would not have anything to *dump* or at least have less. Gerry got snotty when he was challenged, similar to the many others that he had previously criticised. Johnny got accustomed to it; he grew to expect no better.

And with an additional six months under his belt of successfully deceiving Grace, it should have been a bright day the following June in 1984; but instead a silent and sad cloud seemed to lurk over the car as Gerry drove Grace to the airport. She was returning to England having completed her understudy work, and having immediately accepted Gerry's proposal of marriage she departed blissfully with the faithful guarantee of their agreed future together. Gerry was camouflaged with faith, he had only one more month of pain to go before the final showdown – his impending court case was scheduled for Friday, July thirteenth.

CHAPTER THIRTEEN

"Who is 'Tessa the Tempest'?" Morcan asked out of the blue.

"Someone I used to know," I responded easily.

"In Realm One?" he asked.

"Yes."

"What was her Realm name?" he asked.

My mind was elsewhere, I was hoping Morcan would get bored and be quiet. "No idea," I replied truthfully.

"You probably think Fragrance put her name in my mind," he said.

"I couldn't care either way."

"Don't you want to know where I got her name from?"

"No; not really."

"The name just came into my mind all of a sudden – really – you probably think Fragrance planted her name there," he said again.

I had more important matters to consider, we were already six months into our journey and things were getting a little tight in there and I needed thinking room; the last thing I required was Morcan constantly crowding my thoughts. "Nope, I actually do not care," I confirmed more prominently again.

I was starting to put my plans in place; my scheme to get back to Realm One. It was becoming obvious to me that the Realm 'Undercover Movement' was still in operation because mother's 'Psychic Pregscan' conversations were revealing almost accurate information; well, with the exception that mother still thought she was expecting one boy and one girl. For that I could not blame the psychics or their soul contacts in Realm One; mother had made the assumption, and it was a given that no Realm soul in the 'Undercover Movement' would influence the choices of anyone on earth. I made mental notes to make some changes, and introduce some caveats to our undercover operations when I returned. But in the meantime, I lived with it.

"How did you know her?" Morcan asked.

"Know who?" I asked impatiently.

"Tessa?" he asked.

"She was one of the 'Soul Reading Police'," I confirmed, and then I nodded in his direction for quietness.

"Why was she called 'The tempest'?"

"She got that nickname on earth," I replied impetuously.

"She sounds fierce," he said.

"Yes, she was – now can we be quiet?"

"Were you caught by the police?"

"Why all the questions? Can't you tell I want a bit of peace," I said frustrated.

He looked hopeful. "I've nothing else to do, and I'm tired of sleeping, and it's too tight in here to play a game, unless we play something where we have to be in close range; or maybe bounce off each other?"

I sighed. "I tell you what, you think of a game we can play at close range and let me know tomorrow."

"I got it!" he announced almost immediately.

"Got what?"

He looked excited. "We could play Sumo Wrestling, YEP, pretend this ball of fluid is the ring and we are SO huge that we practically fill the entire thing up."

"You are joking, right?"

"No, come on, come on, we could do that, it would pass an hour or so, and then it will be almost feeding time, what do you say?" he said more enthusiastically.

"Why don't we wait until after dinner and then we will have loads of energy for playing, that's a better idea, isn't it?" I asked with disillusioned hope.

"But what will we do between now and dinner?"

"Think quietly and rest, we'll need our energy."

"Fair enough," he said. And then he was silent. Peace at last. That peace only lasted moments.

"What were you up to when they caught you?" he asked.

"When who caught me?"

"The police."

"How do you know they caught me?" I asked curiously.

"Because you said you knew 'Tessa the Tempest' from the police unit," he replied.

"That is correct."

Morcan leaned his face almost on top of mine. "So what's the story then?" he asked.

"Look; Tessa is someone on Realm One, she's not important really, now do you want me to tell you about stuff from Realm One that you possibly shouldn't know about and get you in trouble?" I asked. I had hoped he would pick up on the cue.

"We seem to be doing fine, Fragrance has not bothered us in ages, besides there is nowhere to go now but out, and things are only going to get tighter in here, so I thought since we are going to be siblings we may as well get to know each other," he said with a huge innocent smile.

"We still have three more months in here," I reminded him.

"Not really, we could be early," he said. I smiled at that thought, the thought of separation from Morcan. In the meantime I was certain he would not be quiet.

I sighed again. "Okay; I'll talk to you but if Fragrance starts annoying me about telling stories from the Realm, you have to tell her that you dragged it out of me. Is that clear?"

"Yes," he confirmed.

Secretly I had started to admire him, he seemed to be happy to take risks, albeit tiny risks, I supposed he was starting to learn that there was no way they could punish us in here, or else he was completely bored. "Okay, what do you want to know?" I asked.

He looked excited. "Tell me about 'Tessa the Tempest'."

"It's a short story really and not that interesting," I replied, "a couple of us were hanging out at APES, and one of the lads got arrested and then he met her, that about sums it up."

"What did he say about her?" he asked eagerly.

I smiled. "He had a relationship with her," I said.

"Was she pretty?"

"Not really; she was as bald as an egg," I responded with a laugh.

"Why didn't she choose another look? Did she not know about the 'Freedom of Form'?"

"I assume she took the form of the role she wanted in Realm One."

"Why did he have a relationship with her then?"

"Because he knew she would be useful."

"Useful for what?"

"To help him out."

"To help him doing what?"

"He had some plans," I confirmed. "And, oh yeah, this is the hilarious bit; you'll love this; he wanted a challenge. I mean, of all the challenges you could take on, I mean seriously, would anyone in their right mind want to take on the summons of a relationship with someone in the 'Soul Reading Police'?"

I felt I was in stitches about to tear as my laughter built up. Morcan seemed unaware of my humour, "maybe he liked her," he suggested.

"He actually did after they were better acquainted; but he played the game well at the beginning."

Morcan leaped up. "What game?" he asked with enthusiasm.

"The game to help him with his plans."

"I love games! What was he plotting?"

"He was involved in the 'Undercover Movement'."

"So that's how you knew him?"

"Yep, that's about the size of it."

"What was his name?" Morcan asked.

"He was known by one of his earth names," I replied.

"What was he known as then?"

"What's it to you anyway? – Are you a spy?" I asked with a half-serious laugh.

Morcan looked innocent again. "You said he played a game, I love games; what games did he play?" he asked.

"Undercover stuff."

"Oh go on, tell me; stop holding back, please tell me, I'll have it forgotten soon anyway when we get out of here," he pleaded.

"To be honest I am forgetting lots myself by the day, so my memories are a bit sketchy on the subject."

"You seem to still remember lots about the 'Undercover Movement'," he said.

"I suppose that is because our strongest memories are the last to go." I knew that I was loaded with such warped memories and past experiences that I found it difficult to shake them off, but at least I was aware that I carried them, even if I did allow them to influence my actions and behaviours. And I also played them out, it was important for the purpose of this mission. I had asked myself on several occasions, how many times I had to think the same thing over and over before deciding it was really what I did not want. It's was a human trait, making the same things happen again and again before acknowledging that we do not want those events to occur, yet continuously focusing hard on what we do not want.

I knew there are an infinite number of choices, and eternity meant just that; unlimited time to play out an immeasurable number of decisions and an endless number of experiences. The choice is whether the majority of the infinite are joyous thoughts or miserable ones, and that's where my free will came into play. And that is the journey I had chosen to experience.

"What are your strongest memories?" Morcan asked.

"I think love is number one, and involvement in the 'Undercover Movement' comes second," I confirmed with serious reflection, "I'm not sure how I will handle it when I forget those memories in a few months when we are finally born."

"You won't have to handle it, you'll have forgotten," Morcan reminded me. We both smiled.

"So what was the 'Undercover Movement' stuff that was so funny?" Morcan asked with genuine interest.

"Oh, we used to draw things, we had lots of theories," I said reminiscently.

"Drawing sounds fun. I love fun. What did you draw?"

"Equations – symbols."

"What symbols?"

"We were working out how to raise the consciousness of souls arriving to the Omega region of Realm One," I said truthfully.

"That's ridiculous," Morcan replied.

"I know," I agreed.

Morcan started giggling. "I can see now why you thought it was so funny. Imagine thinking that there is something higher in the Realm than the Omega region," he said.

"What?" I said.

"That is funny," he giggled again.

"You think that that place ruled by the Realm guides is normal?" I asked with slight disbelief.

"Of course it is," he gasped.

I looked on him with pity. "I suppose you know no better, I won't blame you, I blame the teachers and guides there," I said.

"Don't patronise me," Morcan piped up, "if it was not the idea that Omega is the end point, the highest place a soul can be; what was it that you found so funny then?"

"The drawing of the symbols, it was hilarious."

"What's so funny about that?" Morcan asked innocently.

"We drew them on earth," I said.

"That's not possible," he said dismissively.

My body started to tremble with more laughter. "It is, it certainly is, that's what's so funny."

Morcan seemed confused by my amusement. "Did you play a game? A fun game, like?" he asked.

"We hadn't intended to but that's kind of the way it turned out; we wanted to raise the consciousness of mortals on earth so that we could reduce the amount of souls getting grabbed by those Realm guides, which meant over time the growth of the number of souls they held power over would stop. We were clever enough to get to the root cause of it all and what better way than to communicate directly with earth? But of course we also had to work on raising the consciousness of the souls already trapped on Realm One so that the Realm guides would finally lose their power, so that they would be outnumbered," I explained truthfully.

Morcan looked seriously dumfounded. "You can't do that, it's not possible to communicate with earth from Realm One," he said.

"I think we have already established, dear brother, that it is possible. Have you not been listening to our mother's 'Psychic

Pregscan' lady? Where do you think she's getting the information from?"

Morcan looked as though he was thinking hard. "I still don't get the joke though. What was so funny about drawing stuff on earth, if that is what you did?"

"Because earth people came in heaps to see our drawings."

"But isn't that what you wanted?"

"Yeah, we did our drawings in nice big fields of wheat or barley, any crops where we could make an impression that was easy enough for us to see, and any field that was big enough to hold our full drawing; but that's not the funny part," I said. Morcan nodded and agreed with a still and serious expression.

"Well, we'd have a bit of the drawing done, and then we'd go away and sleep on it, and then come back a few earth days later to do some more, and we'd find people sleeping there, and dogs trampling all over our creation," I continued.

Morcan looked bored. "And I'm still waiting for the funny part," he said.

"Well, one time, my friend in the 'Undercover Movement', the one who liked 'Tessa the Tempest' decided to draw her face in the middle of one of the symbols, it was hilarious, he told her he was making a portrait of her, the portrait didn't do her justice at all. He got the bald oval head fairly spot on, but he slanted her eyes in the drawing also. He told her it was a caricature and that it was important to find humour in ourselves. She seemed flattered that he wanted to draw her, but she nearly had a fit when she saw it, and a dog was after doing a number two right on top of where one of her eyes were drawn," I explained as I shook with laughter.

"Hang on," Morcan interrupted, "'Tessa the tempest', the one you said was in the 'Soul Reading Police' actually knew you were communicating with earth and she let you?"

"Yes of course, we needed someone on the inside, everyone has a price; don't you find the story funny though?"

Morcan looked unconvinced. "Ha ha," he said.

"Agh come on, it is funny, and if you knew Tessa you would find it funny too."

"I suppose it would only be funny if I also knew who this friend in the 'Undercover Movement' was," he said innocently.

"Do you know what the most ironic thing of all was?"

"What?"

"We wasted so much time doing this when we had the solution inside ourselves all along," I said. Morcan stared at me in confusion. "Oh, never mind!" I added dismissively.

"You're a geek," Morcan stated suddenly with a stiff back as he started to laugh hard, and I realised our sense of humour had not been synchronised. Being a geek was a good thing.

"I'm surprised Fragrance didn't drop in," I said as I composed myself.

"She probably didn't need to," Morcan replied.

"She'd normally be here reprimanding us," I said, and then wondered seriously why she had not.

"She didn't need to because she probably knows I don't believe you," Morcan replied.

"What?"

Morcan stared right through me. "Okay, so you and your imaginary friend drew on crops on the earth, and the 'Soul Reading Police' knew and did not do anything about it?" he challenged.

"It was no imaginary friend, and yes the police did know about it, well 'Tessa the Tempest' did," I confirmed.

"Ariel has an imaginary friend," he sang, "Ariel has an imaginary friend...."

"I do not," I stomped.

"Yes you do," he sang.

"No I don't."

"Yes you do."

"NO I DO NOT."

"You know there's nothing wrong with having an imagination," he said.

I frowned at him, "I know that!"

"Everything starts in the imagination," he said.

"I know that," I replied again, "everything starts with an idea."

"And you have loads of ideas about what seemed to have happened to you in the Realm."

"Yes, and there is no such thing as a notion being out of our reach."

"Exactly, if we can imagine it in our minds, we can manifest it, we can make it happen," he said, "just like the games I invent."

"Exactly," I replied, "but you are the creative one."

"Everyone is creative," he said.

"Okay, but only some let that creativity flow, you are one of those."

"I think we all do that. If depends on what we create," he said easily.

"I know this, since when did you become Mr. Wisdom?"

"It's obvious, you say these things constantly to yourself but yet you don't practise them."

"I know that," I said again more impetuously, but I did not care to explain the detail of the thoughts I carried, the experiences I had inherited, such ones that can suppress any constructive mind creations. Morcan did not know my burden.

I knew it was my own choice whether hellish or joyous illusions come to be; and I know that imposing a reality based on a majority of deconstructive conjectures from the infinite number of possibilities was a more plausible definition of hell should I have ever decided to believe in one. I knew it, yet I was trapped by the past thoughts I held; and knowledge and practise are entirely different stories as I was learning.

Morcan started singing his mantra again. "So, Ariel has an imaginary friend.... Ariel has an imaginary friend..."

"No I don't, in fact you know him, so there, Morcan!" I sang back.

"From where?" he asked, and he started to sing again.

"You met him in SPOCC," I said as I smirked. "So there!"

"I know your friend from SPOCC; your 'Undercover Movement' friend, really?" he said with a tone of disbelief.

"Yes; you were in SPOCC with us both."

"Okay, which one was he?"

"Alfie," I confirmed in evidence, but Morcan nearly fell out of the womb laughing.

"Alfie? You're joking? Alfie is an incredibly nice soul but please; please; I'm not that stupid, I couldn't imagine Alfie messing up one hair on his head, and you're telling me that Alfie was drawing in fields, now THAT IS hilarious." Morcan giggled loudly.

I had to admit that I did see the funny side of that one, Alfie had liked to look perfect so we both laughed hard together; and our mother threw up. "So there," I said for the umpteenth time as I laughed smugly. "It was no imaginary friend."

"Unless of course I am part of your imagination also," Morcan teased with a half-serious tone.

"Stop it!" I warned him.

Morcan's eyes lit up. "That would be cool," he said. "It would mean that you are my imaginary friend also."

I attempted to kick him gently. "Is that imaginary then?"

"Ouch," he said.

"See, I told you so," I said as I winked fondly at him, "besides, it's starting to look like we'll get on well as brothers."

"But everyone says you're a girl," Morcan answered in a fit of giggles. "Yes," I responded dismally. I had not forgotten that.

CHAPTER FOURTEEN

Gerry kept his head down as he worked the next twenty-five years in the APES afterlife facility. He had not seen nor heard of Alfie since that day he had been arrested by the 'Soul Reading Police', and Gerry had conducted his duties quietly as he was unsure what to do with the information that Alfie had given him. Everything Alfie had said seemed to make sense, but he wondered if it had been the whole truth, after all he had not known that much about him, they had only met briefly.

Gerry had learned quickly to control his thoughts because he knew that Fragrance could drop in whenever she chose. But Fragrance appeared to be nice; and he wondered whether all this information had been nonsense about the board of Realm Guides. Was it really true that the Realm Guides created a process to assume power? Were they really primitive souls 'tied' to the earth and still believing that power was something that you held over others? Had he actually unconsciously chosen to trap his soul in this place? Was it true that he had chosen his own destiny through wild and unknowing choices from the thoughts he held on earth? And besides, what did Alfie mean when he said that Fragrance was not as clever as she thought?

Gerry grew afraid to think. He had wanted to think but his thoughts became self-deprecating enemies and his self-questioning only left him more confused and uneasy; so to camouflage his bewilderment he consciously made his next choice. Gerry decided that the only thing he could do was put the whole incident out of his mind.

He resolved to think no longer and Gerry continued to spiritually deteriorate since the day that Alfie had been taken. He also continued to ignore the greater presence of his soul, he had forgotten to believe he was more, rather than he could've been more; in essence, he had forgotten to truly believe. Gerry had conceded at the cost of his soul.

Gerry saw Uncle Joseph twice during his initial time in APES but on both occasions he had swiftly ducked from his view. In fact, he saw many others from the community of Upperton and he always did the same thing, he had hung his head each time in shame. Memories from earth overshadowed him, they became him, he became them and he had forgotten who he really was. He grew accustomed to depriving himself of any new thought patterns, until in October 2032, twenty-five years post his death, he got a glimpse of her, and even though it was only momentarily, he could have recognised her energy from anywhere.

Her outer appearance had mattered so little to him that he could not recall afterwards how she had actually appeared externally. All he had remembered was her smell, her hands, her aura and her voice. Her energy was the daemon; it distributed her scent with her being at the core. Her vibes were like a thousand twines extending outward with swirling movements demanding attention to her centre. It was captivating; her energy was magnetic and as he drew himself towards her, a thousand excited goose bumps appeared on his torso and with the thought of her slightest touch they all exploded in a domino effect. And so did Gerry.

Gerry had reached out urgently but Grace did not appear to see him. He had been so close, but instead he experienced an epileptic episode of the Realm equivalent of heart failure and another unfinished story with Grace. Heart attacks and Grace became the bane of his existence.

When Gerry finally opened his eyes the intense light of his surroundings was unfamiliar. The semi-darkness of the APES facility no longer loomed. The room was brighter, its ceiling resembling an extensive blue sky with intermittent clouds crossing which dulled the light at times, enabling him to see briefly. He had blinked his eyes several times adjusting to this new light; and it appeared to him that the dull atmosphere of APES seemed to have dawned into a new day. He looked across the room and between flashes of blindness he saw several others, there were at least fifty of them; and one on his far right, a young brown-eyed, blond German soul was speaking. He felt perplexed, he had no idea where he was or who this German soul was; but a tiny spark of peace resided within his being, it was a glimmer of hope which could burst into a bright flame with the right choice.

"I was a woman who believed she was kind, yes," Gerry heard the German soul say, "I thought that doing favours for others meant that they would give me favours too – yes – I expected those I helped to help me back the minute I asked. And it's taken me years; years to realise that I was not being kind; I was not being helpful, my acts were not generous ones. I was making an investment which I thought I could draw on anytime I wished; it was like I was building up credit in others which I expected to claw back whenever I chose. I wanted to control others this way. So to speak, when I offered to scratch someone's back I demanded they scratch mine whenever and however I chose. I only gave with the expectation of receiving, and I got angry when I did not. I spent my life constantly reminding others how I had been generous to them. These were not the acts of a kind lady."

A group of souls that had immediately surrounded her reached out to stroke her hands gently, comforting her before she said with long, deep breaths, "Beatrix Holst was that controlling lady, the name my parents gave me when I lived my last earthly life and I am now trapped as a ghost because of the choices that Beatrix made, but I know now who I really am – I am greater than Beatrix." And she looked around at all the souls as she concluded in one breath, "I am the soul called 'Verity' and I am a 'Soul Anonymous'."

All the souls cheered and Gerry thought he had seen a glimmer of relief flush across Verity's (or was it Beatrix's?) entire being. "A soul – a – what," he said to himself with disbelief, but the room revolved back to a silent order; and although Gerry could not see him clearly between the bursts of this unusual light, he heard an English soul speak next.

"I was a man who believed my highest value was my family," the English soul said quietly though confidently. "I believed I did everything I could to help them, I had so many ideas on how they could experience the perfect life as I thought I did, I organised events which I perceived as ideal, I was a perfectionist, I wanted everything exact without flaw and I wanted to demonstrate my absolute proficiency to help my family overcome their shortcomings. Through my correctness which was single-viewed, I lost complete perspective on their view of the world and how they wanted to experience events, I misunderstood how my nearest and dearest found their own joy.

"And even though I didn't realise it I continued to enforce my tunnel vision view on them. I was not being kind, I was not being helpful; I was insecure, a lost and misguided soul and I lived my life deluded in my own shortcomings. When my family did not conform or did not appear to appreciate my efforts, I thought them selfish and inferior. And when they made their own choices and did their own things, I sat back with malicious thoughts such as being resolute that unless they conformed to my ways of maintaining close relationships, they could not count on me. When they did anything out of the ordinary or made what I viewed as a mistake, I was resentful of them. In essence, I expected them to be exactly like me, exactly like the deluded self I was.

"And I was blurred by my own false beliefs; choosing to constantly forget how I had made so many blunders also. People had told me several times, people had told me we are all different but I always found excuses to justify the way I conducted myself. I constantly remonstrated that my ways were what I liked to do, how I found joy, and claimed there was no impact on anyone else; and moreover if others did feel an impact it was of their own doing. I had forgotten that I was unconsciously forcing my ways on others. I chose to forget that I was always trying to prove I was better than the next.

"I was talented; and I was genuinely wonderful at organising events but my insecurity shrouded my highest intentions of goodness. When people did not understand me I got angry with them, and my uncontrolled thoughts grew into those of fury and I was left feeling out of control. I oscillated between niceness and nastiness and I never understood why – I continued to blame others. Anger overcame me. And the more I tried to cloud that terror with external appearances of extreme pleasantness, the more I tortured myself inside.

"Richard Jones was the name of that tortured man, the name my parents gave me when I lived my last earthly life; but I know now I am greater than the thoughts and memories of Richard; I am the soul called 'Lovian' and I am a 'Soul Anonymous'."

Everyone cheered with another air of empathic forgiveness as more flashes of light appeared; and the more souls that spoke, with each one ending their speech with the same words, 'I am a Soul Anonymous', the brighter the room grew.

Gerry had observed carefully and with his eyes adjusting to the reality which appeared before him, he realised that each soul had only a spark of bright light in the core of their forms when they started to speak, but as each one acknowledged their mortal behaviours, each solid soul grew brighter and shone like a scorching sun. He wondered if he had unconsciously chosen to join some sort of cult and his fear returned; and the spark that was in the core of Gerry's own being started to dim slowly.

The silence that followed seemed prolonged, and then Gerry slowly noticed that everyone in the room had turned to look at him as though he was the next to go on stage.

"I see we have a new arrival today," a tall and slim female soul with distinguished cheekbones said softly to Gerry, "welcome to Souls Anonymous, the SA, my name is Trinity and I am the group leader."

All the souls cheered 'welcome' in response.

Trinity smiled. "And would you like to tell everyone your name?" she asked.

"Am – am," Gerry coughed, "my name is Gerry."

"Hi Gerry," everyone said happily.

"Hi," he said quietly with a slightly worried wave.

"And in your own time, would you like to tell us all here today why you have come to the SA?" Trinity asked kindly.

"I'm not sure," Gerry responded uneasily.

"That's okay," Trinity assured him, "coming here is the first step and is often the hardest."

"I have brought him here," Alfie interrupted with loud authority, and an immediate lingering 'wow' echoed the room as all the souls glared at him like adoring fans, but Gerry looked shocked. "I have brought Gerry here to 'Souls Anonymous' for a wake-up call."

Gerry continued to stare at Alfie in disbelief. "Gerry, you are here because I want you to see what can be achieved in a short time," Alfie said.

"He must come here of his own free will," Trinity insisted. "We cannot choose this for another."

Gerry looked anxious. "Come where? What is this place? What is the SA?" he asked.

"Let go of your fear," Alfie ordered. "This is only one part of the 'Undercover Movement'. This is the one part where a soul can raise their consciousness."

Gerry emphasised Trinity's words with an air of self-pity. "I didn't choose to come here," he protested.

"Unconsciously you have," Alfie said calmly as everyone listened in eager silence, "deep down you know there is more than the 'process' of the Realm guides which you seem to have embraced so easily."

"I saw Grace," Gerry said bitterly. "Why did you bring me here? Why take me from her?"

"Whether you may or may not have seen the woman you call Grace is of no consequence," Alfie responded easily, "I have brought you here to realise grace is everywhere if you can only see clearly."

"YOU took me from Grace," Gerry spat out, "you took me from the one thing I have always wanted."

"The ONE thing you have been obsessed with," Alfie said firmly. "I brought you to the SA to open your eyes. Your obsession with memories and miseries is killing your soul."

"I was with Grace!" Gerry persisted.

"You continue to create your own dismal reality, Gerry; you have chosen the woman called Grace as your highest objective.

Do you really believe Grace to have the same behaviours as the woman you remember? Everything changes here. When you learn to choose something higher than a human love, then everything else falls into place. Choose to free your soul, to be all that you really are and everything you want comes from that," Alfie said with authority.

Gerry was not convinced. "You mean peace?" he asked as he winced.

"Yes."

"I will have peace when I am reunited with Grace," he persisted.

"Really? So you chose to believe the cart comes before the horse still," Alfie said curiously.

"No; you know I don't," Gerry insisted. "They come together."

"Oh Gerry, I had better hopes for you, everyone here realises that the horse existed for centuries before the cart was invented," Alfie responded.

"Alfie," Trinity interrupted cautiously, "I don't think you should be doing this."

"But there is still a glimmer inside Gerry," Verity verified, "there is hope, there is still one small spark lighting in him."

"Yes," Lovian added heartily, "he only has to see his real soul and he too can be an SA; he too can light up like the rest of us."

"What is an SA?" Gerry asked bewildered.

"The SA, the 'Souls Anonymous' group is for souls who know who they are, they know where they have come from, and they admit any mortal shortcomings," Alfie explained.

Gerry sniggered. "Then if they know who they are, why do they call themselves anonymous?" he asked.

"Because we are still undercover Gerry, I have told you before, do you remember? There is a difference between knowing and experiencing and we are all on the journey still," Alfie replied in a softer tone.

"The journey to overrule the Realm guides? Is that it? That is not choosing something higher," Gerry remonstrated.

"We are doing our best; we are doing what we can to raise the consciousness and internal peace of souls who are here. Why do you think this room is brighter?" Alfie asked.

"The more we want to free our souls the brighter we become," Lovian answered persuasively for Gerry's benefit.

"We are freeing ourselves from the darkness and we strive to shine like the bright souls that we really are," Verity added with enthusiasm.

"We are sparks that become burning flames but you must choose it for yourself," Trinity stated.

"What part of the Realm have you brought me to?" Gerry asked suspiciously.

"The place that you have unconsciously chosen," Alfie affirmed, "to continue your journey."

"Where?"

"You know where you are," Alfie responded calmly. "You are where you have been for twenty-five years; you are trapped where the Realm guides call the Omega region of Realm One."

"I'm still in APES?" Gerry questioned.

"Yes, you are in APES," Alfie confirmed. "But you are being exposed to what souls can achieve here, what the 'Undercover Movement' can do, what we are doing, to raise the consciousness of souls, to override the Realm guides."

"No," Gerry insisted, "I am not stupid; this room is too bright to be in APES."

"As more souls strive to free themselves of the process of the Realm guides, the more our internal dimness becomes a new light. This is what we can do unknown to those who continue to choose to live in that semi-darkness. This is why you are here; you are seeing for yourself what we can achieve."

"You can't do that; you can't do that without the 'Soul Reading Police' knowing?"

"My dear friend, I think we have already proved that we can," Alfie responded with serenity.

"And this is only one part," Lovian added with excitement.

"Gerry is on his own journey, he must discover for himself," Trinity insisted.

"As your leader and founder," Alfie interrupted, "I tell you all that Gerry already knows who he is, and he now has to decide and be that." And everyone upheld Alfie's words as the true loyal followers that they were.

"I am a soul and I can be more," Gerry insisted, "but I want to find Grace."

"You *are* more," Alfie insisted. "Decide now who you *are* and *be* that."

"What about the 'Soul Reading Police'?" Gerry continued to ask anxiously.

"As long as you hold onto fear, the longer you will trap your soul in obscurity," Alfie replied.

"Why should I believe you? You were captured by the police, where have you been until now?"

"Doing this; setting up the 'Undercover Movement', obviously."

"How do I know you are not one of the police? How do I know you are not brainwashed?" Gerry said suspiciously.

"You have asked me that before," Alfie responded, "you only need to declare that accusation one more time and my promise to you will be to withdraw my help."

"But you were captured! How did this come about and how did you set this up under your captivity?"

Alfie smiled. "I was released, actually sooner than I thought; and in only a few weeks we have achieved what you can see now," he replied.

"And we can do more than this," Verity added with enthusiasm.

"And imagine what else we can do in time," Lovian said joyfully.

"How?" Gerry cried out.

"I don't think Gerry is ready for the SA," Trinity pleaded to Alfie.

Gerry stared at Alfie. "How did you get released?" he asked.

"There are ways and means, in all good time," Alfie said slowly.

"Then what do you want from me now?" Gerry asked.

"What I wanted since the day we met. You will join our 'Undercover Movement'."

"But Alfie!" Trinity exclaimed, "this is against what we stand for."

"You do not understand yet Trinity, but Gerry will be of enormous use to us," Alfie declared loudly.

"He has not made that choice," Trinity continued in despair.

"He will," Alfie confirmed.

"How do you know?" Gerry gasped.

"Because you want to find Grace," Alfie said calmly, "that is who you were thinking about when I grabbed you, isn't it?"

"Yes," Gerry admitted.

"And you thought you saw her when I grabbed you? I saved you Gerry; I saved you from the human memories that haunt you. I have introduced you here because you are starting to think again, you started to yearn for more again, and the more I am speaking to you the more you realise that you will find Grace easier in alliance with us."

"You know where she is?" Gerry asked quickly.

"Yes; join us on this journey and be who you really are, and finding grace will be easier than you think."

"Where is she?" Gerry asked urgently.

"The woman you know as Grace is at SPOCC," Alfie replied.

"How do I get to SPOCC? I have to find her," Gerry blurted in haste.

"You have work to do first," Alfie said.

"I want to find Grace," Gerry insisted.

"Then you need to get into SPOCC and you know that there is only one way to do that," Alfie said calmly.

"Evolve in APES. Follow the process. Assisting the growth of the souls that arrive here each day, by letting them know the process, by doing the job assigned to me, and by pretending to follow the rules of the Realm guides," Gerry said drolly. "There MUST be a quicker way?"

Alfie smiled again. "Yes, my dear friend, there is," he confirmed.

"How?" Gerry asked enthusiastically.

"All in good time, all in good time," Alfie repeated calmly.

"Alfie," Trinity called, "Gerry must say his soul name to join us, and he must acknowledge who he is."

"Gerry is not joining the SA for the moment, Gerry will join our movement in the other area," Alfie replied patiently. All the souls gasped with eagerness. "Gerry will work with me to raise the consciousness of the souls still on earth."

"I'll do what?" Gerry asked in surprise.

"It's called 'grabbing the bull by the horns'; you and I, Gerry, will work on the root cause and we will work on raising the consciousness of mortals on earth and reduce the amount of souls getting grabbed by these Realm guides; and Trinity will continue to do the same thing with the souls already trapped here," Alfie ordered.

Gerry glared at Alfie with astonishment. "But I want to get to SPOCC? You said there was a quicker way to get there, a quicker way to find Grace," he said rapidly.

"There is and you will experience more if you let yourself, we are all on the journey together; once you experience all that you are, Grace will come easily."

"Okay," Gerry replied with uncertainty. "But I still don't understand how you know she's at SPOCC."

"Because I heard," Alfie replied.

"Where did you hear?" Gerry asked.

"I can't tell you, not yet," Alfie said.

Gerry grew anxious. "Where did they take you? How did you get released?" he asked impetuously.

"In good time," Alfie replied.

"What happened then?" Gerry asked.

"Not for the moment, have patience - please."

Gerry welled with frustration. "What *can* you tell me?" he cried out.

"Nothing yet, I want you to be ready when you hear and only then will you listen."

"Why are the 'Soul Reading Police' not stopping this?" Gerry asked as he looked with amazement upon all the other souls in the room.

"Because we have an insider," Lovian piped out without permission.

"A what?" Gerry asked.

"We have converted one of the police to our ways and that is the truth," Alfie confirmed, "but you, Gerry, are not ready to hear the whole truth yet."

"That could take another twenty-five years," Gerry protested.

"The timing of that is entirely up to you," Alfie replied softly, "for now have trust."

Even though Gerry felt perplexed, he placed his trust in a human longing to meet Grace again, and he would do whatever it took to make that happen.

CHAPTER FIFTEEN

Gerry objected loudly. "You want me to what?" he shouted.

"Please; listen," Alfie pleaded as he moved closer into Gerry's aura, "this is why I didn't want to tell you sooner, I suspected you would react like this."

"I'm not working with her, Alfie."

"It's important for our work, Gerry, at the least consider it."

"No way!"

"You want us to be found out then; is that it?"

"You're the one with the theories and you're roping me in on your mission," Gerry insisted.

"I have to admit I was wrong, then, I thought that when you understood the hope of the souls at SA you would soon realise that bad feelings from earth are easily released here; maybe Trinity was right after all, maybe you are not ready," Alfie said dismissively.

"You're using me, and I'm not working with her," Gerry said as he pointed at Tessa.

"'Her' has a name," Tessa retorted.

"How could I forget it," Gerry responded.

Tessa folded her arms. "Well, whether you like it or not, you need me if you want your plans to work," she said.

"They are not MY plans; they are Alfie's plans," Gerry reminded them both.

"Gerry, it is our duty to all souls in Realm One to give them back their free choice and not be ruled by the Realm Guides," Alfie pleaded.

"I have no duty," Gerry retorted.

"Obviously; you never believed you had," Tessa responded sharply. "But some of us DO exercise duty to others; it is called loyalty."

"Loyalty, my backside! I suppose you were being loyal with all your lies on earth," Gerry argued.

"Earthly feelings no longer matter," Alfie insisted.

"They do, I'll tell you that; I have no problems working with Trinity or even the controlling Verity but I am not working with HER."

"What? Have you learned anything? Verity is not controlling, Beatrix was and Verity acknowledges that she is the released soul," Alfie spelled out in disbelief.

"They are the one and same thing," Gerry said.

"Oh my God, you have a lot to learn, Gerry," Tessa reinforced before she turned to Alfie. "Alfie, to be honest, I'm not sure I can actually work with him, he hasn't grown one bit since earth."

Gerry smirked. "That's right and you have each other now, and I am happy for you both," he said.

"Sarcasm doesn't help, Gerry," Alfie responded, "and if you didn't want to be with Tessa back then, I don't see your problem with Tessa and me making a union."

"I have no problem with that, it's your free choice, Alfie, my problem is that I don't see why I have to work with her," Gerry retorted as he stared at Tessa.

"You're still obsessed with Grace," she said smiling. "I bet you are!"

"You are both going to work together whether you like it or not," Alfie ordered.

"Really? But tell me first, Alfie," Gerry enquired snidely, "was that where you were for the past twenty-five years? Canoodling with Tessa all along? And I had been worried that the 'Soul Reading Police' had done something to you, worried they wiped your memory, or tortured you, or worse!"

"He's lying," Tessa said as she laughed, "Gerry has been too afraid to think, let alone worry about your welfare. Nothing changes; he locks himself up continuously in his own misery and self-pity."

"Gerry, listen," Alfie called, "Tessa IS the 'Soul Reading Police'."

Gerry laughed. "Oh, my dear Lord, this gets better! Tessa will trick you, I know her," he said.

"And I would still be under arrest with the police if it had not been for Tessa's help," Alfie started to explain.

"So now you think you owe her one," Gerry spat out, "I know all about that, she's tricking you Alfie, she tricked me on earth, she made me believe that I had to marry her as an obligation, that it was my duty, that I owed it to her, it was all a lie, and now she is doing the same to you."

"I wanted to marry you, and if I remember correctly you wanted to marry me too," Tessa interrupted.

"Stop it now," Alfie shouted at them both. "Tessa and I only met recently if that is your concern, Gerry, and she has not been here that long. But that doesn't matter now; all that's important is that we work together."

"So how did Tessa help you get free?" Gerry enquired suspiciously.

"She is assigned as my probation officer, they let me free on this condition, and Tessa is to report my every thought back to the 'Soul Reading Police'," Alfie explained.

Gerry laughed again. "That's exactly what she will do," he said. "She will set you up, you do know that? Don't you?"

"Shut up," Tessa shouted at Gerry.

"So why did you join the 'Soul Reading Police' then?" Gerry asked her sarcastically.

"THEY chose me," she replied defensively, "they said I would be perfect for the job."

"They were right there," Gerry agreed.

"I thought it was for the best," Tessa continued. "When I returned to the Realm I was rehabilitated into the police unit and they said I was specially chosen for that work."

Gerry shook his head with a sarcastic smile. "So, you just abandon your specially chosen work because you suddenly believe in Alfie who detests the sight of the police," he said.

"Yes," Alfie confirmed. "Yes; that's exactly what happened."

Gerry shook his head, "you two think I was born yesterday," he said dismissively.

"No, Gerry," Tessa spat back, "no-one ever expects you to be re-born; you are far too immature."

"Gerry," Alfie called more calmly, "this is why I couldn't tell you in front of the souls at SA, I knew you would react like this and the souls there would not see you fit to be part of our movement. You would cause more trouble than it was worth."

"I didn't ask to join, it would have made no odds to me," Gerry remonstrated.

"We need you," Alfie admitted slowly and aroused further suspicions in Gerry.

Tessa turned away. "I don't," she said indifferently.

"Tessa, please," Alfie called out as he touched her gently.

Gerry rolled his eyes. "The truth is coming out, need me for what?" he demanded to know.

"We need you to handle Fragrance," Alfie confirmed uneasily, "but first I need you to get along with Tessa." Tessa and Gerry avoided each other's eyes.

"Tessa, will you explain to Gerry what has happened to you? And Gerry will you listen? And can everyone remain calm while we sort this out?" Alfie pleaded to them both. Gerry nodded cautiously as he wondered what Fragrance had to do with their movement, but instead, and for once, he made the sensible choice and decided to listen.

Tessa searched Alfie's eyes before she spoke. "Okay," she finally said calmly. "I didn't know any better at first, Gerry, but when I met Alfie he changed everything, I don't want to be the person I was on earth, and you see I have changed. I want to make amends; I want to do what is right for all souls," Tessa blurted out with passion.

"I don't believe you," Gerry interrupted.

"Listen!" Alfie instructed.

"When did you meet Alfie?" Gerry asked.

"Only recently, I came back to the Realm only four months ago," she replied truthfully.

Gerry laughed again. "So you lived to the ripe age of seventy-four then and there was me thinking that you would possibly die of a broken heart after I departed," he said sarcastically.

"You're right, Gerry, I did feel freedom after you died, and yes, I had an absolute ball spending your money, I was lonely though and I did miss you in my own way," she explained with an honest look.

Gerry turned to Alfie. "She'll report me, I know she will; she may not report you, but I bet you anything she'll report me," he said.

"I won't," Tessa protested, "I'm not totally happy to work with you, Gerry, but I will do it for Alfie and for all souls, and to betray you would be the same as betraying them all."

"It's true, Gerry," Alfie assured him.

"What's truth?" Gerry asserted. "Everything here appears so real but yet does not feel real. How do I even know both of you are real? And if you are, how do I know if what you say is the truth?"

"That's the catch twenty-two," Alfie said calmly, "nothing's real that seems real, and yet everything is real."

"We are going around in circles," Gerry cried, "you are full of contradictions."

"Yes, it is almost like a puzzle," Alfie said calmly, "and I don't know all the answers either." Tessa looked blankly from one to the other while Gerry wound himself into another emotional knot.

"You have made yourself a leader, Alfie, what makes you any better than the Realm guides?" Gerry cried out. "There are souls out there that think you are some kind of God. Does that give you gratification? How are you different?"

"I think we all need to control our emotions, this is very testing and defeats our higher purpose," Alfie continued quietly. "Gerry, do you understand what I meant about knowing and practising being entirely different things? How easy it is for us to forget and let emotions overcome us. We are all in development still; and when emotions run high, intelligence flows low."

"What are you talking about, Alfie?" Tessa asked suddenly, "you said you knew, you said that we could free ourselves, you said it was about truly believing."

"This is priceless," Gerry sniggered, "even the lovers who proclaim they stand for the truth have secrets from each other."

"Come down from your own high horse," Alfie shot back. "You're no stranger to secrets. Why else do you torture yourself in shame?"

"I'm still paying for it," Gerry started to explain, but Tessa quickly over-shouted him, "For ONCE, can this NOT be about Grace? I've spent a lifetime living in her shadow. What's going on Alfie?"

"What's going on is that it is so easy for us all to fall into traps that are carefully laid out for us," Alfie responded calmly.

"You are trying to manipulate us," Gerry accused.

"Then maybe if you even start by believing that I am manipulating you both, then finally you have something in common and may even begin to agree with each other, something good can come out of anything," Alfie responded.

Tessa looked concerned. "Are you manipulating us?" she asked.

"No," Alfie replied fondly, "I am continuing my journey also." Gerry and Tessa looked perplexed.

Alfie sighed. "Let me give you the example of the mortal who spent his lifetime searching for the higher truth, a man who considered himself on a journey of spirituality," Alfie commenced to explain. "This man believes that all the answers are already inside of him, his soul knows all the answers, and he believes there is a higher truth that will be revealed to him as he starts to walk his spiritual path. He meditates and self-examines for at least an hour a day, and always searching within. He knows and sees heaven everywhere, the glory of God and His creations; and he makes it his higher purpose to know himself, know his soul, and the part his soul plays in the greatness of this universe and the other universes beyond. Yet he is still a mortal and with humanity there are many flaws. He is so involved in his spiritual searching that he ignores the most basic of his duties. He fails to spend quality time to have fun with his children, he neglects to wash the dishes after his wife has spent hours doing housework, he forgets to call his mother regularly and he even omits to pay the bills. His inner reflection and thoughts are so deepened in his meditation that he develops a tendency to forget the physical reality in which he then existed."

"Are you saying that meditation and inner reflection are bad, though they appear good on the surface?" Tessa asked curiously.

"No, I am not; this is where the catch twenty-two comes in," Alfie said firmly.

"There is also the man of complete opposites," Alfie continued to explain. "He believes everything before him in his mortal life is real; the arguments, the resentment, the bitterness of doing a job he does not like, the stress of public transport, disturbing incidents he hears and believes, and even the most basic tension associated with dealing with difficult people. He never once thinks about the other realities which he cannot physically see; he never thinks beyond the physical world into which he is born, in which he lives and dies, and he believes that life brings you trials and troubles and that it is not designed to be easy. He thinks he knows it all, and when another human positively encourages him to look beyond what appears real in his physical world, he dismisses it as illogical."

Alfie inhaled a long breath. "I am the first man I described to you; my earthly father was the second. There were flaws in both ways because we were both people who lost sight of another reality. I am not saying that all spiritual people do this and equally I am not saying that all non-spiritual people do this either; the point is that we both fell into a trap of our own unshaken and solid beliefs. It is about balance; the balance of living to experience the reality which you perceive on earth and also allowing yourself to grow spiritually."

"Is this only about you continuing you own spiritual journey then?" Gerry enquired.

"Not only that," Alfie admitted with a look of honesty, "it's about striking momentum and doing our best within the knowledge that we currently have. It's about knowing we are more than the limits of this place while dealing with the challenges imposed on us while we are here; and importantly, accepting that we do not understand everything yet as we continue our journey."

"So which approach should we take?" Tessa asked logically, "do we purely deal with the physical reality of this place in the example of your father's behaviour, or do we reflect internally on our souls and search for answers beyond the limits of this place?"

"There is no either/or conundrum, there are truths to be found in all things and approaches. It is no different to the religions created by mortals, there are some truths in all of those institutions, and it's about marrying beliefs with faith. So we will take the 'and' approach. We do both. We deal with this physical reality we are faced with, while we acknowledge we are not bound by the limits of this apparent reality. That is the catch twenty-two. And to do that, we start with the common denominators of love, kindness and forgiveness. This is about going back to basics, starting with genuine kind behaviour towards each other and our environment. It is no different here than it was on earth," Alfie concluded.

"And it is no more difficult here than it was on earth, which means it won't be easy," Gerry added, "which explains the knowing versus practising."

"Yes," Alfie agreed, "and we will continue to fall into the traps set before us whether we take a purely spiritual approach or a purely practical approach, which means we take the approach of the commonalities of both, which is the common language of *kindness, love and forgiveness* – everything boils down to the practise of this trilogy. Experience the apparent reality before you and simultaneously grow spiritually knowing you are not bound by that reality."

"Which is why you want Gerry and me to work together?" Tessa asked.

"Yes," Alfie smiled, "we are starting with the most elementary ingredients, and if you both can practise those on each other, you can practise and demonstrate on any soul where ever they exist."

"What about you, Alfie? How do you grow here?" Gerry enquired curiously.

"I combine both the physical and spiritual with love, kindness and forgiveness, as you both will do also; and with time we will start to truly believe. We know we *are* more and with action and practise we will truly believe and then we can be set free."

"So you are saying that you have genuine love for Tessa?" Gerry asked.

"Yes I do, maybe not at first when we met, but I do now," Alfie replied.

Tessa looked disgruntled. "How do you mean 'not at first'?" she questioned sharply.

"Serenity please," Alfie said calmly, "this is what I mean about the traps. We must be honest about our past, yet we must not be offended when we hear the truth."

Gerry smiled. "She didn't get the name 'Tessa the Tempest' for no reason," he said.

"Who called me that?" Tessa asked with an astonished look.

"Everyone," Gerry said as he grinned.

"Not me, I have never said that," Alfie added easily.

"Everyone on earth," Gerry said as he corrected himself. Tessa looked shocked, and Alfie sensed another tension growing. "Remember; kindness, love and forgiveness," he repeated to settle the mood, "it will not be as easy as you think, so we start with reminding ourselves to remember these three words. Once we remember, we will practise, the more we practise the more it becomes habit until we no longer have to remind ourselves; then we will be in fact '*being*'."

Tessa and Gerry both nodded an indication of understanding, while both regarded each other sheepishly in the knowledge that it would indeed be a trial for them both. Gerry sighed, and for the first time he truly understood the significance that knowing and genuinely practising were entirely different things. There was a lot more to it than the obviousness of this simple statement and the simplicity of the language in which it is expressed.

"Alfie," Gerry called after a gentle reflection, "what did you mean when you told Trinity that I will be of enormous use to the 'Undercover Movement'?"

"There are two reasons," Alfie replied. "The first is gentler and spiritual in motive, and that is if both you and Tessa can do this as a team, it will demonstrate to all souls what can be achieved in terms of forgiveness and pure love."

"Gerry and I will fall in love?" Tessa enquired with a look of disbelief.

"Pure love, I repeat," Alfie said, "not human love, not romantic love; but a pure love, again there is an enormous difference."

Tessa blushed. "Is this the kind of love you have for me?" she enquired softly.

"The love I have for you is genuine love similar to the human romantic kind, the love that is based on sincere affection," Alfie replied fondly. "Love based on affection is the easiest of all loves to have, believe it or not; but my aim is to have pure love for all, as you and Gerry will have for each other and for me and for all the other souls. We are on our journey yet, and our biggest enemy is the longing for the human definition of purpose, those memories are the demons that are trapping us here in this place."

"And the second reason is?" Gerry interrupted softly.

"The second reason is equally as important, and it is in fact the reason why I had been waiting for you to arrive," Alfie said, "it is the more practical reason, it relates to dealing with this reality in which we currently exist. I need you to handle Fragrance."

"What does this mean?" Gerry asked with confusion.

"Fragrance brought you back early, Gerry, that is why I have been waiting for you," Alfie replied, but Gerry remained confused.

"Fragrance was meant to take you in your sleep, and not in the pub where you finished your earth life," Alfie continued to say.

Tessa smiled. "If I was still the same Tessa I was on earth, I'd say that Fragrance did me a favour then," she said.

Gerry rose to the bait and challenged her. "Johnny is living in guilt because I died in his pub, he feels responsible somehow and I bet you let him," he said, "when I should have died at home in my own bed."

"Gosh, Gerry, I was only making a light-hearted joke," Tessa said appearing shocked by his outburst, "I do think it is important to see things on a lighter note at times."

"You were her first, Gerry," Alfie said, "the first soul Fragrance transported back to Realm One."

"So she got the timing wrong, is that what you mean?"

"Yes," Alfie confirmed.

"So you were waiting for Gerry because Fragrance messed up on the timing of his departure," Tessa reasoned, "which means if the board of Realm guides were to become aware of this then Fragrance would get dismissed and lose her precious position in the Realm."

"I was not waiting specifically for Gerry, I was waiting specifically for the first person that Fragrance would deliver and get it wrong," Alfie admitted.

Gerry understood. "And that's what you meant when you said that Fragrance was not as clever as she thinks," he said, "and her actions caused my friend Johnny more pain."

Alfie sighed again. "Gerry, the sad practicalities are as follows," he said, "the very minute Fragrance is suspicious of our movement, you will inform her you know her secret."

Gerry felt shocked. "You mean blackmail?" he questioned, "what about your lecture on the trilogy of love, kindness and forgiveness?"

"As I said, our methods are a mixture of both the spiritual and the practical; the practicality is that we have to face the reality of this place where we currently exist."

"But why would Fragrance monitor us?" Tessa asked. "They know that I am assigned to this job. Why would they interfere?"

"They will interfere when they become suspicious, we must be prepared for any eventuality that may occur," Alfie stated firmly.

Gerry felt uneasy. "I am not entirely comfortable with this mixture of the spiritual and what you call the practical," he said quietly.

"Yes, just like the example of a spiritual man that neglected the ordinary duties, and the man of opposites that failed to see what is not physically in front of him," Alfie said, "our only hope is to do our best to combine both ways; to do our best with the highest possible intentions. Just like there are a great many mortals that claim they know the truth whether it is from a purely worldly or spiritual way. We can only learn from experience, and by knowing that our experience is still limited as we grow, and accepting that we do not understand it all."

"I'm confused," Gerry said quietly.

Alfie smiled. "Confusion is good," he said, "it helps you to open yourself up to a new understanding. And when we are open to understand something new, we realise that in fact we do not know all the answers; and we grow. In the meantime we must push on and deal with the apparent reality of this existence, in the best way we can. As we grow and raise our own consciousness I am sure there is an easier way. That is what I believe."

"How can you be sure that Fragrance would be fearful of her secret being exposed?" Gerry asked.

"Because institutions of beliefs that are rule and process driven exist for those who live with fear. Why do you think they need a process?" Alfie asked rhetorically, "the process exists to control fear, the Realm guides are consumed by fear and Fragrance is no different."

"Fear is their biggest enemy then," Tessa said.

"Yes, and that is the only practical tool we have to use in our movement; using their fear to end all fear," Alfie added.

"Using the cause of all of this to end it, by mirroring it back on them," Gerry summarised in a more upbeat tone as Alfie smiled. And Gerry relaxed as he sat back, wondering how this may work to his advantage. This new knowledge meant he could easily snare Fragrance, and he marvelled on the idea of bartering this information in exchange for an express ticket to SPOCC, his passport to find Grace. He smiled at Tessa; she reciprocated his smile, both genuine for the first time since they had met nearly fifty years previous. But Gerry suspected that Tessa had monitored his thoughts.

CHAPTER SIXTEEN

"I need you to stay quiet for a few hours," I said.

"Okay," Morcan said.

"That was easy!"

"I'm busy myself."

"Doing what?"

"You said you wanted quietness and you're the only one talking," he replied.

"Okay, quietness starts now," I agreed.

"Okay."

"This is really far too easy, what are you up to?"

"Creating a new game," Morcan replied.

"Oh, okay," I said.

"What are you doing?" he enquired.

"I'll tell you later, I need a few hours quietness now."

"Tell me now, I told you what I was doing," he insisted.

"I want to listen to Mother and Daddy Joe," I said.

"Why?"

"I said I'd tell you later."

"Was Mummy Charlotte on the phone to her psychic again?" he asked.

"Not yet today, she wants to go to a gallery," I said.

"Where?"

"Listen to them and you'll find out and you won't have to ask me."

"I'm busy inventing a new game, I told you."

I sighed. "Then I'll tell you later if you can't be bothered to listen in yourself."

"My work is important also," he stated, "things are getting very tight in here, we need more new games we can play within the limits of this space."

"Shush," I prompted.

"Charlotte, are you sure you should be travelling?" Daddy Joe asked our mother.

"It's okay, Joe, don't worry," she had told him.

"Darling, I can't help it, your blood pressure is up, and you have gotten extremely large, the twins could pop out at any-time," he said fondly.

"I'm sure they have hospitals in Cornwall also," she said quite calmly, "oh come on love, just because I am pregnant doesn't mean I am an invalid."

"No it doesn't, but Cornwall is over three hundred miles from Hampstead and I am not sure you should be taking a train in your condition," he said.

"What condition? I suppose you are referring to the fact that I look like the size of a house and my legs are swollen up like tree trunks," she said, getting worked up.

"No, no; you know I don't mean that," he protested softly, "I am worried about you."

"Then come with me, you are supposed to," she said.

"Is that what the doctor said?" he asked.

"Not exactly."

"Oh Charlotte, please tell me that the doctor confirmed it was okay for you to take a train when you are seven months pregnant," he begged.

"Oh Joe, sometimes I'd swear from the way you speak that you were born in the twentieth century. Joe, it's the latter part of the twenty second century and Cornwall is only ninety min-utes by fast track train," she confirmed as she sighed.

"Charlotte, what did the doctor say?" he asked again.

"Nothing exactly," she replied quietly.

"You didn't ask him, did you? The doctor doesn't know that you are taking the twins on a train travelling over two hundred miles an hour, does he?"

"We're fine, Daddy Joe," I assured him, but he did not hear me.

"No, Charlotte, you are not going, why can't you do the sensible thing and go visit a gallery closer in London?" he continued.

"There's a medical team on the train," she said persuasively.

"I don't care, you're not going."

"If you are so worried, why don't you come with us?" she asked, before she added quietly, "you're supposed to."

"Because you only announced you were going this morning. Oh, please Charlotte, I have to go into London for work, and I'm going to be late if you keep this up," he said very firmly.

"Just because I only said so this morning doesn't mean I have not wanted to go for ages," she suggested.

"Charlotte, this is ridiculous, you have decided only this morning and now you are telling me that I have to go with you," he said loudly. Mother started crying.

"I know you think I am hyperactive, easily excited and slightly vain, Joe, but I want to do this, my heart and my soul are crying out for this; call it intuition, please Joe," she begged between sobs.

"You led me to believe that the doctor said it's okay; look, love, I know you are very intuitive, but really, now you have the twins to consider in addition to your own health," he said more softly.

"I know that, I'm not silly," she said quietly, "I just know we have to go there."

"Charlotte, please tell me this has nothing to do with your 'Psychic Pregscan' adviser?" he asked with concern.

"Well, it does," I said, "and you know she'll go there with or without you, Daddy Joe."

"I know myself," she continued to say.

"For what reason do you have to go there?" he asked in a more serious tone.

"I'm not sure, but we have a connection there. Oh, please Joe, you know I'll be right, I generally am," she cried softly.

"Oh God, Charlotte, I have to get into the bank today," he said with a sigh. "We'll go to the gallery at the weekend."

"Call in sick," she suggested.

"No, Charlotte," he responded firmly.

"Why do you have to be so logical about everything, Joe? Sometimes we have to live for the moment," she continued.

"My logic, my job as a computer engineer, my work in one of the world's biggest banks is what enables us to live in this lovely house in one of the nicest parts of London," he reminded her.

"Just call in sick for one day," she pleaded, "they won't know, just for one day, please Joe."

"I want to know why you suddenly woke up and a gallery in Cornwall becomes so important? What will it be tomorrow? Will I have to take another day off work then?"

"Okay then, go to work, I'm going without you, so either way you will have to take a day off work if only to monitor me, so what do you choose?" she threatened quietly. Daddy Joe remained quiet.

"I know your work is important, Joe, but sometimes I feel you need to lighten up, and not take everything so seriously, stop living your life like it's one of your work processes," she continued in a plea.

"But why now?"

"My adviser said.." she started to say.

"I knew it, this has to do with your psychic adviser," he interrupted loudly.

"Yes, it does Joe; she said it would be good for me, good for us both!"

"When did she say that?"

"Yesterday, when I spoke to her."

"And did she advise you about your health and the babies' health?" he asked.

"We're fine, Daddy Joe, let mother go, I want to go," I cried. Daddy Joe did not hear but Morcan did.

"I'm not fine, I'm in a quandary, and I can't think of a single new idea for a game, do you think I am becoming more human too soon?" Morcan asked in bewilderment.

"Shush," I said quietly again, shaking my head in his direction.

"My psychic said the babies are very healthy," Mother confirmed.

"And you believe her?" Daddy Joe asked.

"Yes," Mother replied confidently.

"Daddy Joe, the psychic has been fairly right so far, Morcan and I can confirm that," I said in mother's defence.

"Shush," Morcan instructed, "I am focusing on a new game."

"But you have to agree that the psychic has been right on lots of stuff so far, isn't that right?" I asked him.

"I suppose, but it doesn't really matter."

"Okay, I suppose it doesn't really matter in the huge scale of the universe, but are you not in the least bit interested why the psychic told mother that there was a connection with this gallery in Cornwall?" I asked with hope.

"I suppose, but Fragrance does have an issue with your interest in this 'Psychic Pregscan' organisation, she could be here any moment," Morcan warned.

"Fragrance cannot stop our mother making her own choices," I concluded abruptly, and a newly curious Morcan joined me to tune back into the outside noise.

"I can't go in to the office now, can I? If I go to work, you'll get the train to Cornwall, so I have to stay with you one way or another," we heard Daddy Joe say.

"I knew you'd come round," Mother said through happy sobbing.

"I think you two should rest," Fragrance warned Morcan and I suddenly, "you will both be making your journey out soon and you will need all your energy for that."

"Okay," I said.

"Okay?" Fragrance said with surprise, "I know what you are up to, Ariel."

"What's Ariel up to?" Morcan asked.

"Ariel has been making plans to leave you on your own," Fragrance told Morcan.

"Are you?" Morcan asked, as his big, round eyes glared me in the face. A shot of sadness hit me in the pit of my stomach.

"Not exactly, Morcan, don't listen to her," I said dismissively.

"Ariel is thinking about returning to Realm One and leaving you to be born alone," Fragrance added.

"Don't listen to her, Morcan," I pleaded again.

"Listen to me, both of you," Fragrance said, "you are both being born, there is no way back, you have no option but to go out and the time is coming soon."

"Would you really leave me?" Morcan asked with sad eyes.

"I would make sure you are safe," I reassured him gently.

"She's right then, and you are planning to go back," he cried suddenly.

"No one is going anywhere but out," Fragrance repeated sharply.

"You still owe me," I reminded her slyly.

"Let go of your mind, Ariel, that has always been your biggest problem," Fragrance said.

"What does she mean by that, Ariel?" Morcan asked confused.

"She's trying to confuse you, Morcan," I replied, "think about it, she is full of contradictions."

"You will be born, Ariel," Fragrance remonstrated.

"What's going on?" Morcan asked perplexed.

"Ariel wants to return to Realm One to search for someone that Ariel thinks is there," Fragrance told him.

"Searching for whom?" Morcan enquired immediately.

"You're not as clever as you think," I said to Fragrance in a gentle reminder of our secret.

"And you are not as clever as you think, Ariel," Fragrance said confidently as she departed.

"Searching for whom?" Morcan enquired again, but I remained silent.

"This is freaking me out, you don't want to be born for some reason, your interest in Realm One soul contact with humans; your comments about your Realm involvement with the 'Psychic Pregscan' organisation; your interest in this trip to Cornwall; and saying that you had someone on the inside in the 'Soul Reading Police'; are you getting me involved in something sinister?" Morcan gasped with several tones of frustration and worry.

"No, I am not, there is nothing sinister, STOP hanging onto every word that Fragrance says," I pleaded.

"Then help me understand," he cried.

"I have been. You just haven't been listening."

"Why don't you want to be born?"

"I am happy to be born, and I haven't decided that I would renege on it yet, it's just that I am better use in the Realm," I replied truthfully.

"Why?"

"To help the other souls there."

"Like this soul you are searching for?" he asked.

"I don't know where that soul is now," I confirmed sadly.

"So Fragrance was right, you are looking for someone and you think you will find them in Realm One."

"It's just that we have a better view of all life from Realm One, it's my best chance."

"Then why did you agree to be born in the first place?" he asked innocently.

"I didn't," I replied.

"So you really don't want to be here."

"I didn't say that."

"What are you saying?"

"It's complex," I said.

"Then start at the beginning," Morcan suggested.

"Don't you have a game to create?" I asked, hoping to divert him.

"Yes, it's called truth and I want to know it."

"Okay," I shouted exasperated as I threw my hands in the air fluid surrounding us. "I was in the Realm and I wanted to contact a friend of mine who lived on earth, I learned quickly that I could contact people on earth, and this guy was a great friend to me in a past life, he had lived in Ireland. One day when I started to tune into him, this woman called Doris DaValle came through instead and started talking back, it freaked me out to be honest when she spoke to me," I recalled truthfully.

"Doris DaValle, the woman who started this 'Psychic Pregscan' organisation on earth, you contacted her directly by accident, is this true?" he summarised suspiciously.

"Yes," I confirmed.

"We heard from Mummy Charlotte's psychic adviser that Doris was based in San Diego, so you expect me to believe that you were contacting a human in Ireland and someone almost on the other side of the globe came through to you?"

"Yes," I shouted.

"I don't believe you," he said.

"Then if you don't like the answers stop asking the questions," I said impatiently.

"It doesn't make sense, if you contacted the woman called Doris from the Realm then why don't you want to be born? If you were born then you could meet her in person," he said innocently. And I wondered seriously whether his hearing was impaired or else he just could not perform simple addition.

"Incorrect, Doris lived on earth in the last century, we contacted her in the summer of 2033, by accident I confirm; she was in her sixties at that time so it is a fair assumption that she is no longer on earth, or if she is reborn as someone else now then she would have little or no recollection of ever having been Doris," I stated factually.

"What was so important about contacting Doris?" he asked.

"It wasn't, it was by accident."

"Then why are you looking for her?"

"I'm not," I said, astonished by his naivety.

"Fragrance said you were."

"STOP listening to Fragrance," I shouted.

"Then who are you searching for?"

"Why don't you answer some of my questions instead," I said, "how did you know about 'Tessa the tempest'?"

"You said you didn't care before."

"Well I do now, what else do you know that you are not saying?" I questioned.

"I only know the thoughts that come into my head and I don't even know how some of them get in there; the other stuff I know is what you tell me; I also don't know what is truth and what thoughts are misleading and untrue," Morcan said with a hint of frustration.

"I have told you the truth about Tessa, about Alfie, about the 'Soul Reading Police,' and about contacting Doris. I have told you the fact that it is wrong to experience semi-darkness in the Realm, and I have told you that the place the Realm guides call the Omega region is not the end point. I have told you the truth, why do you not listen?" I asked, reciprocating his frustration.

"Because your presence here is a lie if you are planning to go back to the Realm and not be born," he sobbed.

"I never said that," I replied more softly.

"You didn't deny it when Fragrance said you were planning this."

"Oh, Morcan," I called gently, "can we just enjoy the day out to the gallery today?"

"I don't have the same interest in the gallery as you," he said.

"Galleries are for creative people, like you," I said, hoping to coax myself back onto his list of friends again.

"The visit to the gallery is connected to all of this, isn't it?" he asked suspiciously.

"Genuinely, I don't know, all I know is what we both heard the psychic adviser say yesterday, that mother has a connection to it somehow," I replied honestly.

"What connection?" he asked innocently.

"I don't know," I shouted with frustration, "if I was in Realm One I could find out, but we both know we cannot find out anything new while we are in here, unless we hear new stuff from the people on the outside around us."

"So you really don't know?" he questioned.

"No, I don't; look, why don't we find out together? You could invent a new detective game," I suggested, though I suspected strongly that detective work was not his forte. Morcan began to smile.

"And you will tell me about the other stuff later?" he asked.

"I'll tell you whatever you want to know, but you have to learn to accept my answers."

"Okay, so where are they now?" he asked.

"Who?"

"Daddy Joe and Mummy Charlotte," he replied.

"OH MY GOD, please, oh no, please don't tell me you have done this again," I shouted at Morcan.

"Done what?" he asked innocently.

"Diverted me, diverted my attention with more pointless questions, please, oh please, don't tell me we have missed their trip to the gallery," I cried.

"Why on earth would you think that I would divert your attention on purpose?" he asked innocently.

"Maybe not on purpose, but you said that thoughts come into your head and you don't even know where they come from," I said with paranoia.

"I wouldn't do it on purpose."

"Maybe not your purpose, but I bet anything that Fragrance is planting thoughts in your head, thoughts to divert my attention," I accused.

"Wow, look who is suspicious now, maybe Fragrance was right when she said you were primitive."

"I am not."

"It's a possibility," he said.

"No."

"Could be."

"Not possible," I concluded confidently, as though I had evidence to support this belief. I was definitely more human than I had thought.

"Whatever; where are they in any case?" Morcan asked before we both listened in silence.

"I think they've just arrived at the gallery," I said finally with enormous relief.

"See, there you go, I did you a favour," Morcan said proudly.

"How do you make that out?"

He smiled. "I helped pass the time," he said.

"Don't you have games to invent," I reminded him.

"You have to admit it, you jumped on a pedestal, jumping to conclusions about me diverting your attention, I did you a favour, you didn't miss anything, and now you get to listen to the important bits, I helped you," he said merrily.

"Remind me to buy you a medal when we are born; but for now, be quiet."

"You can thank me later," he said.

"For what?" I asked.

"For making time literally fly while Mummy and Daddy travelled to Cornwall," he said proudly.

"Time doesn't exist," I teased.

"You're welcome," Morcan said. And finally we had silence on the inside.

CHAPTER SEVENTEEN

"Charlotte, look here," Daddy Joe called with an air of excitement, "this marble sculpture is just like you."

"You seem enthusiastic for someone who thought this trip was pointless," Mother said with a teasing tone.

"I'm surprised myself to be honest," Daddy Joe said fondly. "But this piece of art is absolutely amazing; it reminds me of ... well... It reminds me of love; it reminds me of you." Morcan and I were suddenly forced into a familiar squashed ball so I suspected he was embracing her again firmly on the outside.

"It is exquisite, Joe," Mother exclaimed. "You are right! It really oozes love, wow!"

"It is an original from a famous sculptor who was born in this village," a strange female voice said with authority.

"Imagine that, a famous sculptor from this tiny Cornish village, 'Torsands'," Mother said reflectively. And my ears perked up suddenly at the mention of Torsands.

"Yes, she was born in March 1953, it is believed she was in her early thirties when she created this sculpture 186-187 years ago. In fact this entire section is devoted to her sculptures; they are incredible really," the lady continued with an enthusiastic voice.

"It is so beautiful, such an elegant piece of art, is it a love scene?" Daddy Joe enquired.

"It is one of her first sculptures, and also one of her more famous ones, she never sold it, apparently it is a self sculpture, but since she had no family remaining after her death, we do not have the entire facts, other than knowledge gained from her inscriptions, some notes and diary entries," the lady explained.

"If this is a sculpture of her then she was a remarkably beautiful woman," Daddy Joe said softly.

"Yes, she was very beautiful indeed; we have recovered some old pictures, some letters along with a few of her diaries and journals in the cabinet on the far side of this exhibition," the lady continued.

"There is a slight sadness in her face," Mother said, "do you believe that was intentional?"

"There are lots of theories surrounding her emotions expressed in this piece, some say there is sadness due to loss of love, some say it is not sadness but more reflective of her inner serenity. We are not entirely sure, but from the letters there is also a possibility that the gentleman by her side in the sculpture is her lost love, she never married," the lady replied.

"She has hair like yours, Charlotte," Daddy Joe said.

"The sculptor's hair was actually quite red, and not blonde; but other than that I would say that, yes, her flowing hair was very similar to your wife's," the lady said encouragingly. "Are you looking to purchase a piece today?"

"We had not planned to, but this one is exquisite," Daddy Joe said clearly.

"You seem to have changed your tune, Joe," Mother reminded him fondly.

"Charlotte, I feel like I know this woman, I feel a lovely warm connection with this piece, it is almost haunting," Daddy Joe said in almost a whisper.

"See, I was right, Joe," Mother said joyfully, "I told you that we both had to come here for a reason. I told you there would be something special for us. My psychic advisor said so."

Daddy Joe laughed. "I'd rather not talk about your psychic friends, Charlotte," he said, "but I'd like to know, and I'm fairly sure this won't be a weird question for you, but do you feel an extraordinary connection with this piece of art, or is it just me?"

"No, I feel exhilarated, it is proof that we were meant to come here," Mother said.

"That's not what I asked, I feel connected to this art, do you?" he asked again.

"I knew you would, I knew you would," she confirmed, "I just knew, I knew you were meant to come here with me, every fibre of my being told me."

"Your psychic advisor told you," Daddy Joe reminded her.

"No; she didn't tell me specifically to bring you," Mother replied, "and don't say I am loony, but the deepest feeling within me tells me that there is a huge connection to you. Seriously, the connection is with you, it has nothing to do with me. My decision to bring you here was based on a very strong feeling I had from the depths of my being, a feeling I knew I had to follow."

"Charlotte, I feel slightly shivery looking at this art, it is becoming more and more haunting," Daddy Joe said quietly.

"Shall I leave you to browse?" the lady asked.

"Thank you," Mother said politely, "however, we would like a little more information about this piece here, please?"

"Well, as I said, little is known about this woman's art other than what we have learned from her notes, some letters and her diaries. We know she lived a very quiet life, her parents died at an early age and she was brought up by her aunt. When this sculptor died she had no relatives to inherit her belongings so most of her unsold sculptures were donated to this gallery as per her last wishes. In fact it was the opportunity to display her sculptures that placed this gallery on the map of the art world," the lady said.

"She must have been a very rich woman," Mother said.

"With lots of admirers," Daddy Joe added.

"No, apparently she lived most of her life alone, she died at the age of sixty-two, and she died as she had lived, barely making enough money to make ends meet," the lady confirmed in a sad tone.

I felt numb as I listened.

"That is so sad, how could such a talented and beautiful woman live alone and poor?" Mother asked.

"Apparently she had revolved her life around love, though from the letters we understand that some unusual circumstance parted her from the love of her life," the lady replied. "She has engraved all of her sculptures with the initials GDC at the base, her birth records do not indicate she had any middle names, it says she was christened Grace Carter, we assume the 'D' came from the surname of the man she loved, a man called, Gerry Daly."

"How romantic," Mother said, as I relaxed quietly into a deep reflective mood.

"How poetic," Daddy Joe said softly, and as he did his tone sent my mind racing back in time, a time when I had once heard that exact phrase said in the same manner before.

"You can see some of her letters and diary entries in the glass cabinet over here. It appears to be an incredible love story," the lady said.

"Can we read one?" Mother asked with excitement as her heart raced to the same beat as mine.

"Yes, of course, you cannot touch them but you can read them through the glass top." My heart thumped as she started to read.

"Monday September 24ᵗʰ 1984.

Oh Gerry,

I am so sorry it has taken me this long to reply to your letter. I received it three weeks ago, and I was so angry on reading it. I could not believe the words as they jumped from the page, I could not believe you broke your promise. I felt my heart break into thousands of fragments. My anger revolved into a numbness and uncertainty. I have been so confused, and knew if I replied instantly I would say things I would later regret. It has taken me this long to realise that you made a mistake, one which you openly acknowledge and are truthful about, and I write to say that I hold no resentment.

I trust you still now, even though you say you have changed. As for the circumstances you wrote about, and I do feel that what I say in this reply comes from a place of self-interest but my heart misses you so much; it has been too long without you and I cannot bear it for much longer. So I write with the promise to support you in all the 'mess' as you have described it in Ireland. I do feel selfish accepting your offer to leave everything you have behind you, and your request to come and be with me in England. But I'm not sure how I can bear to go on without you. I know we will make it work.

Aunt Joyce has seen me so upset since the arrival of your letter, and insists I do not reply. Oh Gerry, I have to tell you that when you come to Cornwall, you will not be welcomed by her, but I will welcome you with my open heart.

I miss you so much. Remember that day when we met on the plane, remember what you told me, that we live in a world that is a magnificent palace? Then remember also that we sleep under the same stars, the same sun and the same moon every night, nothing can separate us, we are one, we will always be one, our thoughts are always the same, our thoughts are one.

There is so much I can write but it is easier to speak, I want to hear your voice. I want you to hear mine; I want you to know that it can be okay. I know you want to change these habits you say you have developed, and once you are committed to making those changes in your life I will help you as much as I can, I love you far too much not to. But I cannot support you unless you want to help yourself, no one can, the choice is yours to make.

The past can be dealt with and put safely to bed. You are already living through the pain of that, and it is not the smartest thing to continuously go through it again and again through your memories; living through any pain once is enough. Everyone can change for a better life and in doing that you can move forward, and we can move forward. Moving forward in love and that starts with loving yourself.

Should anyone wish to drag up that past, as I am sure my Aunt Joyce will do, and whether they do so with or without intention, it only encourages you to relive that pain which can

*hinder us. Focus on who you want to be, opposed to getting
away from who you believe you are now.*

*Please ring me as soon as you receive this letter. There is
nothing to be afraid of. I am impatiently waiting to hear your
voice.*

Yours forever,

Grace, xxx"

My eyes had welled with water as mother finished reading. I
was overwhelmed with sadness, love and regret simultaneously,
and it seemed surreal how Gerry could have been so obstinate
not to realise any of this before.

"That is amazing, isn't it Joe?" Mother said, quietly sobbing
as she finished the letter, "and to think that they didn't end up
together, I wonder what happened?"

"Grace's diary entries indicate that there was never any response from Gerry. She waited for weeks, months and even
years in hope that he may one day find it in him to reply," the
lady replied.

"It sounds like he was the one that did something terrible
and she was welcoming him back with open arms. Why on
earth would he not respond to such a forgiving and beautiful
letter?" Daddy Joe asked.

"Her diary indicates that when she wrote this letter, her Aunt
Joyce was furious that Grace would even think about responding. The entry says that she sent the letter; however, we know
that Joyce stopped this letter somehow without Grace's knowledge at that time. Whatever it was that was in Gerry's letter
must have been terrible in Joyce's eyes," the lady answered sadly. "This letter was found in an old tin box which was owned by
Joyce, and obviously inherited later by Grace after Joyce's death.
We don't know whether Grace actually discovered this or not.
Grace was fifty years old when Joyce died, so if she found this
letter then she may have already moved on with her life, but

equally she may have never seen it. The box was so rusty by the time the gallery got it, that we assumed it had not been opened in several years. It was stuffed tight with several newspaper clippings and writings on Grace's parents' death, so maybe Grace did not delve further into the details of its contents. We don't know why Joyce never disposed of this letter, maybe she did want Grace to find it eventually or maybe she had forgotten that she still had it. There is nothing in Grace's journals that reference this discovery, so we are not any wiser on the circumstances. All we know is that it never reached Gerry.

"We have spent years searching archives to piece her story together, and we know that she travelled to Ireland a few times, but those travel dates were before the date on this letter. All we know is what I can share with you today. I have also been fascinated by both the creative and spiritual mind of this lady, most of which appears to be lost now."

"Do you have his letter?" Mother asked. "Do you have the letter that she was responding to?"

"No, we never found a copy of his letter; she kept very few of his letters in the end. Her notes tell us that after five years of no contact from Gerry that she burned a lot of the letters," the lady replied.

"I can imagine that," Daddy Joe said. "She must have been very angry. I mean if she never knew the letter was stopped by Joyce then she would be undoubtedly upset that he had never replied. Also, if she did find this letter amongst Joyce's belongings after Joyce's death then she must have been very bitter with her aunt for interfering with her life."

"No, we have not detected any anger in her writing, a lot of her latter diary entries clearly indicate that she had let go; she had found a peace within herself. Mostly her notes refer to her art and her observations in nature and how she reflects those in her sculptures. We found no later references to the man called, Gerry Daly."

"She sounds like an incredible lady," Mother said seriously and quietly, "very calming, much centred and very balanced."

"I guess if we don't go through stuff in our lives, we have nothing to experience, and stories like hers can be an inspiration to others," the lady said. "She forgave, she moved on and she found peace; and she knew she was the only one that could do that."

"It sounds like she did move on; but since she never married her heart must have remained with him always," Daddy Joe said softly.

"Yes, it sounds like she stayed true to her promise, older entries in her notes tell of a promise she made to him, and that she would always stay true to him," the lady said. "You two are certainly a very curious couple; none of our visitors have had such an interest in this love story."

"I guess we feel a connection," Daddy Joe said fondly, and I felt a hint of sadness in his voice. And then there was another huge silence on the outside and I suspected he was holding mother against him again. "I have an enormous warm feeling about this art and this beautiful woman," Mother whispered.

I started to identify with mother's strong feelings as my overwhelming emotions prompted me to ask myself the sudden question over and over, 'Could the beautiful sculptor, the wonderful lady that was Grace Carter, could she have been reincarnated in my mother?' That thought had been both exhilarating and shocking simultaneously as I felt an instant connection with my mummy; Mummy Charlotte.

"How come you are so concerned about this couple, Gerry and Grace?" Morcan asked gravely in response to my quietly spoken thoughts.

I looked seriously upon Morcan. "It is my mission," I replied sadly, "Gerry is about to get a second chance." Morcan looked bewildered so there was no change there.

"I want to buy that sculpture for you, a present for being the future mother of my children," I heard Daddy Joe say quietly.

"It's very expensive," Mother whispered, "but it does feel right, it feels like it should belong to us. I believe it will find its way home with us."

"Thank you Mummy Charlotte, I understand now why I chose you," I cried softly, as I surmised my reason for having picked her. And even though my memories from my time at SPOCC, the place where I would have selected her, had faded completely then, I decided to promote her from 'Mother' to being my 'Mummy Charlotte'.

CHAPTER EIGHTEEN

"I hear you're the fellow to talk to if we want to contact someone back on earth," Bertie announced as he walked towards the otherwise empty space where Gerry had been sitting.

"Where on hell did you spring from?" Gerry asked in shock as he swung around with surprise on hearing his old friend's voice again.

"Certainly not hell, apparently it does not exist; I came directly to APES," Bertie responded excited.

"When?"

"A few months ago," Bertie replied merrily.

"Wow, it seems so strange yet wonderful seeing you again," Gerry said with enthusiasm.

"It's certainly strange my old friend, given the circumstances like, both being dead and all," Bertie said smiling, and the wrinkles streamed between the sagging skin of his elderly face.

"Well, we all know it's the inevitable, for me sooner than expected, but you Bertie, gosh, I hardly recognise you," Gerry said with surprise.

"What do you expect, Gerry? I'm seventy-eight!"

"But we are ageless here; we can choose any form we like."

"They told me that alright, but I said no, I said Marie would hardly recognise me if I changed my appearance, and Jaysus, Gerry when they told me who the leader of the 'Freedom of Form' initiative was, I said 'no way, boys, no German dictator is getting his hands on me', they'll be asking me to have dinner with Napoleon next. No way Gerry, I said I was happy the way I was."

"And how is Marie?" Gerry enquired as he laughed fondly.

Bertie moved closer to Gerry. "That's who I am here to see you about. I understand you're the fellow that can help," he replied in a whisper.

"So Marie is still on earth?"

"She is for sure, and Johnny is too, he's not married you know, and now some greedy cousin is 'caring' for him, erra, she's only after the pub, the pub and his money. But Marie is Johnny's only sister and my family should have that pub. I've been telling Marie for years but she said she wasn't able for a family battle over money, especially after what happened with you and the famous Uncle Joseph."

"We all strive to move on from those kinds of memories in this place, Bertie."

"Have you?"

"I honestly don't give Uncle Joseph a second thought anymore."

"Good for you, good for you, but if it's all the same with you, I thought you could show me how to do what you do, you know, show me how to contact Marie; I thought I might be able to give her a bit of guidance and a few tips from this place."

"Tips for?" Gerry asked confused.

"To get rid of that greedy cousin of course, Marie calls her 'the cleaner' because she'll clean Johnny out of all his money given half a chance, and, well, she actually is his house cleaner also, it's metaphor Gerry."

"I understand what metaphor is, Bertie, but why have you really come here?"

"I told you, I've been looking for you everywhere to help me, and I knew you'd understand my view point. The gang down the SA didn't."

"You've been to the SA?" Gerry gasped with surprise.

"I've been all over asking about you, I've been telling everyone we're great friends and very similar, and a truthful soul asked me if I was ready to know who I really was, and sure you know me, I'm game for most things (once there's no dictators involved), so I went along with her."

"Who was that?"

"The truthful one, I told you."

"Bertie, the SA is for souls to open up and be truthful, they are all truthful there."

"No, this one was especially truthful, she was named after it, now let me think, what is another name for truth? Beginning with 'w' or maybe 'v', she was German so it was hard to tell."

"Verity?"

"That's the one, fierce nice altogether she was. Anyway, I didn't think the SA was ready for me yet, so I asked Verity to let me know where you were, and since she was someone I trusted and with a name like that I knew she could not tell me a lie, so here I am."

"So you forced her to tell you, by using the very essence of her nature to be true."

"Because I knew you'd be thrilled to see me, and sure you were, you were beaming like the Cheshire cat when you saw me. And I knew you'd understand my reasons for wanting to contact Marie."

"Bertie, we are different here than we were on earth, I will help as best I can but really we should only do it once it is for a higher purpose."

"The higher purpose is to save our good friend, Johnny," he rationalised.

"And how do you think I may be able to help?" Gerry asked cautiously.

"Help me talk to Marie behind their backs, so that I don't get found out by the 'Soul Reading Police'."

"I'm not sure," Gerry said tentatively.

"Gerry, I know you're the man to talk to," Bertie insisted.

Gerry challenged him. "How do you know that? How do you know I can contact earth? If I could, wouldn't I have known that you had died and that Johnny and Marie were still there?"

"Because knowing you, you've probably been glued watching Grace the whole time."

"She's not on earth anymore."

"Where is she?"

"Apparently she is in SPOCC."

"I haven't been there yet; but anyway Gerry, I'm no fool, I know you can contact earth, Johnny told me."

"Johnny?"

"Yeah, he said that after you died you were planting all sorts of things into his head. And I want to do the same with Marie now."

Gerry inhaled deeply, "Bertie, listen, I didn't know any better then, a lot has changed since I first died, we are part of a movement now and our initiative is about raising the consciousness of humans via contacting them but we do not interfere with their personal choices."

Bertie looked disappointed. "What's the point in that?" he blurted out, "we only want to help them."

"Yes," Gerry agreed, "but not by interfering with their own choice. We contact mortals now to let them know there is more than the reality they perceive on earth, we contact them so that they can start to believe in what they cannot physically see or touch, our movement is to raise the spiritual beliefs of humans so that they do not fall victim or unknowingly choose to be grabbed by these Realm guides upon the process of death."

"So you've gone all spiritual again? I thought all that stopped after you lost Grace."

"Bertie, we *are* spirits now."

"I know, and I reckon we could have some fun with that."

"This is not a joke and, yes, there are some souls, some spirits that actually do that, their intentions are not for the best, they do it because they do not realise they exist in fear themselves and are effectively 'tied' to the earth still, and what's worse is that the 'Soul Reading Police' allow these spirits to trouble mortals in this way, because it enforces more fear into humans about the afterlife and more humans become targets for the Realm guides. Bertie, do you realise what you are involved in now?"

"So that means that the police won't be bothering me then if I contact Marie because they'll know it's about the money. Gerry, you've been a great help," Bertie said happily as he attempted to shake Gerry's hand, but Trinity burst suddenly in between them. "Gerry, I couldn't stop him, he shouldn't be here, he's not ready," she gasped in short breaths as she flew anxiously towards Gerry with Alfie, Verity and Lovian in tow.

"He said he was your friend, I thought he knew about the movement," Verity cried defensively. And Alfie motioned his hands palms outwards to both Trinity and Verity for calmness and silence.

"Most of us believe that others behave in the same way that we do, in Verity's case she assumes that others are truthful also, I'll handle it from here," Alfie said firmly before he turned towards Bertie. "What do you know about our 'Undercover Movement'?"

"What's the 'Undercover Movement'?" Bertie asked in reply.

"It's about helping souls to free themselves of this existence without the 'Soul Reading Police' or the Realm Guides' knowledge," Alfie explained calmly.

"So we're trapped?" Bertie questioned.

"Yes."

"I'm not trapped," Bertie said confidently, "after my stroke on earth I couldn't walk or speak properly and I was always forgetting things, but in this place my body is healthy, I have full freedom back in my body and mind."

"It's about body, mind and spirit," Alfie corrected, "and even our minds are not free here, we are deliberately connected to earthly memories and we are enslaved to the beliefs of these Realm guides, that is not freedom."

"So, we're in hell?" Bertie gasped.

"No."

"Purgatory?"

"No."

"Limbo?"

"No, we are in APES," Alfie confirmed, "and APES only exists, has only manifested itself out of the fearful thoughts of the Realm guides. This appears real, and has become the reality in which we exist, but it is not real."

Gerry, Trinity, Lovian and Verity regarded each other briefly before they slid back and relaxed; Gerry had suspected they were in for the long haul as it generally took Alfie days to explain the concepts and apparent existence of APES to new souls that arrived to join the movement. And usually those souls had joined in search for a higher truth and by their own choice, but this did not appear to be the case for Bertie; his motives were earthly monetary ones. "The irony is that souls arriving to APES have already unconsciously chosen to be here, and yet they do not realise it. We are trapped in this unreal reality," Alfie said.

"I get you," Bertie said casually. Gerry glanced from Trinity to Alfie and back to Trinity again with confusion, and both Alfie and Trinity reciprocated his expression. "No, you don't, Bertie," Gerry insisted, "this is more complex than your current understanding."

"It's not," Bertie replied, "it's easy, isn't it the same as you drinking yourself to an early death, Gerry, instead of choosing to find Grace when you had the chance."

"We are not on earth now," Alfie reminded him firmly.

"I know that," Bertie replied, as he looked at Gerry, but Gerry felt his old earthly resentments well-up as he stared at Bertie with offence. "Agh, don't get me wrong, Gerry, we were all happy out down the pub, you made the best of the situation, we had some great laughs, didn't we?" Bertie asked.

Gerry nodded.

"Exactly," Bertie said, "so it's easy, I say we make the best of the situation. We made the best of it then, so we should do what we always did, and we'll be grand. It's not normal to reach for the stars, so why start now?"

Everyone stared at Bertie with disbelief. "Bertie, you misunderstand," Alfie replied with authority, "reaching for the stars is exactly what we should do."

"I've no desire to be famous," Bertie replied, "I just want to have a chat with Marie."

Alfie sighed. "It's not about being famous, it is about growing and evolving, learning from past mistakes, trying to do better, otherwise we never find heaven, a peace within ourselves," Alfie said loudly, "that is exactly why we should *not* do what we always did before."

Bertie looked offended, "I appreciate the help, but if it's all the same with you all, I came here to find Gerry."

"It's ok," Gerry said, "I'll handle it."

"No!" Trinity protested, "Bertie shouldn't be here, Gerry, no! You are barely ready for the movement, and you still haven't forgiven Tessa, I don't have a good feeling about this. Bertie is only here a few minutes and already he is stirring up more of your earth feelings."

"Trinity is right," Alfie agreed calmly, "Gerry, you have done so much work on yourself, you don't need more distractions."

"I'll handle it," Gerry insisted.

"If you've all done so much work on yourselves, to evolve so you say; how come you are all disagreeing?" Bertie asked.

"Nobody is disagreeing," Alfie said with compassion, "it is normal to have challenges, Bertie. We just had not expected this one so soon."

"Bertie, do you know where you are now?" Lovian asked with equal compassion.

"Of course I do, I'm in APES," Bertie replied as he shrugged his shoulders.

"So you understand that you are not in heaven?" Lovian questioned.

"I got that part," Bertie replied.

"Do you believe that heaven exists as a place then?" Lovian asked.

"Of course I do," Bertie replied instantly, "I listened to the priest at mass every Sunday, I'll tell you."

"I believe it exists also," Lovian said, "because we believe that in heaven we experience pure love and forgiveness, in this place we are consumed with earthly memories and fears."

"So we are separated from heaven and most souls don't actually realise it," Alfie added, "do you understand that, Bertie?"

"Yes, we are in APES," Bertie confirmed again as he nodded hard.

"So as long as we are separated from heaven, as long as we exist somewhere other than heaven, you could say we were in limbo, or purgatory or even hell, couldn't that be right?" Alfie said, "I mean they are only words or labels at the end of the day, but it's the meaning that is important. So you could say if we choose to stay here in this existence forever then we are in fact in the reality of hell, but if we choose to leave this place then in effect we have been in purgatory or limbo for a period before we moved into heaven. Does this make sense, Bertie?"

"Those other places you mention do not exist, you already said it before," Bertie insisted and nodded again.

"Exactly," Lovian said, "in the same way that APES does not exist, it appears to exist, it appears real, APES has become the reality in which we exist but it is NOT real. So APES is not real, hell is not real, purgatory is not real, limbo is not real; the only thing that is real is the fact that we are separated from heaven, so we can label this current reality any way we want, it boils down to the same thing. If we are not in heaven we must be somewhere else, the Realm guides just chose to call it APES."

"Okay then, I understand - you're saying the clue is in the name," Bertie replied, "we are apes if we choose to stay here."

"Well, yes," Alfie said as he smiled, "you could explain it like that."

"Your explanation was simple too though," Bertie replied as he looked seriously at Alfie and Lovian, "but I suggest in future it may be easier for you if you went straight to the punch line and explained to souls where they are not, instead of where they are; only a suggestion."

Gerry observed that Trinity appeared offended by this comment to their leader. "That's exactly what they just did, Bertie!" Trinity insisted, "you did not choose to join our movement, you are not ready."

"I must have unconsciously chosen it," Bertie responded with his continuous nodding, "wasn't that the reason given for most souls ending up in APES, so by the same logic I must have unknowingly chosen to come to the 'Undercover Movement' as well."

Gerry noticed Trinity stare at Alfie as though she had wanted him to defend her, but Alfie continued to smile, "I think there may be hope for Bertie," he said, "Trinity, we must not turn our backs on anyone. I'm sure we can find a job here for him in the 'Undercover Movement'."

"No one mentioned anything about work," Bertie replied quickly.

"Everyone in the movement works, we work to support each other as we continue this journey together," Alfie confirmed.

"I'm not one to take a job from another, there's no honour in that," Bertie suggested anxiously.

Alfie smiled wider. "It's not work as you define the term on earth, you will work with Gerry and me in this part of the movement," he said.

"What's 'this' part of the movement?" Bertie asked as he looked at Gerry.

"Our part of the movement is to communicate with the highest intentions with the mortals on earth. And while you must also work your own evolvement, Bertie, you can help us recruit more souls in APES to help our movement," Alfie replied.

"Like human resources, except with souls?" Bertie asked in confirmation.

"Yes," Alfie confirmed.

"And what's the other part of the movement?" he asked curiously.

"The SA," Trinity replied, "that is the part that I operate, where Verity and Lovian are also."

"So I get to communicate with Marie," Bertie said happily.

"Not in the manner that you want to," Alfie replied quickly, "you will be able to communicate with mortals with the intentions of letting them know that there is a heavenly place where their souls can go, we work to encourage them to strive for joy and eliminate fears such that they don't get trapped here."

"But in the meantime, would there be any problem with having a chat with Marie and giving her a hand to get rid of that greedy cousin?" Bertie asked hopefully.

"Marie can be supported emotionally, you can assist her to gain strength, you can help her to enrich her life and others' lives, but not for her personal gain, if she wants personal gain she must do it herself. You cannot influence mortals, they make their own choices," Alfie responded. "But I warn you that even if she does hear you, she may not be receptive, many mortals are not!"

"I can't get her out of my head...." Bertie started to plead when his jaw dropped suddenly as he looked in shock at the soul that unexpectedly appeared behind Alfie. "I know," Tessa said softly in agreement, "it is the process here, we are left to grieve, feel bitterness and hang onto earthly memories, which is the reason why we have to get out."

"Where...where... where... did you spring out of?" Bertie stuttered as he pointed at Tessa.

"I can be anywhere I want in an instant," she answered softly.

"Tessa works with us," Alfie explained.

"Don't tell me you're still married to her here, Gerry, are you?" Bertie asked as disbelief started to mix with the shock on his face.

"No," Gerry responded, "we all work together for the same cause; Tessa is undercover in the 'Soul Reading Police'."

"Is she ... is she...monitoring our thoughts now then?" Bertie stammered again, and he looked as though he had aged another ten years.

"You can ask 'she' directly," Tessa responded nicely, "and the answer is yes, I don't always do it but I can when I want."

"I don't know," Bertie said as he started to shuffle, "I don't feel so good all of a sudden, if it's all the same with you all, I'll turn down the job."

"Tessa helps us, Bertie," Verity assured him, "she protects us from the police and the guides, you trust me, and you know I tell the truth."

"And all of you have untoward thoughts in any case," Tessa added, "it's not a problem for me; there's no shame if you are worried about Marie and her money; we are all evolving still."

"I don't know," Bertie said uneasily, "but I'm not... I'm not working with her," and he pointed at Tessa again.

"I'm not going through all of this again," Alfie said with a hint of annoyance, "we are all working together."

"We are in development yet, don't you see, Bertie," Verity said passionately, "we all still struggle with our thoughts, so we support one another. That's the truth."

"It's true," Tessa said encouragingly, "I'll give you an example, Gerry's dominant thought is still Grace, and he is one of the leaders here, none of us are better than the rest." Bertie managed a faint smile.

"My thoughts are not dominated by Grace," Gerry said as he moved forward, "I have the highest integrity like everyone else."

"We know," Tessa said as she patted him backwards, "but you can't get Grace out of your head just like Bertie can't get Marie out of his."

"And we already know how we can do that," Alfie said as though it was a caution against any unpredictable behaviour, "the solution is to practise genuine kindness and forgiveness, and experience pure love."

"How do you know that?" Bertie asked casually.

"Because that is what God says," Alfie replied.

"I thought you said we were separated from heaven, so how did you find all that out from Him?" Bertie asked as he looked at Alfie. Everyone relaxed except Gerry, who started to take more of an interest in Bertie's questions. He felt confused suddenly and looked to Alfie for a response also.

"Heaven's everywhere," Alfie said calmly.

"But if everywhere is heaven then why are we not experiencing it?" Bertie asked. Gerry felt further bewilderment as he searched Alfie's face. Gerry had once thought heaven was everywhere, yet even he had struggled to believe it with all his conflicting thoughts from his experiences, believing in a God, a heaven that had abandoned him when he needed Him most.

"I said heaven's everywhere, that doesn't mean that everywhere is heaven, it is up to us to see it or not, it is something from deep within us, it is about evolving," Alfie explained.

"Do you believe you are separated from God, Bertie?" Lovian asked with compassion.

"Well, yes," Bertie replied, "because He is in heaven and we are not. We are the apes."

"When you were on earth, did you believe you were separated from God?" Lovian asked.

"Well, yes and no," Bertie said, "it depended on what was going on in my life."

"Did you believe God was in heaven then as you do now?" Lovian questioned.

"Of course, yes I did," Bertie said as he started nodding furiously again.

"And were you able to talk to Him?"

"Yes, well yes, I could," Bertie replied.

"Then it's no different here, we may not be in heaven but we are not separated from God because He's everywhere; heaven's everywhere," Lovian concluded.

"We believe that God is in us and when we truly accept Him, heaven is an experience which takes you to a glorious place, a wonderful state of being independent of your physical location even," Verity added.

"I never thought of it like that," Bertie said quickly as Gerry listened attentively, "I understand completely. I knew I must have chosen to be here. Thanks lads! Now that's sorted, when can I tune into Marie?"

"Gerry will help you," Alfie responded, "it will help divert his dominant thoughts from Grace." Gerry felt offended again, but said nothing. Alfie, Lovian and Verity embraced Bertie with a large smile, Trinity remained neutral, and Tessa regarded both Bertie and Gerry suspiciously before they all departed leaving Gerry and Bertie alone again.

Bertie rolled his eyes. "I thought they'd never leave," he said to Gerry, "you don't believe all that stuff, do you?"

"I'm struggling again, Bertie," Gerry said, "but the thing is, I used to believe this firmly when I was a young man."

"When you were with Grace?"

"Well, yes," Gerry replied seriously, "but before I met her also, I just never shared my views with anyone."

"Grace and her faith all over again, there we go, and you already know what happened there," Bertie said, "she never replied to your letter. She left you."

"It's different here, Bertie," Gerry said, even though he started to feel uncertainty again. Why had Grace not responded? He bore his heart to her. Gerry felt despondent.

"Erra, they're off their heads, Gerry," Bertie said as he started nodding again.

"You agreed with them," Gerry reminded him.

"You know me, I'm not one for confrontation; I don't think it's holy to disagree with anyone. I'm doing my best."

"I'm not sure," Gerry said as he felt more confused. 'Was Bertie right? Should they make the best of their situation now?' he thought.

"Of course you're sure, we're best friends Gerry, now where were we?" Bertie asked oblivious to Gerry's perplexed reflection.

"You wanted to contact Marie," Gerry replied.

Bertie smiled widely, "I knew you'd understand my view point, I was right when I said you were the fellow I should talk to."

CHAPTER NINETEEN

"How in the name of God did you manage that?" Bertie blurted out.

"Have you told your mother?" Johnny asked urgently.

"No, no," Gerry said quickly and quietly. "Please be quiet, I don't want the whole pub to find out."

Bertie put his hands behind his head as he leaned back on his barstool. "That's some mess," he said, "and it was only less than six weeks ago we were celebrating your triumph in the court case."

Gerry sighed. "I know, I know," he said, "I thought everything would be clear cut and dry from there on out."

"What's happening to you?" Johnny asked with serious overtones.

Gerry dropped his head. "Tessa told me yesterday," he said, "she told me she was pregnant and that the baby was mine. I didn't believe her. She said she had to tell me as soon as possible so we could make some arrangements and avoid the shame. She said that her father would literally kill me if I don't do the decent thing. She said if we don't arrange a wedding as soon as possible it'll bring huge shame on both our families, and that my family has been through enough shame as it is."

"Tessa seems to say a lot of things, Gerry. What do you think?" Johnny asked as he seemed to study the panic on his friend's face.

"I don't know what to think," Gerry said frustrated.

"Gerry, how did you manage to put a bun into Tessa's oven?" Bertie asked.

"We don't need the nitty gritty," Johnny assured him firmly.

Gerry sighed again as he buried his head in his hands. "You may as well know," he said, "the night I won the legal case against Uncle Joseph, Tessa said we should celebrate, you know me, I'm not one to turn down celebrations. And sure I was only thrilled that I could finally go home when the court ordered

Uncle Joseph to move out of the family home. Tessa took me to one of those expensive hotels and ordered champagne; I had to pay for it of course, even though she was going to get a large sum of the winnings eventually. But I was just relieved and I was looking forward to getting drunk, I felt free, I was over the moon, and I had just rung Grace to tell her that I had some free time coming up and that I would be over to visit in a few weeks. Grace still doesn't even know about all the trouble we've had at home. I was planning to book a flight to see her the following day."

"But that was the thirteenth of July, how come you have not been over to visit Grace yet?" Bertie asked with his usual bluntness.

Gerry felt frustrated. "That is because one thing led to another with Tessa that night, I was as drunk as a skunk, and we were in a nice hotel, and Tessa took me to a room, and something happened and I woke up with her in the morning. I felt sick and I was disgusted with myself, and of course after being unfaithful I could hardly go over to Grace pretending nothing happened. And now I have another guilty secret to keep from Grace. I thought if I made an excuse and let the dust settle for a few months, the guilt would wear off and then I could go and find Grace. But then yesterday Tessa told me she was pregnant," Gerry explained with defeat.

"What are you going to do?" Johnny asked as they all leaned in towards each other.

"He has to marry her, of course," Bertie blurted out.

"It's 1984, Bertie, wake up man, people do not forcefully marry each other because of pregnancies anymore," Johnny said firmly.

Gerry felt confused. "Tessa says I have to marry her before she's three months gone, and that then we could pretend the baby was premature or something like that," he said.

"And you trust her, do you?" Johnny asked.

"I thought you didn't even like her," Bertie said easily, "though I have to admit she is fairly easy on the eye, if you could learn to ignore her abrupt ways."

"Gerry, listen man," Johnny said seriously, "Tessa didn't care who she trampled on in court or what she did to win your case, and now all of a sudden she seems concerned about shame, it doesn't make sense."

"Johnny, I'm not sure, all I know is that my mother has had enough grief to last a lifetime and doesn't need anymore," Gerry replied. "Besides, you saw Tessa in court, if I don't marry her, she will probably sue me, she'd take everything I have, and she would chew me up and spit me out in bubbles."

"What about Grace?" Bertie asked.

"I don't know. I don't know what to do," Gerry cried out.

"Gerry, you can't marry Tessa, please tell me you won't marry Tessa," Johnny pleaded.

"It would be the end of my mother if she knew I had a girl pregnant and didn't do the right thing," Gerry said.

"Get a back bone Gerry, man, for God's sakes, snap out of it, get some courage, you have just won a huge legal battle and now you are afraid to approach your mother and explain the truth. Tell her that you got Tessa pregnant by accident and that you don't want to marry her," Johnny lectured.

"How do you know that Tessa is not tricking you? How do you know the baby is not belonging to some other fellow?" Bertie asked coyly with folded arms.

"I don't; but Tessa said I will know from the scan because they will give the exact date of conception which would be the night she spent with me. Tessa also said that the scan happens at three months and that would be too late to plan a wedding if we were to avoid shame, she wants to get married in the next few weeks and pretend we were dating all along," Gerry said as he felt more disbelief at the events he was describing.

"She's tricking you, Gerry," Johnny declared, "she knows what you are worth; she is after your money. Does she know about Grace?"

"I think I told her about Grace when we were drunk," Gerry said truthfully, recalling as much as he could remember.

"That's a theory then," Johnny said, "maybe she knew she had to snare you into her trap as soon as possible, because she knew you were now free to do as you please and would probably marry Grace."

"That's possible," Bertie said reflectively.

"I bet it is," Johnny said.

"Okay," Gerry said with deep breaths, "so let's just say that I don't marry her and Tessa tells everyone and puts the family into more shame whether it is my baby or not, what do I do then?"

"You face the music," Johnny said firmly.

"You can't blame me if Tessa is lying," Gerry said defiantly.

"That is correct, we have no control over other people and you know that," Johnny replied firmly. "Whether Tessa is lying to you or not is not important now, be more concerned about what you are going to do now, we're blue in the teeth from hearing that you only want to be with Grace."

Gerry protested. "Gerry," Johnny said more calmly, "if you object continuously when someone talks sense to you, what does that tell you about yourself?"

"That's easy for you to say," Gerry said, "I'm weakened from all the issues, you have no idea what it's like."

"All I see is that you seem to be constantly inviting more issues into your life," Johnny said courageously.

Gerry sat up straight, detesting what he had heard. "What do you mean?" he said loudly.

"Since this business started with Joseph, it sounds like you are not happy unless you have a problem."

"I do have problems," Gerry shouted. "You don't seem to be listening?"

"Don't I?" Johnny said in a challenging manner. "I've been listening to you constantly for the past six months and to be honest my ears are burnt from it all. You're the one that has to do something about it, and not bite my head off when I try to help you and give you friendly advice. It sounds to me like you are indulging yourself in misery. And Gerry, I'm starting to have enough."

Bertie moved back from the firing line of Johnny's words as he looked towards the floor. Gerry scrunched his face, "Johnny, it is easy to see that you've never had a problem. If you did, you'd understand."

"What do you think I've been doing?" Johnny asked rhetorically. "What do you think other people do with their problems?"

"They have friends that help them."

"So you think that others agreeing with you and helping you dive further into the problems is the definition of help, is it?" Johnny said. "You know this, Gerry, but you refuse to listen when it applies to yourself."

"What do you mean?" Gerry said again, as disbelief spread across his face with disappointment at Johnny.

"Take a look at yourself, Gerry," Johnny said.

"Johnny, I'm weak enough as it is," Gerry replied as he shook his head slowly from side to side, "and I don't need you causing me more grief."

"Someone needs to say something to shake you out of your rut."

"No," Gerry protested again, "it's not my fault if Tessa is lying."

"She probably is, but if you keep thinking about those issues then you'll be doing the stupid thing."

"How the hell do I not?" Gerry shouted. "I have to deal with it!"

"You're not dealing with it; you're terrified of it and the outcome."

"Of course I am. How else would you expect me to be?"

"Get some courage."

Gerry laughed. "That's easy in theory," he replied sarcastically.

Johnny shook his head. "Where has the man that we all used to know gone to?"

Gerry felt afraid as he heard Johnny yet he refused to listen to the message, "so what do you suggest? That I tell Grace, is it?" he asked as he folded his arms.

"If you want Grace to be part of your life, you do the clever thing and talk to her, if you don't want Grace in your life and are indifferent to her then you don't have to say anything that may cause further grief," Johnny said.

"Grace will dump me," Gerry said with self-pity.

"Get off that chair and stop feeling sorry for yourself," Johnny lectured. "You are already drinking more than you ever did, you don't want to get worse. If you marry Tessa, you'll drink yourself to your death. I couldn't imagine any man being able to have a bit of peace with a busy-body tempest like her. Tessa seems like a vengeful type person on the surface, yet Grace does not. Be clever and trust yourself."

"That's a good one," Bertie said with a hint of light-heartedness, "Tessa the Tempest. Nice one!" Johnny and Gerry both ignored him.

"Gerry, you will never know whether Grace will dump you or not unless you talk to her. And if you contemplate marrying Tessa, well, you will have lost Grace forever anyway. Catch yourself on," Johnny said.

Gerry's face softened as he started to absorb Johnny's words. And Bertie looked slightly relieved as he leaned towards Gerry and Johnny, with a slight glint in his eye as though he was taking the opportunity to change the subject. "Was she good?" he asked.

"What?" Gerry asked with confusion.

"Was Tessa good in bed?" Bertie asked again.

"Shut up, Bertie," Johnny ordered as he shook his head again.

Gerry relaxed as he reflected on Johnny's words. He looked unemotionally at Bertie. "I don't know, I actually don't remember much after the drinks, and I remember little or nothing about the room," he answered truthfully.

"Forget Tessa," Johnny said firmly, "you are a free man now, and you have no restrictions. You can call Tessa tomorrow and assure her you will provide for her and the baby in every way, after you find out from the scan that the baby is actually yours."

Gerry looked away momentarily. "My father would be ashamed of me," he said remorsefully.

Johnny stared into the pupils of Gerry's eyes. "Your father would be proud of you for standing up for yourself," he insisted.

Bertie managed a faint smile. "Do you want to marry Tessa?" he asked.

"Of course not," Gerry and Johnny shouted together.

"I was only asking," Bertie said as he moved back and folded his arms again.

"Look, Gerry," Johnny said, "the solution is simple, if you're afraid of telling Grace, write her a letter explaining what happened and ask her to write back if she still wants to discuss things with you. If Grace is as good as you say she is then she will view this reasonably without repercussions. And then you'll know. Grace may not want to be with you but at least she doesn't sound like the revengeful type. It's as easy as that."

Gerry stared at Johnny as he realised the sense that he made. "Not a word of this goes anywhere," he said, as he felt an intense fear return.

"Sealed lips," Johnny assured him.

"Bertie?" Gerry asked cautiously.

"Me neither," Bertie replied.

Gerry stared at Bertie again. "Promise, not even Marie," he said carefully.

"Promise," Bertie said as he crossed his fingers.

Gerry stared into open space for a few seconds, "Okay," he said finally, "I'll write to Grace, and I'll see her response before I do anything else."

Johnny relaxed. "Good man, Gerry," he said.

"Great stuff," Bertie said, "do you want us to help you?"

"No," Johnny said sternly, "let the man have some peace and privacy, for once he is agreeing to be honest with himself."

Gerry even managed a faint smile for the first time that evening. "No," he said to Bertie, "I have written enough letters to her, I think I will find the words on my own."

"You have to do what's right for everyone to move on, and please don't cause any further pain to anyone else," Johnny warned. Bertie nodded, and Johnny looked carefully at Gerry as though he was curious as to how honest Gerry could be with himself.

CHAPTER TWENTY

"Sunday August 26th1984.

Dear Grace,

This is my fifth attempt at writing this letter. Bertie says that I should stop beating around the bush and finally post it to you. He hasn't seen this letter, I promise you, but I want to be honest and tell you that both he and Johnny know the contents of what I am about to tell you.

I am so sorry I haven't been entirely truthful with you to date. Things got so messy here at home, and I have been involved in a court battle over my father's will. I didn't want to share this with you before and I would be lying if I said it was purely because I didn't want to worry you. You have been so trusting and I feared you wouldn't have been if you knew I had a legal battle with my own brother and uncle. I feel embarrassed and ashamed that it came to that – a hostile conflict over land. I feared if you knew I was going down a legal route with my own family, you would not have liked the man that I have become, and you may even have encouraged me to walk away from it, and it's no excuse but I didn't want to lose my father's land to a money-grabbing uncle who manipulated my brother and mother. But now I know that it is so insignificant to the thought of losing you. And in truth, I don't even like the man that I have become.

If only I had known what it would all have led to, I would not have got myself involved in this whole mess; and now I regret to say that it is worse than I could have ever im-

agined possible. Because of the struggle at home I had moved into Johnny's pub, it wasn't because I was learning independence as I had led you to believe when you were still here, I had moved out of home due to a lack of courage and I am pained by the amount of deceit I have caused you. Living under the same roof as Guinness and whiskey has not helped; alcohol became my temporary solace to escape the reality of my life. Alcohol is the enemy of all men, and I let myself fall into its temptation. Gladly I have moved back in home again but the tension in my life remains between my brother and I, and I have also caused myself even more trouble.

To say I am ashamed and disgusted with my behaviour wouldn't do it justice. I fear for my sanity, I don't like what I have become and I write to ask for forgiveness even though I have no viable excuse for what I am about to reveal to you in this letter.

I love you so much my heart breaks at the thought of losing you as a result of this letter. But I must be totally honest if you are to give me another chance. The court case finished six weeks ago, and I got everything that will be rightfully mine. I should be over the moon but I am not, and I feel sick telling you this, however there is no other way other than to come straight out with it.

The day I won the court case, I got so drunk I spent the night with the solicitor, the woman who had represented me in court. Oh Grace, I am so sorry, but now this woman claims she is pregnant. It was a once off, and I don't even know why I did it. I was so tanked up with drink I don't even remember it. I don't want her, it was a huge mistake. I want you; I want to marry you as we promised.

I know it may be too much to ask, and I know this must be a devastating shock to read this, but if you can please find it in your heart to forgive me, I will give up everything without a second thought and I will leave instantly to be with you in England. Please say the word and I will phone you and explain everything, there is so much more I want to say about how I feel for you, I will never hold anything back from you again.

Oh Grace, in my foolishness I am so afraid I will lose the only thing that has ever mattered. I am fearful of losing you for eternity, and I fear deep down in my heart that I already have.

I'm so sorry for this letter. I'll do anything for you. I have truly learned from my mistakes. I love you so much I'll never forget you, no matter what you decide to do. My heart is set on being with you if you'll still have me, and if I don't hear from you again, I want you to know that my heart is with you for eternity.

I love you Grace.

Gerry. x

P.S. It is after ten pm in the evening and I am completely sober writing this letter."

Gerry placed the letter on the top of his bedside locker and he instantly fell back against his pillows. He felt every pore in his body was excreting the guilt and the shame that had become him, his self-honesty was an exhausting process.

His mind felt void of all the internal conflicts that had been self-inflicted, and with that relief he started to relax, peace entered his mind as it wound itself down, and as he drifted off slowly and deeply into a silent repose, an intense trance overcame him.

There were still millions of thoughts floating around in his head, but they were silent presently with none shouting above the rest for his attention. But one little niggling thought lay amongst those throngs, and though it disguised itself momentarily as having no more importance than the rest, that little thought was moving its way up the ranks to become his most dominant one. That thought was created out of his fear of Grace's reaction to his letter, and if that thought was left uncontrolled it would consume him.

CHAPTER TWENTY-ONE

There are only three scary experiences of being born, and the only reason they are alarming is because you are becoming human, and with humanity comes apprehension and fear. The first is that you consciously forget everything your soul already knows and you start a human life with a blank template. The second is that you fear you will not learn to remember who you really are during your process of a new life, and all souls want the reassurance that they will evolve spiritually on earth. And the final frightening experience is the blinding process.

The blinding process is the final blinding before birth, the wiping of the sense of sight. All babies are born blind, and that privilege is taken in the moments before final rebirth. Even though existence in the womb is dark, all unborn babies' eyes adjust to the darkness, like an instinctive inbuilt night vision. However, in the final moments in the birth canal, the sudden intensity of the bright light from the external world is so intense that internal protective mechanisms shut down the sense of sight, and so the baby is born blind.

Immediately following the blinding process are the developments of the only two known natural fears that all babies are born with. The first natural fear is the fear of loud noises and bangs; this is generally due to the sudden turbo increase of volume as you emerge, like someone suddenly added a woofer to the commotion on the outside. The second natural fear is the fear of falling, since you are heading out head first you have no idea which way you will land or who is ready to grab you when you emerge.

"Can you see anything?" Morcan asked the day before we were finally born.

"Just some shadows still," I said.

"What's the blinding process like?" he asked.

"Okayish," I lied.

"How much do we get to see before the blinding process starts?" he asked.

"Why are you always concerned with questions about what we should expect? We'll be out of here soon," I said in a very tired manner, and I felt as though I was the one that was eight months pregnant with twins that were about to drop out at any minute.

"I'm mentally preparing myself," he said.

"It happens in a fraction of a moment, a flash of bright light to an instant darkness," I said as I yawned.

"Do you know what positive hallucinations are?" Morcan asked strangely, I assumed to get my attention.

"Of course," I replied, "why do you ask?"

"Just wondering."

"Are you hoping to positively hallucinate that you will be able to see when you emerge?" I asked.

"Not really, I am happy in the knowledge that I will grow sight after I am born."

"Then why ask? Is this a game?" I asked with confusion.

"No."

"It's squashed in here, positive hallucinations of space would be good now," I said happily as I stretched and yawned some more.

"That's not what I was getting at," he replied promptly.

"Then why all the cryptic questions, Morcan?" I asked.

"I am just wondering if you know what positive hallucinations are, and what you will actually see properly before the blinding process."

"I'm not sure how this is relevant."

"It's very relevant."

"How?"

"Just is."

"Maybe I can help you if you are a little more specific, is there something that you want to see before the blinding process?" I asked, and despite my intentions of sleep I grew more awake from his constant chattering.

"Not me, I don't want to see anything specific, I just want to help you avoid any upcoming shocks."

"How are you helping me? Remember I have been here before," I said confused.

"I want to make sure you will be okay with what you see; if you do see."

"I think I'll survive."

"Okay, if you insist, but don't say I didn't try to help you," he replied.

"What has this got to do with positive hallucinations?" I asked.

"I think you positively hallucinate," he said calmly.

"What?" I laughed as I attempted to turn onto my side.

"It's true, I think you hallucinate, like you are hypnotised by your own thoughts, you imagine things that are not there," he replied seriously.

"What proof do you have?"

"You see things that don't exist," he said.

"I told you before that everything I told you about the Realm is true," I insisted.

"I'm not talking about that," he replied as he attempted to shake his head.

My interest was aroused. "Then what are you on about?" I asked.

"I've known for ages," he said.

"Known what?"

"At first I thought it was a game, and then I thought you were just deluded, and then I realised you were being true to yourself and that it was possibly just a hallucination," he said as though he had thought that he was explaining thoroughly.

"What hallucination?"

"Take a look down."

"I can't, I'm squashed against you."

"Can you see anything at all down there?" he asked.

"Shadows; and the outline of your toes curled above my knees," I said with confusion.

"Anything else?"

"No."

"Can you see your fingers?" he asked.

I got annoyed. "Yes, of course I can see the outline of my hands, because they are beside my face," I responded quickly.

"So you know what fingers and toes look like?" he asked.

"Are you being simple? Of course I do."

"And if you had to describe fingers and toes to an alien, how would you describe them?"

"Little 'sticky out' bony things...." I started to explain before I stopped myself, realising how ridiculous the conversation was becoming.

"And what other 'sticky out' things do we have?"

"Ears, nose; Oh Morcan, this is getting ridiculous," I replied impatiently.

"What else?" he persisted to ask.

I stared bewildered for several moments until the thought finally dawned on me like an epiphany, "Agh ha! I get it now, you are afraid to say the word 'penis' in case you get in trouble; and you want me to say it, you want me to say the word; well of course we have one of those also, it sticks out down there, don't worry about saying that word; only humans avoid using the correct terms for our private parts, they use silly names like 'pee wee' and 'little man' and the likes, it's pathetic really, humans get embarrassed when people use the correct terms. Don't worry."

"Forget about humans in general, I am talking about you," Morcan said calmly.

"I'm not afraid to say the word 'penises'," I remonstrated.

"I know that," he said, "it's just that you don't have one." He completely threw me with that comment and I suspected that it was that one instant shock which induced Mummy Charlotte's labour so early.

"What are you on about?" I demanded to know.

"Let's just say if you were a boy, you'd have one down there, just like I have," he replied calmly.

"I KNOW THAT – what are you on about?"

"Positive hallucinations."

"Maybe you are having negative hallucinations and you are NOT seeing things that are there, HUH; did that ever occur to you?"

"I don't think so," he said.

"I am NOT a girl," I said forcefully.

"Then why don't you have the same little extra bits like I do?"

"You mean a penis, Morcan, is that it? Stop using baby talk, we're both two mature unborns!"

"Just check, and ask yourself what you know about positive hallucinations," he continued.

"You think I imagined that I am being born a boy," I said with disillusion.

"No, I don't think, I know it."

"I must have requested to be born as a boy in this lifetime," I said with despair though I actually could not remember.

"If you did, maybe you didn't get your wish, I've known from day one," he said softly.

"You're saying I'm a girl?" I said loudly with disbelief.

"Yes, I'm saying you're a girl. Even Mummy Charlotte is saying you are a girl, and the 'Psychic Pregscan' also confirmed it," he stated firmly.

"'Pregscan' got it wrong," I replied instantly with defensive worry.

Morcan shrugged his shoulders as he rolled his eyes. "Really? You choose to believe everything else they said, but not that you are a girl, and we both know that Mummy Charlotte is highly intuitive, following her heart and the yearnings of her soul. We both know that. And you still choose to believe you are being born as a boy," he said.

"If you're looking for an argument then I'm not going to play with you anymore," I replied.

"You are the one that is arguing – again!"

"What can I say? I've got issues, we both know that."

"Yes; I have realised that over the last eight months, even if I have forgotten most of them. But I can't forget what I see with my own eyes."

"Why are you doing this?" I asked perplexed.

"Because you are confused about your human identity," he said in a more concerned and soft tone. "But I didn't want to upset you, are you okay?"

"Why would you have not said any of this before?" I asked with suspicion.

Morcan looked downwards sheepishly. "Because I thought it was a game, and it was kind of fun from my point of view," he replied softly.

"Fragrance has told you to say this, hasn't she?" I said with a false accusation.

"I have done no such thing," Fragrance said suddenly as we both shook from the sternness of her voice, "my only concern is that you are both delivered safely to the outside."

"I don't know what to believe," I replied in frustration.

"You still hold on to those human emotions – let them go," she said firmly and her presence faded as she left me with my thoughts and Morcan's revelations again.

"Are you okay?" Morcan asked after several minutes.

"Yes," I replied sulkily, and I had hoped he would pry further and provide me with the consolation and sympathy I felt I deserved. He did not, he said nothing.

"So I am really a girl?" I asked sadly, with the expectation that it may prompt him to donate some empathy.

"Yes," he confirmed, "are you okay with that?"

"Of course; yes," I lied with a disheartened tone complete with disappointment, as I hoped again he would probe further and provide a hint of compassion. My hopes were lost when he did not.

"Great stuff," he said enthusiastically, "now, do you think we have time to create one new game before they shove us out?"

I acknowledged his request with a forced smile but he had certainly left me with food for thought. I had choice. I had the choice to like it or lump it.

It was an enormous shock and I was left with an option of resentment towards Morcan for pointing out a new truth to me. Equally I could thank him, even though the news was not necessarily pleasing for me. So I could accept or I could continue to justify and defend myself. I asked myself which option would serve me best. It made my decision easy; I made the choice based on what I really craved which boiled down to how I wanted to be. My mind had grown so tired and what I most desired was internal harmony, so I eventually decided to embrace the change with curiosity as I knew I could create a new future for myself as I continued my journey. My journey into the future as a woman!

CHAPTER TWENTY-TWO

People tend to talk casually about 'getting comfortable in the job,' or 'if you cannot beat them, join them,' and that is the essence of what happened in the Realm. I am also certain that Gerry will dispute that statement and add it to our growing list of conflicts. But no different to the politician with the ideals and ideas for global improvement that joins his chosen party only for his endeavours to be plucked from him, Bertie and Gerry relaxed into their roles.

Bertie had found his niche. He had assumed a managerial role and for the first time throughout his existence he had found a function that he excelled at. All he had to do was organise the new soul recruits and they did the actual work. It was second nature to him, creating new jobs to keep the other souls busy, and the less he had to do the better he got at his job.

With Bertie on board, Gerry easily settled back into his non-action orientated conversations, reminiscing on the days at Johnny's pub as they spoke fondly about Marie and Johnny. I had no problem with that, it is what they could have taken action on but did not that was cause for concern. The outcome for me was heavily dependent on the memories and attitudes that Gerry developed and chose to carry. But Gerry seemed to be mindful to continuously reverse the opportunities that appeared before him. How everything could easily have changed in such a short period of time, but then again thoughts manifest themselves more quickly in the Realm than they do on earth.

When Bertie was not sleeping on the job, both he and Gerry flicked quick glances to check on both Johnny and Marie on the earth, and despite Gerry's shortcomings he held true to his focus that they would not interfere with any mortal choice. Tessa started to grow edgy and uncomfortable with their continuous contact with earth for their own personal reasons, warning that it may cause outcomes that were blindly unknown to them. And unlike the background of the human she had once been, she asked regularly when they would begin to implement the concepts that Alfie had so easily explained, but each time Gerry would respond that they were doing their best. Bertie remained neutral on the issue, flat out busy in his new role doing nothing.

"Johnny, can you hear me? It's your old friend, Bertie," he was saying quietly as Tessa moved towards him and Gerry.

"I don't like this," Tessa interrupted, "something feels very wrong about it; I feel we are making a choice which will have consequences beyond what we comprehend now."

Bertie turned suddenly in reaction to the sound of her voice. "Are you monitoring my thoughts?" he asked suspiciously.

"I don't need to, you speak them always!" she confirmed, "it must have been the consolation prize being married to you."

"And me?" Gerry asked. "Are you monitoring mine?"

"Yes," she confirmed, "and don't look at me like that Gerry, I thought we had made our peace, but in your mind I see that is obviously not yet the case."

Gerry ignored Tessa's comments as he focused hard, taking control from Bertie, "Johnny, it's us," he said.

"*Yes, I hear something faintly,*" an alien voice suddenly replied.

"That was a female," Bertie said with anticipation and surprise as he moved closer to Gerry, "do you think it's Marie?" Both Gerry and Tessa shook their heads.

"I think we quit while we are ahead," Tessa said, "something is not right about this."

"Are the Realm guides onto you? Is that what you are worried about?" Bertie asked.

"No, I don't think so, but this could be a trick, we don't know who or what we are contacting," Tessa pleaded with concern.

"Like you tricked Gerry," Bertie piped up, "pretending that you had been pregnant so that he would marry you."

"I don't need reminding," Gerry said sternly.

"We are different here," Tessa cried, "earthly deeds of misfortune no longer matter."

"*Hello, I can hear you,*" the strange female voice said suddenly again. Gerry acknowledged the voice which interrupted the icy debate that may have brewed up with Tessa. Bertie shrugged and Tessa continued to reflect a look of uncertainty.

"My client is looking for a John, are you John?" the female voice said.

"No, I am looking for Johnny," Gerry replied firmly.

"I think we have made contact with your John," the female voice said quietly.

"Great," Gerry said, "can you put him through directly to me?"

"He wants to speak with you directly," the female voice said.

"I'm not sure, I don't think I could," a second female voice said, and Gerry and the others heard someone softly weeping through the open communication channel.

"No, we should stop," Tessa interrupted with panic, but remained unheeded.

"She's feeling a bit tearful," the first female voice said, *"can you communicate through me?"*

"Is she talking to me?" Gerry asked Bertie, but Bertie only shrugged again in reply.

"It's obviously not Johnny," Tessa stated firmly, "I think we should quit this."

"Maybe you should have quit when you pretended that Gerry had actually slept with you," Bertie spat out bluntly, "instead of leading him down the garden path with your deceit of pregnancy when there never even was a conception in the first place. Fooling him when he was too drunk to remember!"

"Gerry knew that I wasn't pregnant before we got married. He knew nothing had happened between us. Gerry married me of his own choice, he was insecure, he was afraid of being alone, and he had thought that Grace had abandoned him when he heard no more from her," Tessa replied firmly, "but I don't see the relevance right now!" Gerry's face twisted. "And there's no point in continuing this communication either," she said, "this is not Johnny. Am I the only one that doesn't see the sense in this?"

"Are you still there?" the first female voice said.

"Yes," Gerry replied abruptly as both he and Bertie continued to ignore Tessa's plea.

"*Do you have anything you want to let her know?*" the same female voice said.

"I'm not sure," Gerry said tentatively, as anger, confusion and resentment welled up inside him, brewing a prospective storm with Tessa.

"*He seems overwhelmed to have made contact with you,*" the female voice said.

"Who is she talking to now?" Bertie asked casually, choosing to remain oblivious to the sentiments he had stirred between Tessa and Gerry.

"Not us," Gerry barked in reply, "but I think I know something about the other female that is with her."

"*He's saying that he wants to tell you something,*" the first female voice said.

"I wasn't talking to you," Gerry confirmed bluntly, "besides, I said that I know something, I didn't say I was going to tell you."

"What do you know?" Bertie asked.

"Don't say anything," Tessa warned.

Gerry was defiant of Tessa's caution. "I think the second female is pregnant, listen, there is another soul in there, he's in there alone," he blurted out to Bertie, "listen for yourself and you'll detect him."

"*Oh my God,*" the female voice screeched with joy, "*he's telling me that you are pregnant.*"

"No, I was telling Bertie," Gerry replied.

"*This is wonderful news,*" the female voice said in exultation, "*John, your late husband is telling me that you are pregnant with his baby, isn't that amazing? Did you know that?*"

"Is she talking to the other female?" Bertie asked.

"I'm not her late husband, look, all I want to do is speak with Johnny, and I was talking to Bertie and not you," Gerry stated firmly through the open channel, but the sound of flooding tears came rebounding back. Gerry suddenly felt slightly remorseful.

"You all seem upset on that end, I'm going to go now," he stammered out with a temporary regret.

"He said he's sorry for upsetting you, but he knew you'd want to know," the female voice said.

"No, I didn't say that," Gerry protested. "He didn't say that," Bertie repeated.

"He seems upset, I think he is missing you," the female continued.

"This is pointless," Tessa said with confusion, "no-one knows who they are talking to."

"Who am I talking to?" Gerry thought to ask suddenly.

"My name is Doris," the female replied.

"Okay Doris, I'm Gerry; and I'm looking for Johnny, so do you know where he is?" Gerry continued stubbornly.

"My contact is passing me messages for someone else now," Doris said innocently, apparently talking to the other female, *"I will have to leave it at that for today."* Silence followed for several minutes while Gerry and Bertie waited eagerly.

"My client has left now," Doris finally replied, *"I thought you were John."*

"You mean you led your friend to believe that I was," Gerry replied quickly.

"No harm has been done," Doris said, *"my client wanted to contact her husband John, he died recently at a young age. Do you know where he is?"*

"No, I am looking for a John myself, we know him as Johnny, normally I get straight through, but you interfered somehow," Gerry said.

"She is pregnant though, I heard correctly, didn't I? Is it true that my client is pregnant?" Doris asked Gerry.

"Yes, that's true, so I have helped you out, now can you help me? You must be near my friend Johnny if we had interference, do you know where he is?" Gerry asked.

"Where does he live?"

"Upperton, he has a pub there."

"Which state is Upperton in?"

"South coast of Ireland, of course."

"I don't know anyone in Ireland. I am in San Diego," Doris confirmed.

"Is Johnny in San Diego?" Bertie asked with surprise.

"*I am sure there are plenty of people called John in San Diego. What specifically do you want from him?*"

"I think you are a bit confused." Gerry replied cautiously, "I'd prefer to talk to him directly myself about our own business, so I'm going to leave now."

"*No; wait,*" Doris said urgently. "*Will we have contact again? This is huge, giving women news of pregnancies.*" But Gerry turned immediately to Bertie, "that was strange, very strange, the fact that I detected an unborn soul; isn't that strange? I mean, a soul on earth before he became fully human, imagine that, this is fairly amazing, don't you think it is?"

"It wouldn't have been so strange if Doris had been around in your days on earth, Gerry," Bertie replied casually, "it would have been wonderful in fact, she might have been able to contact someone in the Realm and confirm to you whether Tessa was pregnant or not."

"It was Gerry's choice to marry me," Tessa insisted.

"Only because you tricked him," Bertie replied.

"How many times do I have to say this?" Tessa spat out, "Gerry thought Grace was gone forever; he had already forced me to tell him the truth, the truth that I was not pregnant and he still agreed to marry me. Had I known he was on the road of self-punishment I wouldn't have gone near that marriage with a barge pole! And whether there were tricks or games involved or not, we are responsible for our own decisions."

"*Gerry, Gerry, are you still there?*" Doris asked as her voice continued to pipe through the unclosed communication channel.

"Gerry, close the channel," Tessa requested firmly.

"Gerry's still here," Bertie replied to Doris.

Gerry stared at Tessa. "Closure?" he said.

"Yes, close the channel, she can still hear us," Tessa said urgently.

"No," Gerry replied firmly to Tessa, "I want closure with you."

"This is about what Bertie has decided to stir up again," Tessa said as she shook her head.

"Yes," Gerry said and smiled, "and I want you to undo what you did to me."

"You are behaving like a child, Gerry," Tessa replied, "I thought we had made peace, nothing that happened on earth matters, Alfie has explained all of this, and I cannot undo something I originally told you in deceit when we were on earth; we've been over this several times, and you knew the truth before we got married! But I am very happy to help you find your Grace again."

"We're looking for Grace still?" Bertie asked confused.

"No, we know she's in SPOCC," Gerry confirmed.

"Gerry's primary concern in the Realm is to find Grace," Tessa added.

"Closure," Gerry said quietly, "Doris will help me get closure."

"Did you call me?" Doris asked with a hopeful tone. *"I'm still here, is there something you want to tell me?"*

"We already have closure, Gerry," Tessa cried. "Now we want redemption, and peace, and joy, and love; what is happening to our movement? We have made one step forward and about twenty steps back!"

Gerry thought long and hard before he spoke. "If you want redemption and peace and everything that comes with it, then you will have no objections with what I am about to do," he said as he glared at her, but Tessa only reflected confusion.

"I'm going to work with Doris from here on out," Gerry said firmly, "and we are going to work our hardest to make sure no man is fooled ever again by any woman's claims to snare him." Tessa threw her eyes to heaven and looked at them both with despair.

"How will you do that?" Bertie asked.

"Doris can round up the clients, and I will confirm the pregnancies, and Bertie, you will help me," Gerry concluded. Bertie gulped.

"When?" Bertie asked.

"Now," Gerry ordered firmly, "the channel is still open."

"So we would be like a Realm pregnancy scanning agency?" Bertie asked.

"Yes," Gerry confirmed.

"I don't think this is right," Tessa warned, "but I promise you I will not interfere."

"'Pregscan', that's what we could call it," Bertie said enthusiastically, "that sounds right, I'll recruit the souls to do the work."

Tessa looked more concerned. "Are you sure this will not make you even more bitter and resentful?" she asked Gerry.

"No," he stated loudly, "it will give me some sort of release, a satisfaction."

"I think this may take you away from what you really want, Gerry," Tessa continued, "if you don't do this from the place of your best intentions and from a peaceful mind, we could have catastrophic results."

"I'll take my chances," he replied as he dismissed her.

With Bertie's influence, Gerry's insight was obscured; no different to a rabbit in lush woods where the sun cast a shadow on the part where he had been crouching, yet shining so brightly within a foot of him. He was on the borderline of that shade and with one leap in the right direction he could expose himself to the light that awaited there. But yet the foliage was so dense in his immediate surroundings and his view so low that everything appeared the same to him in all directions. He had arrived at the edge and one move forward could free him, yet one step in the opposite direction would take him further into the obscurity of the comparative darkness. Unlike the rabbit that would undoubtedly move in search of fresh juicy grass, Gerry decided he was comfortable enough on the spot he had chosen for himself. Staying on the familiar patch was the choice he made, he decided to do nothing different and continued to pursue his endeavours in the way he knew best, he did not like change, and his fears still devoured him. It was the definition of madness and he knew it; and I would carry the impacts of his decisions.

CHAPTER TWENTY-THREE

D oris DaValle founded an earth organisation called 'Psychic Pregscan', while Gerry and Bertie operated the Realm side of the same 'Pregscan' initiative, the latest branch within the ever growing 'Undercover Movement'. And this movement started to resemble a multi-functional organisation with many departments, roles and responsibilities hidden under layers of hierarchical management; and with so much focus on its structure and planning, its members worked diligently to form an efficient breakdown of communication and a forgetfulness of its original purpose and mission. And it was also no surprise when Alfie lost touch with the shenanigans of Gerry and Bertie, as Alfie appeared to trust their intentions.

Under the mist of this movement, there was not much interference from either the 'Soul Reading Police' or the Realm guides; it had appeared that Gerry's original enemies were no longer required in the reality that both he and Bertie had then collectively constructed, and these external hostile forces seemed to disappear from the universe in Gerry's mind. And it is only my conclusion that through his own design, Gerry's outward fear revolved into such a powerful and introverted one, it meant he did not need any exterior foes because he had himself; allowing himself to be influenced by Bertie, and happy to stay put in the cushy number that he had created and where he was as important as he could choose to be. Sadly, Gerry grew unaware that he was even doing it.

New opportunities for his development were handed to him left, right and centre, but Gerry chose to continue his path of blindness with similar uncontrolled thoughts that he had held in the latter half of his life on earth.

His existence in the Realm mirrored that life he had lived; on first arrival and in the earlier years when he had hope, when he was curious and when he had been open to new ideas and insights, yet lost in the process of the rules driven by others and the new regulations he started to enforce himself; forgetting he was more than the actions he carried out.

Alfie had been there to guide Gerry on a new path, and even 'Tessa the tempest' had chosen a path of evolution, but Gerry neglected to see these new enhancements as he was consumed and driven solely by his one obsession, an obsession so powerful that he deprived himself of all the grace he could have ever experienced.

The vast and quick growth of the earthly 'Psychic Pregscan' business meant that centres were opened up worldwide through the creative initiatives of Doris, as guided by both Gerry and Bertie. Doris was an honest and thorough woman, and followed their advice to perfection as she targeted more men worldwide as potential clients. But despite her marketing campaigns, the majority of her customers continued to be women, the mothers who wanted to know all they could about their unborn, the prospective mothers who wanted to 'get it right' with the false belief of being unlike what their parents had done before them.

Not surprisingly, the lack of male clients did not upset Gerry too much, as his new-founded self-importance overshadowed his original intentions of the 'Pregscan' arm of their movement. With Bertie's encouragement, Gerry thought his self-made position defined who he was, and he equally assumed that Grace would undoubtedly fall at his feet when he would gallantly sweep through the entrance of SPOCC with this upheld social standing. He had yet again clearly decided that everything he did was for her.

Gerry felt proud and satisfied with his achievements because he did not understand them. And the only thing I remember was a dilapidated outline of what he could have been; he had lost touch with his own self-worth and remained oblivious to his real internal power. He had forgotten what power meant, he had forgotten who he really was; and he immersed into a bubble further than anything he could have imagined on earth. He began to lose the plot; letting the power of his fear overrule.

Not only did Gerry and Bertie operate in a farcical environment, they existed in an apparent paradox. They encouraged others to 'think outside the box' with an understanding that rules were only built for the majority, but Gerry and Bertie did not even understand the dimensions of their own box to even begin looking outside it. They enforced rules within their organisation which they considered were for the wellbeing of others, forgetting in the process that those others had joined by their own choosing and did not require such discipline; Gerry and Bertie had forgotten that others learned to experience for themselves. Had they exhibited such trust they would have understood trust.

Not surprisingly, Gerry gained thousands of followers as others loved to be led in this way, as it meant they had less to think about for themselves. And Gerry considered himself a leader because of the growing number of supporters; he had forgotten that a leader is not someone who has followers, but rather a leader is the one that breaks new ground, paves the way while overcoming the barriers, demonstrating the message they wish to convey; in essence, a leader being someone who goes first. That was the paradox.

Gerry found himself satisfied with the growth of the 'Pregscan' organisation which was originally formed out of his animosity towards Tessa, he believed that through his efforts he had found forgiveness and he decided that he had found peace of mind via the false importance of the role he held; so it was obvious that he would next delude himself with the ambition of finding love.

Impatience grew to being one of his virtues when compared to his vices, and it was a conversation that Gerry overheard about SPOCC which accelerated events when he decided to transport himself there with the idea of reuniting with Grace. Gerry knew that the unreal reality in which he then existed, allowed him to create any other new reality he wanted through the power of focused thought. The answers were already inside him. So Gerry focused his thoughts towards SPOCC, and from the instant he arrived there, he was like a knotted ball of wool looking for an angle of release in his pursuit of Grace.

Gerry had found himself immediately sitting in a SPOCC class where the teacher was asking the class to complete their application forms. Gerry looked in front of him and saw a thick yellow pad of questions. He looked at it with annoyance, he wanted to waste no more time, and he had already waited long enough. He knew his thoughts could create any reality he wanted, so he closed his eyes and focused on Grace. Almost instantaneously he opened them, and eagerly anticipated seeing her, but all he saw was the same yellow pad and class of SPOCC pupils in his immediate surroundings. He did it again. Nothing happened. He tried it again but his environment stayed the same.

He panicked. He made rash accusations towards his soul. He believed his soul had deceived him as he started a battle between the thoughts that had consumed his mind with those of his soul. Internal dialogue started to overwhelm him.

Gerry pleaded loudly that he wanted to find Grace. But the voice of his soul asked him to question what he wanted most at that point in time. Gerry was overwhelmed with anger, he charged his soul with manipulation; but his soul only told him to release his suppressions. Gerry hit boiling point. His soul reassured him that Gerry was where he had intended to be. Gerry broke, and his soul pledged it was to his benefit.

Gerry cried. He was overwhelmed with negative emotion. And so it was, his soul told him that was what he had in fact chosen. Gerry yelled why. And his soul replied fondly that it was because Gerry refused to listen to his soul.

His soul held his true direction and his mind held all the capabilities to carry out the actions and decisions to take him there, but Gerry had not yet understood how to balance his mind and his soul. Gerry was choosing to turn his back on his own soul, and in that dumping he was actually finally acknowledging its existence, the existence which is a part of the whole of him. A soul cannot be discarded, it is eternal, and although he did not realise it yet he had only chosen to neglect that part of him temporarily. He was being prepared for his transformation.

Gerry looked perplexed. As he surveyed his environment, the thick yellow pad remained in front of him and hundreds of smiling SPOCC students still surrounded him. He noticed a fresh, bright-eyed young male pupil sitting beside him but Gerry only glared at him in silence. He then scanned the classroom again to search for Grace but she was still nowhere to be seen. In desperation, he called on his soul again. But there was no response; he decided it had abandoned him.

"Are you okay?" the friendly boy beside him asked. Gerry turned to look at the source of the happy voice. "It can be confusing," the boy continued to say, "they give us so much choice. I can help you if you want."

"I am looking for someone in particular," Gerry replied quietly.

"Me too," the boy replied enthusiastically, "I want my mother to be creative and spiritual and loving." Gerry looked confused. "Pardon?" he said.

"My next set of earthly parents," the boy said, "I have filled out all of my requests and answers for my mother, and I am almost finished the description of the father I choose when I am born on earth."

"In this yellow form?" Gerry asked with confusion, as he searched inside for his soul again.

"Of course," the boy replied as he smiled continuously, "the incarnation application. Have you not completed yours?" Gerry shrugged indifferently.

"Please get ready to hand up your completed forms," the teacher announced from the top of the classroom, but Gerry stared vacantly at the incomplete yellow forms that were still sitting in front of him as he acknowledged what he had done. He smiled at his own foolishness. He knew this event was happening because of his decision; his refusal to listen to his soul had yet again created a new reality from his thoughts and desires.

His soul was always there to guide him, he only needed to listen to the answers he received; yet with his conscious mind bombarded with such strong destructive emotions, and whether he was aware that he was consumed with such negativity or not, it meant the voice of the soul was lost in the web of his unconscious. His soul lay dormant momentarily, exercising kindness under the cloak of apparent destitution, knowing that Gerry had in fact chosen to feel soulless to enable him to choose an alternative.

In desperation again, Gerry called wholeheartedly and honestly for Alfie's aid and was stunned when he suddenly saw Alfie immediately appear behind him. He used the power of his mind to invoke a friend, and realising that he still held the power to create any reality he wanted, he tried the same trick to induce Grace again, but she still did not appear in the same way. He delved into further perplexity as he wondered whether Grace may not have been in that part of the Realm after all; immense sadness overwhelmed him, he had done it all for nothing. He felt soulless. And Gerry finally cried honest tears.

"Shush, don't worry," the friendly boy said, as Alfie asked Gerry gently who this new boy was. Though disheartened, Gerry introduced them and they seemed to engage in joyful conversation immediately. The young boy seemed impressed with Alfie's perfect form and impeccable manners, and Alfie demonstrated an interest in the young boy's dreams and hopes as he enthusiastically told Alfie that he was applying for his first lifetime to be born on earth, and that it was soon coming. He was full of curiosity and joy on all that awaited him.

"Application forms, please," the teacher repeated as Gerry stared at his blank yellow forms, he looked to Alfie and the friendly boy for guidance, but they were too engaged to notice. Gerry took his opportunity. He sneaked the young boy's application form under his own to copy the answers. It seemed the easiest thing to do. He thought he could not be born again; it was only the soul that could be reborn so it was of no consequence what his answers and requests were because he was choosing parents for his soul, a soul that he believed had abandoned him.

Once he had completed his mischievous cheating, my opportunity arose. To an onlooker we resembled one spirit consisting of a soul combined with memories, experiences, attitudes, thoughts and behaviours. Gerry was a spirit that had two voices with which it spoke, one was the mind voice and the other was the soul voice. He knew I was the soulful part, and he defined himself as the mind; and yet his body still lay peacefully on the earth. All three elements combined defined the existence of Gerry Daly. 'Gerald Michael Mary Gabriel Anthony Daly' was the name our parents gave their eldest son in the twentieth century when I was born into that body and mind which defined the whole of Gerry. But there was an internal conflict that only Gerry and I experienced. That conflict between mind and soul was the struggle in his being.

Internal dialogue overpowered him again. "So there," he said to me forcefully, "I signed the contract, you're free, take your chances and find yourself another body and mind to inhabit." The friendly boy beside him regarded him strangely.

I explained I was not free. I would carry his blueprint, he may have signed himself over to reincarnation, but he certainly had not released his soul. He got knotted up in more bewilderment. "Is this a trick?" he asked. I knew he did not understand. As long as he held onto the memories, thoughts, attitudes and behaviours of his former life, the issues would remain unresolved in both the aura and DNA of whatever new body we inhabited.

"Why?" he asked, "why me?" I replied that it was because we were both parts of the whole; we co-existed.

He sighed. "I'm not going back to 'Souls Anonymous'," he said. I explained we could start with a new template, our clean slate.

"Are you trying to delete me?" he asked suddenly. I explained not. But it was important that he acknowledged the voice of his soul because it would become more difficult for us once we inhabited a new human body, and that would begin from the moment of conception. "Why?" he asked again. And I told him calmly it was because to be conceived is to experience mortality, to understand more instances of humanness. And in that process, we would not always be mindful that we consisted of body, mind and soul.

"But," he persisted, "you already know all of this, you can remember!" I explained that may be true, yet once I embarked to reincarnation, I would begin the process of mortality, yet also clouded by the aura of his not yet relinquished fears. It mattered none what our external representation was, or in what form or appearance we had, born or unborn; I would carry his unresolved behaviours in the new baby foetus that we would occupy.

"Are you not worried that you will be viewed as a badly behaved soul?" he expressed with a tiny hint of concern. I said I had become accustomed to it.

"So what do we do?" he asked. I requested we hand up the form. I explained we were going on a journey to birth; the soul that was I, was being reborn with the memories, experiences, attitudes, behaviours, fears and thoughts of the mind that he clung onto.

"Then how do we become free?" he asked. I concluded that it was our mission to become free. And despite his unresolved confusion, Gerry nodded slowly.

"You're welcome," the young boy beside him said, with a huge smile. Gerry looked more confused until he realised he had been talking aloud. "It's okay," the boy continued, "I didn't do anything, sometimes it's best to get it all out in the open, talk it out and come to your own conclusions."

Gerry smiled briefly, the young boy smiled again and I smiled. Yet Gerry's fears loomed in the background. I told Gerry to prepare himself and allow his unhelpful memories fade as we embarked on a journey to birth. I sensed his anxiety increase.

"But what do we do if Fragrance finds out?" he asked concerned. I told him that he already knew that his perception of Fragrance was his creation, which became an unreal reality to him, and I asked him to let go.

He swore he could not. "Fragrance has instigated all of this, I know she has," he accused as I felt the cold draft of more of his horrific thoughts. I assured him not.

"I know her secret," he confirmed, "she took me early to death, Alfie said so." I told him it was his choice to believe what he may. It was his decision which memories would fade easiest for us both; but I already knew what he would choose. I also knew that as soon as we became one with a new baby body, I would start my journey to mortality again and I would not know how to discern the truth anymore. I would be consumed with Gerry's past-life thoughts, his desire to return to his created comfort in the Realm, his obsessive search for Grace, and always being overruled by his fears.

The teacher moved around the classroom collecting the forms, and a sudden new thought occurred to Gerry. Urgency made him scan his copied answers quickly. He saw requests such as 'intuitive, enthusiastic, easily excited, overwhelmed with joy, beautiful, creative, whimsical, friendly and talkative,' for the proposed new mother. And thinking of the possibility that Grace may arrive back to earth also, Gerry quickly added an additional line on his application that said, 'P.S. I want mother to help me find Grace.' The teacher snapped up his form as his thoughts returned to the vision of meeting Grace.

Everything that followed happened at an accelerated speed of time distortion. Every event seemed to occur simultaneously and several dimensions of activity appeared to exist in SPOCC. Gerry had flashes of a large red book with thousands of pages and gold writing entitled 'The Realm Bible,' he had visions of limbo and millions of other frightful circumstances seemed to appear all at once. He had insights that everything he saw and experienced was the manifestation of every thought that he had carried with him, and it was terrifying to him when he realised what his mind contained. He had no idea how long he could have been in SPOCC, it could have been a day, a year or even a hundred years; the passage of time no longer existed.

Suddenly, in a flash of 'lightening', Gerry spiralled down a tunnel of warped time. When he arrived at the end everything was dim yet something was familiar, Gerry looked around with uncertainty as to where he was. "We are removing you from the Realm," Fragrance said firmly in response to his thoughts. It seemed that Gerry's mind had clearly decided that Fragrance would accompany us on our journey. "It is clear you have not let go of your human emotions, the panel fears for your sanity and you are going back to earth to be reborn," she continued to say, leaving Gerry convinced that he was being punished some-how, and his fears persuading him that Fragrance continued to be his foe.

Instantly, Gerry's mind clouded the aura of a new baby foetus; and every memory, every thought, every experience, every reality, every attitude and every behavioural habit that consisted within the mind of Gerry Daly merged again with me as I, the soul, occupied the new baby body. I felt mesmerised temporarily.

"Hello," a little sweet voice suddenly said. Startled, I looked around nervously.

"Over here, look over here," the little voice said. I turned and looked to the opposite side of the balloon where we had been dumped. I realised the familiarity of the place I was in, except this time someone else appeared to be with me. I was in the womb and I had a friend.

"Who are you?" I asked surprised.

"I sat beside you in class once," he responded with excite-ment. "It's me! It's Morcan." He had large, wide smiling eyes as he bounced around the sides of our new home.

"I'm Ariel," I responded quietly. "I know," he replied, "and you talk loads to yourself." He started giggling. I felt sudden paranoia.

"It looks like we are travelling companions," Morcan said joyfully, and I could not help thinking how my new companion liked to state the obvious. I was also aware at some basic level that my view point was thwarted with the disturbance of Ger-ry's mind, so I decided I would explain myself before Morcan got to know me better.

"This may sound strange," I found myself saying, "but you may find my behaviour a bit weird or untoward at times."

"That's okay," Morcan replied. "Have you been here before?"

"Many times," I replied.

"Cool," he jumped enthusiastically, "then you already have games we could play."

"Not really," I replied dumbfounded.

"Surely you must."

"No," I insisted.

"Then what do you suppose we do in here for the next nine months?" he asked innocently.

"What would you have done if you were alone?" I asked in response.

"I knew I wouldn't be."

"How could you have known that?"

"Because I specifically requested a twin," he confirmed, "so that I could have someone to play with."

"But I didn't," I assured him.

"Really?" he said, "I saw you copy my answers, so of course you did; in fact in doing so you have equally requested me for company, and we're getting the same parents also. Isn't that just fantastic?"

"Yes, I suppose," I said slowly.

"Great," he agreed, "so what do you think we could play?"

"I'm not sure."

"Okay," he replied almost too quickly, "I have already thought of one. Do you want to play it?"

"Depends on what it is."

"I have only just created it, so it's in conception stage, just like us, isn't that funny?" He laughed, "so, it's the first time my game is played with another."

"What is it?"

"It's called 'Space Chairs'."

"Huh?"

"Let me explain, it's fun, I was practising on my own before I saw you. I'll show you."

He did show me, and we bounced for hours on end with Morcan having the advantage of winning each time. I had the advantage of allowing myself to create some new joyful, child-like memories, and I knew that in time as the memories of old would fade, new room would be made for these unborn innocent ones. I also knew that there was a rocky road ahead as I would continue to struggle between myself, the soul and the thoughts that had become me. Morcan, on the other hand, had no idea what he was in for. He had no clue he was accompanied by the cranky memories of Gerry Daly.

CHAPTER TWENTY-FOUR

Morcan had volunteered to be born into the world and like the many first timers the poor mite had spent a few hundred years standing in line waiting for his turn to be transformed to bodily form. That is what he told Alfie the day he met him at SPOCC. Of course, I was expelled from SPOCC and was being sent back to the world to expand my comfort zones, at least that is what I believed as I was clouded by the torment of past-life memories. In reality, I knew deep down that I was being guided into a rebirth with the hope that another lifetime would give me the good shove up the backside I so desperately needed. I knew who I was, deep in my psyche I knew I was a pure soul, yet as expected I was blinded by the harness of the burden that I had carried.

"Weeeeeeeeeeeeeeeeeee – I'm on my way," Morcan sang in a crescendo, which suddenly stopped. And then there was a pause. It was our final day in the womb, the morning of our birth and we were about to be born. We were both pointing outwards head first, and Morcan had made more headway than I, his eagerness had propelled him. His navel was adjacent to my eyes when he called back, "you haven't moved."

"I'll be there in a bit," I lied.

"You're changing your mind again."

"What do you know about minds?" I laughed nervously. "You haven't lived your first life yet."

"You're still planning to go back," he said.

"No-one's going anywhere, except out," Fragrance reminded us both.

"Sure," I muttered. Once Morcan moved on, I had planned to start the negotiations with Fragrance. She still owed me though I was not sure if I could play that card again, or if even it was a card I could play, had I imagined it all? Our secret had worked well in the Realm and a large part of me still wanted to get back there, and there's no second guessing as to which part that was. As far as I knew Alfie was still in SPOCC and since Bertie was left in charge of the Realm 'Pregscan', they needed my help more than ever. Besides, I had a purpose back there, or did I?

"I'll see you on the outside," Morcan piped up cheerfully. I transferred a false 'thumbs up' signal into his mind and he reciprocated with the image of a large, round delusional eye winking.

"Full steam ahead," I encouraged, despite my arduous sack of thoughts. He must have heard me think when he suddenly shifted into reverse.

"Why are you so hesitant to be reborn?" he asked tactfully.

I felt pity for him, and said, "I told you, it's great."

"You go first then," he announced, as he half looked me up and down at very close range. Suddenly the screams further sharpened on the outside and I feared that if he reversed any further, he would drive his foot into Mummy Charlotte's thudding heart. Consumed with past-life thoughts, it would mean a meal ticket for me, a free ride back to the Realm, but I knew that was not what he wanted.

"Shift a gear, you're making them panic," I said panicking.

"You shift a gear, you're making me panic," he said.

"I'm watching your back for you," I lied again. And then I really panicked when I truly recognised my guilt of deception, and it was with that acknowledgement that I knew I was fully human again. There was no turning back.

"Drive on," I shouted. Defiantly, he flipped completely around with a somersault that almost blinded me.

"One of them is a breech," someone from the outside shouted. And as the external cries intensified, not only was I brewing up a migraine from all the hysterical commotion but Morcan also bopped me on my shin. "Ouch," I cried like a baby.

Morcan rotated roughly around again and another bolt went through me. His foot used my stomach as a trampoline that propelled him with such a force that I expected him to land in the middle of next week. His ricochet routine delivered him half way down the passage, opening it up and encouraging more light to enter. For the first time in the womb, I got a good view of him and, though white haziness veiled my vision, he looked like a cowering, drowning puppy, anticipating his first life. Simultaneously we were both blinded in a fraction of a moment.

I felt a wing clip my ear, it was Fragrance.

"Okay, okay; I'm going too!" I said, realising my predicament.

"Alive?" Morcan asked.

"Yes, alive."

"Sure?" he asked.

"How many more times; yes!"

"Silence," Fragrance said calmly.

"I'm excited for you," Morcan said.

"Just keep going," I replied hurriedly.

"You're afraid," he challenged.

"Not!"

"Why cannot you be excited for me?" he asked innocently.

"I am; look, it's tough; okay."

"We get to meet our soul friends as humans," he continued to say.

"You won't remember them," I reminded him.

"But we learn to remember during our lives," he said excited.

"Of course we do," I answered quietly, and then I knew that I was certainly human, as I worried about what I would actually remember during my next lifetime. My memories were faint. What if I met Grace and did not know who she was?

"Please; just go; you need to learn for yourself," I begged.

"Come with me now," Morcan encouraged with a still unborn innocence.

"It's easier to wait in the Realm for my love to come," my human mind responded.

"But everyone has pure love," Morcan reminded me.

"Human minds play games," I reminded him.

"I love games," he piped back before making a final sprint towards his goal.

"You sod," I said, and I instantly regretted it. He was gone. We parted on those terms, and I knew he was right. His hope propelled him, an optimism that I had dismissed. But I, rigid and still, did not budge for another seventeen minutes. Piercing sounds of glee commenced on the outside and Fragrance smiled inside my mind, but defiant and with nothing else to do, I thought I would make myself comfortable. In truth I felt afraid; Gerry's fearful memories were overwhelming.

I had a huge dilemma, I could move forward to rebirth and create a new blueprint to experience with a newfound innocent joy; or I could grasp onto the last strands of memories that remained. I cried inside, I wanted help, I wanted a friend, I wanted a guide, and I wanted someone to show me how to reshape the fragments of the remaining memories that were shrouded in fear. I wanted it with all my heart. And that was the choice that was made in the mind and that was the decision I acted on, and that pure desire created my next moments of unborn experiences.

"Ariel," Fragrance called out to me softly.

"Yeah," I replied slowly.

"It is okay to let go of those thoughts."

"I'm afraid," I admitted openly as I shivered with anxiety, but huge and warm fluffy wings surrounded me, engulfing me with a sense of safeness and security.

"Is that you?" I asked Fragrance.

"You asked for a friend," she replied.

"But how can it be...." I said with confusion, "you are a Realm guide, you are fierce... and you enforce unwritten rules."

"It is up to you to design what those unwritten rules are, Ariel."

"Are you an angel then?"

"You can bring forth an angel if you want; the angels are always there overseeing you and will guide you. It is your responsibility to ask."

"Are you saying this because this is what I want to hear?"

"I am saying this because this is the reality of your soul, and your mind has finally allowed you to see it."

"I create my own reality through the power of my thoughts," I said reflectively.

"Yes, you do," she replied.

"My mission was to purify the thoughts I chose to carry with me."

"Yes, it was."

"What do I do?"

"Listen to yourself, your true self, and listen to the soul that you are. You are a pure soul, Ariel, underneath the memories you have inherited. You always knew the time would come, you always knew you would reach this crossroads; it was your mission."

"But ... but ... what about you?"

"I am your guide, Ariel, you chose to fear me or embrace me, and the choice was always yours."

"But you wanted to enforce a process? Even Alfie said so."

"Ariel, you have created your own reality, you have created your own experience of the Realm. Your experience of the Realm was the magnification and confusion of the attitudes you brought back from earth."

"Then why am I being reborn?"

"For the same reason as any other pure soul," she replied softly, "you choose to be born to experience being human again."

"It's that simple!"

"It's always that simple."

"What do I choose now?"

"Listen to your heart, Ariel."

"Love; peace, and joy," I said honestly.

"Anything else?"

"Love; peace, and joy," I repeated.

"Nothing else?"

"Grace?" I asked tentatively.

"You may have grace also in whatever way you imagine it to be."

"I choose to know myself, I choose another chance."

"And so it is," Fragrance replied in synchronicity to the soul that was I, the core of myself that I finally recognised again.

I had lived as a man confused by emotion and overwhelmed by negativity and limited self-beliefs. Rather than celebrating my emotions and allowing the power within myself to expand my mind, I chose to block every ounce of creative thought within my being. I neglected the opportunities to follow my heart and allow my mind to take me to where my heart wanted to be. I was consumed by self-pity, choosing to blame others and external circumstances for my own situation. I suppressed intuition to the point of wanting to kill my soul. I had forgotten who I really was. I had decided to no longer listen to the calming voices inside. I was a self-tortured man. The name of that man is Gerry Daly; but I am more than the memories of Gerry Daly. I am the soul called Ariel and I am a 'Soul Anonymous'.

I become anonymous again as I rejoin the masses of others oblivious to the pure internal power. But in my next life, I know that I am willing to find myself again.

I proceeded to undress myself of my negative thoughts, washing my mind of unwanted behaviours and attitudes; and instead created a heaven within the depths of my being that waited to be filled with new joyful and carefully selected thoughts. I felt reborn.

Fragrance carefully eased me forward as the screaming agony again commenced on the outside. I paused; and as I looked back, I said goodbye to my memories. I prayed as I told the remnants of Gerry that we were completing our mission, I explained that the last fragments of his mind was being wiped within moments from birth. I said we were creating a new joyous future together, but he did not respond. I said goodbye to him but it appeared that the distorted mind that consisted of Gerry no longer wanted to struggle.

I had not expected I would, but Morcan had already paved the path, he had taken the lead, he had gone first; so I too with sharp convulsive breaths forced my way towards my next destiny.

"And a little girl," someone announced cheerfully when I emerged. Mummy Charlotte's screams hit my ear lobes instantly at full steam on the outside, I felt dizzy and disoriented but relieved simultaneously. I finally recomposed myself, adjusting to my new breathing mechanisms when I noticed that Mummy Charlotte's commotion had subsided also.

"Let's call them Jane and Edward," Daddy Joe said with excitement. And with an instant shock, I recognised something new about his energy, it all was becoming clearer. He embraced me and the powerful tension of his aura was familiar. The force made itself known to me and the overwhelming electric event I experienced was reunion with the soul of my Grace. "It's me; it's me," I sobbed in delight searching in blindness for his face, but my voice only sounded like a staccato passage that said "Whaaa!!" several times. Daddy Joe kissed me softly.

Fresh thoughts of Grace entered my mind but escaped it as quickly as they entered. I searched around for Morcan but instantly forgot who he was. Everything I barely knew was rapidly slipping away. I repeated "Grace", "Mummy", "APES", "SA", "Gerry", "Soul", "Realm", "Verity", "Fragrance", "Angel", "Trinity", "SPOCC" and "Joe", over and over in my mind, and I gasped and gasped for more and more air as I started to forget what I was doing.

"Daddy Joe, Mummy Charlotte, I love you," I wept, with my newfound innocent joy. Then I tried to say something else but found it impossible. Thoughts vacated me. My head filled up with empty space. Silence echoed my walls inside. Everything went blank. I cried, but I did not know why. I forgot to think.

It was Friday March thirteenth in the year 2172 when I finally arrived to the outside world in Hampstead. And even though a dusty snowfall powdered the outside streets of London, I felt a warm and jubilant glow. Finally reborn and surrounded by angels, I managed a faint smile, a silent one. And then I knew no more.

THE END

ACKNOWLEDGEMENTS

A heart-felt thank you to Lorraine Thomas, a wonderful British author who embraced my writing from the outset despite having no previous or personal acquaintance with me; I thank her for her enthusiasm, support, encouragement, patience, generosity and friendship. She continues to be a beautiful influence in my life.

Deepest thanks to John Dolan, a newspaper Features Editor, who gladly and curiously received my novel despite us being strangers to one another. I couldn't have asked for a better Editor as he played a fundamental role in supporting me; his trust, his efficiency and his belief in this novel have made a great difference. I thank the heavens for sending him to me.

My heart-felt gratitude for the beautiful friendship of Sue Cole and Joan Buckley, as when no one else knew I was writing this novel, they provided amazing support, encouragement, feedback, reviews and praise in all the good times and bad when doubts crept in, all of which I am eternally grateful for. I am proud to call them both my soul mates.

Huge thanks to the wonderful writer, Jonathan Dawson, (www.dervishtrade.com), for his support, his honesty, his dedicated time, his gentle critique and detailed feedback, which helped me to improve the characterisations greatly. His spiritual presence brings a beautiful energy to all who encounter him.

Heart-felt thanks to Brian Mayne, whose mere presence is a true inspiration, and has made a fundamental difference to my life, for he really taught me about *being*. I am privileged to call him a friend today.

To Adam Shaw for the laughter and fun he brings to my life; Pam Lidford for her great encouragement; Sherron Mayes for her generous advice and support; the team at Original Writing Publishing for their guidance and patience; and Colin Lavers for his generosity when he provided me with the beautiful photograph of the white rose which is used in the design of the cover.

A huge thank you to all who reviewed my novel, literary professionals and supporters who provided great praise, once strangers and all of whom I am now happy to call my friends.

My deepest thanks to everyone worldwide who all played a significant role in getting this novel into the top 250 worldwide books from thousands of entries in the Next Top Author international competition. I appreciate your support from the bottom of my heart; all of your generous comments, feedback and emails and the wonderful community you have created together brings enormous joy, excitement and love to us all; hearty thanks to Kate Revins (my sister) for her belief and fun as she enthusiastically rallied so much support for this competition.

My heart-felt gratitude to my sisters, brothers-in-law, nieces, nephews and all my friends who add significantly to my life, and for their support, their friendship and great humour; and most of all for being there.

Finally, enormous thanks, appreciation and love to my parents; my father, Jeremiah Whyte, a wonderful storyteller who passed over in January 2006, who in passing reconnected me with my intuition and changed my life in the most beautiful way; and my mother, Catherine (Kitty) Whyte, who has always believed in me, and whose love could only come from a mother. This means the world to me. My success is theirs.

ABOUT THE AUTHOR

Mairéad Whyte qualified with a degree in Electronic Engineering and a post-graduate higher diploma in Mathematical Modelling in the early to mid 1990's. Having spent more than thirteen years in business and corporate environments, she resigned from her position as a Director of an international software firm to pursue her passion for writing on a full-time basis.

She has been writing for much of her life, and has been a freelance writer since 2006 with several publications in Ireland. She has travelled a path that integrates her scientific background with her intuition and spirituality. She is a qualified Holistic Coach, a Hypnotic Practitioner and a Masters NLP Practitioner who offers workshops and personal coaching, enabling others to holistically connect with their own inner creativity and heart-felt truths.

With her heart and soul driven passion for writing, her creative writing workshops, scheduled for 2011, are designed to encourage others to direct their feeling, vitality and energy into their writing in a uniquely combined holistic and stream of consciousness manner.

Her heart lays in opening up our innate curiosity to the world around us and beyond.

Over the years, she has presented at several international conferences; and she has written a large collection of short stories. She has lived and worked throughout the world and currently resides in her birthplace in Cork, Ireland.

The author may be contacted directly at
allforgrace@maireadwhyte.com

www.maireadwhyte.com